RISEN II

The Progeny

by

Krystal Lawrence

Risen II, The Progeny

Cover design by Telemachus Press, LLC

Cover art:
© Copyright iStockPhoto/113655/nautilus/shell studios
© Copyright iStockPhoto/26712721/Krakozawr
© Copyright iStockPhoto/3337190/XiXinXing

Scene separator © Copyright iStockPhoto/29722028/Giraphics

Published by: Telemachus Press, LLC
http://www.telemachuspress.com

Visit the author's website:
http://www.darksidestories.com

ISBN: 978-1-941536-51-3 (eBook)
ISBN: 978-1-941536-52-0 (hardback)

Ver. 2015.01.01

In loving memory of Robin Williams—
I can hear the angels laughing.

RISEN II

The Progeny

FOREWORD

While I normally don't write forewords to my books, I simply had to thank everyone who asked me for the sequel to *Risen*. Without you, this book would have never been written. I was overwhelmed by how many people wanted to know what happened after we last left Alder Lake. I will even admit to having what can only be described as an embarrassingly *Sally Field acceptance speech moment. (They like me! They really like me!)*

To be honest, my first thought when the subject of a continuation to the story was broached was, *Sequel? What sequel?* I didn't have a clue what fate had befallen the townspeople after the last page of *Risen* was done.

However, as time went on, I found myself wondering the same thing, so I paid Alder Lake another visit. I was delighted to discover that their story wasn't done after all. Francis wasn't quite dead yet, and Kurt, Amanda, and all their neighbors still had a lot to talk about.

There were also requests that I raise a couple of Alder Lake's lost residents from the dead, (may God have mercy on their fictitious souls.) You will find that I took these recommendations under strong advisement.

And just a note to anyone familiar with law enforcement: I hope you will forgive the blatant liberties I took with the AFIS database. I exercised a bit of creative license with what fingerprints are entered into it for the sake of the story.

Having found my way back to town, I was charmed to wander the streets of Alder Lake again. It was fun catching up with all the familiar faces, and meeting a few new ones. I hope you will enjoy your reunion with them as much as I did, and that your curiosity will be satisfied.

One caveat before you enter the city limits, however:

I discovered there is still an awful lot of evil lurking in the shadows of Alder Lake after dark. Enter at your own risk, and don't blame the messenger if you end up sorry you wanted to know how things worked out. Keep in mind, it wasn't all that long ago I warned you, *Be Careful What You Wish For.*

Krystal Lawrence
Seattle, WA
August 2014

CHAPTER 1

The sun was sinking behind the mountains as the dead boy walked on, every bone in his over-taxed body aching from strain. The constant cloud of dust and ash that floated about him like a grimy halo made flagging down car rides impossible. This journey would be made on foot, and there was a very long way to go, especially for a boy who should have been resting peacefully in his grave for some three hundred years.

As the boy felt the rising breeze lift his long hair from his brow, he raised his hands to his face and groaned. He watched in silent horror, as his fingers dissolved into fine grains of ash and floated off into the mild California evening. If he did not find shelter for the night soon, there wouldn't be much of him left to lie down tonight at all.

Five years before, Francis Barclay had been cremated and interred in a vault one hundred miles east of his hometown. Though he was no stranger to rising from the dead, the first time around he was given a fully formed body to work with. This time he was comprised of hundreds of thousands of tiny flakes of burned ash, and they didn't stay put when the wind grew restless. Worse was the odor clinging to him like an unwanted lover. He smelled like a poorly tamped-out brushfire, lingering cinders smoldering on his skin.

Francis stumbled. He watched with dismay as his left foot began evaporating into fine powder, swirling in the air before him. It turned to mist, and rose into the sky above him like a departing soul, taking that miserable burnt smell with it.

Limping now, he did his best to quicken his pace. He reminded himself to find a pair of more suitable footwear tomorrow. So far, all he'd managed to come up with was a pair of beach thongs that offered no protection from the hateful breeze. Their only redeeming quality was how well they matched the haphazard outfit he'd stolen from the same owner: a pair of wildly printed beach shorts and a green t-shirt emblazoned with a surfboard. He would work on his wardrobe tomorrow as well.

Fortunately his dissolved limbs would reform once he was out of the wind. He feared if he lost too much of himself, or if the same limb turned to ash and blew away too many times, it would simply cease to restore itself. He had enough handicaps right now without losing any of his very tenuous body parts.

When Francis awoke from what should have been his eternal slumber a second time, he was convinced it was because he had not completely avenged the death of his family the last time he was forced from his resting place and returned to that wretched town. He hoped it would be done, but no. Not yet.

As his body rose from the ashes in the vault, and he'd stepped into the harsh sunlight for the first time, he was unaware of just how far from Alder Lake he had been interred.

He was horrified to discover when his enemies burned him to dust and placed his remains deep inside a stone mausoleum wall, they'd secured him over one hundred miles away.

Now he was forced to return on foot. He supposed he could not blame the drivers for speeding past him without stopping. No one was going to offer a ride with that dusty cloud constantly swirling about him, and that wretched scorched stench.

As the days progressed, Francis grew to realize his bloodlust had left him. He no longer felt the same animosity or hatred for his enemies. It slowly dawned on him that perhaps he was not resurrected this second time for revenge. Perhaps something else beckoned him home. Something to do with the child, Lorna. The reason would reveal itself soon enough, he supposed.

The sun drizzled through the drawn curtains, as afternoon gave way to evening in the quiet, upscale hotel room. Deputy District Attorney, Carolyn Devonshire stirred from a light doze and reached out to find the other side of the bed empty.

Her lover emerged from the bathroom already dressed. He smiled apologetically as Carolyn reached for his arm.

"Sorry, babe. I have to pick my daughter up from rehearsal. No time for seconds today."

She sighed and pulled the sheet back to expose her full breasts. With a wicked grin, she pulled his hand onto her breast. "You sure, Detective? Not even a quickie?"

The smile left Kurt Dale's face as he bent down and gave her a perfunctory peck on the lips. "Sorry, Car, I really don't want to make Lorna wait."

Sensing his irritation, Carolyn drew the sheet back up to her chin. "Sorry," she mumbled.

She was insatiable. That was one of the things Kurt loved about her at the beginning of their affair—and one of the things he really couldn't stand about her anymore. He could never escape without some type of drama. She didn't have children of her own, and Kurt thought it rather selfish how she always tried to hold him there when he needed to pick up his daughter. She just didn't get it. As a parent, he had certain responsibilities.

An unwelcome voice in his head answered, *Yes, and being a husband carries certain responsibilities too, oh wise one. One of them is not being in hotel rooms doing naughty things with women who aren't your wife.*

He bristled at his own conscience. That irritating voice spoke up more and more frequently over the last few weeks, and he was just now starting to pay attention to it.

The affair was in its second month, and it was already time to end things. The problem, of course, was that ending things was not Kurt Dale's strong suit. He was never very good at letting women down easy. He always remained trapped in relationships he didn't want, far past their expiration date. Manning up and breaking things off seemed to be a skill he could never master. And, well, if he was to be honest, the allure of forbidden sex was just so damn intoxicating.

Historically, his extramarital dalliances never ended well. None quite as unpleasant as the last one; his mistress murdered in a grizzly manner, and he the lone suspect for a while. But that was a long time ago. These days he didn't have to stray from his wife for long before he remembered all the reasons why he didn't need such complications in his life. *Frankly,* he thought, *I am just too damn old for this nonsense.*

"You can make it up to me on Thursday," Carolyn remarked, as she rose from the bed and padded naked into the bathroom.

Kurt sighed wearily. He felt what he'd come to refer to as the "Mistress Migraine" begin forming at his temples.

Where is John Wyatt when I need him? Kurt brooded. There had never been anyone for him to talk to or get any sage wisdom from since John moved to Florida. He still missed his old friend and partner a great deal. Sadly, things were never really the same between them after the horror they went through several years ago.

While they stayed in touch after John moved away, the relationship was no longer a close one. It consisted mostly of cards on birthdays and holidays, and the occasional long distance phone call.

Kurt knew this time he was going to have to navigate his way out of an affair all on his own. There would be no one else to help him do it. He smiled wistfully and thought, *As my daughter would say, it's time to put on the big boy pants.*

Lorna Dale stood outside the school chatting animatedly with two girlfriends. When she saw her father's SUV pull to the curb she smiled broadly.

Kurt reached over and opened the passenger side door for his daughter.

"Daddy, can we give Kelly a ride home?" Lorna asked, waving a hand toward the cute little blonde girl standing beside her.

"Sure, sweetie, but where's her mom?" Kurt answered as the girls climbed into the car.

His daughter glanced away, and Kurt looked curiously at the girl in the back seat.

"I have no idea," she shrugged. "She isn't here, which is totally weird 'cause her car is right there." Kelly Winter pointed to a late model Volvo in the parking lot.

Kurt looked at the car uneasily. "Was it there when you came out of rehearsal?"

The girl nodded. "She's always earlier than the other parents. Maybe she's inside talking to someone."

"Daddy, can we go?" His daughter looked at him with pleading eyes.

"No, honey, we can't. Not until we find Mrs. Winter."

"Do you think something's wrong?" Kelly asked nervously.

"Nothing's wrong, Kelly," Lorna soothed before her father could answer. "She's probably just talking to one of the teachers and lost track of time."

Kurt always marveled at how grown up his daughter seemed, though she was only seven years old.

He told the girls to wait in the car, not seeing the worried expression on his daughter's face as she watched him walk away.

Kurt approached the abandoned Volvo and peered through the window. The doors were locked and there was no handbag inside. Nothing suggested foul play. He entered the school and walked to the main office.

A ghost of disquiet gnawed at him. He had picked Lorna up from play rehearsal numerous times, and Rona Winter was always standing outside the school waiting faithfully for her daughter. He knew immediately something was wrong.

The secretary was just pulling on her coat to leave for the day when Kurt walked in. After he explained the situation, Kurt asked her to check the girls' bathrooms to see if the woman might have fallen ill and was inside one of them.

The secretary led Kurt to the first bathroom and he waited outside while she checked each stall. He heard the click of her heels against the tiled floor, making him even more impatient. It sounded like listening to the clicking of seconds going by.

She walked out, shaking her head. "No one's in there," the secretary said, leading Kurt to the next bathroom.

He listened carefully as she inspected the second lavatory. He found himself nervous even though he dealt with this kind of thing every day.

"Mr. Dale!" the secretary yelled.

Kurt burst into the bathroom, meeting the secretary's wide eyes with his own narrowed ones. Her shaking hand pointed to the body between them; Rona Winter was sprawled on the floor, unconscious, the contents of her overturned handbag scattered around her in an untidy heap.

"Rona," Kurt said loudly, while carefully turning her body face up. He gently shook her shoulders. "Rona, can you hear me?" He put two fingers on her neck and felt for a pulse. His head snapped toward the secretary. "Call paramedics right away. Tell them we found her unconscious in the bathroom and she's not responding, but she's breathing."

The panicked secretary ran from the bathroom to place the call.

A quiet but distinct moan slipped from Mrs. Winter's lips and her brows furrowed together. She was waking up.

"Rona, can you hear me?" Kurt tried again.

She nodded slowly.

"The police are on their way. You're going to be fine. Do you know what happened?" He was trying to keep his voice calm.

She opened her eyes and squinted at him. "I… I don't know how I got here."

"Do you remember anything?"

Mrs. Winter thought for a moment, her brows still knitted. "Yes," she whispered, "I remember opening the door…" She sighed. "I guess that's all I remember. Everything else is just a blank."

"You don't remember if you tripped or fainted? Were you feeling poorly?"

"I was fine. I just… I can't remember anything after walking into the bathroom."

The door swung open and paramedics entered the room, rushing to the woman's side. Kurt stepped out of their way. He saw a couple of police officers standing in the hallway and went to join them.

"No need to take a report," he said. "She doesn't remember anything, and nothing indicates an attack. Her purse was overturned, but it looks like that happened when she fell. The most important thing right now is to see she gets to the hospital." The officers nodded in agreement.

Mrs. Winter was taken to the hospital and determined to have suffered a mild concussion. The doctor examining her found two minute, pin-sized holes at the back of her neck which he could not identify. He questioned her about them, but dismissed them as an insect bite when she could offer no explanation for how they got there.

Several days later, Mrs. Winter experienced a sudden flash of memory. She recalled hearing a noise behind her when she entered the lavatory. The memory was too vague to know exactly what the noise might have been. It was followed by… She wasn't exactly sure what. She only knew she'd been hit by something heavy right after she heard it.

Rona told her husband what she remembered as they were getting ready for bed one night. "Do you think I should tell the school? It could be important."

Mr. Winters stopped drying his face in front of the mirror and considered Rona's question before answering. She'd suffered a concussion during the incident, so her memory couldn't be trusted. It was possible she just slipped and hit her head for all either of them knew. With no description of who hit her, if anyone actually did, what good would it do to raise that kind of panic? Their daughter's play was right around the corner. The performance was a big deal for Kelly, and her father didn't want anyone else's drama to overshadow his little girl's moment of school fame.

"No," Rona's husband replied with certainty. "You aren't at all sure of what happened, and the first thing the school—and the police, for that matter—will ask is what you remember. A noise you can't describe isn't much to go on. I think it would be best to just leave things be."

Rona agreed with her husband in theory, however, in her heart she knew someone struck her as the door closed behind her in that bathroom. It would trouble her for a very long time.

CHAPTER 2

The boy who walked the dark of night on his way to Alder Lake was barely a man himself, and he was no longer human, though he came in search of his child. He knew that now. He dreamt of her the night before and now understood why he'd awakened from his eternal slumber once more. His worst fear had been realized, and the thought of how many miles he needed to cover to reach her was worrisome.

Returning to Alder Lake, a town he despised, murder was not what plagued his mind, as it did the last time he was summoned to those hated streets. What occupied his thoughts tonight, with each excruciating step, was family. His progeny, to be exact.

Francis Barclay had been dead a very long time, still there was no rest for his weary soul. He was summoned once more to Alder Lake, because during his last visit, he not only failed to avenge the murder of his parents, he also, quite literally, created a monster.

It was now his responsibility to return and instruct her. There were many things to teach her so she could get along in the world undetected. He would not allow his child to make the same mistakes his family had made centuries ago. The mistakes that led to their murders, their house torched to the ground, their souls writhing in disquiet for all eternity.

Francis Barclay would do right by this child of his, and then, maybe, he could finally rest.

Amanda Dale loaded the dinner dishes into the dishwasher as she listened to her husband recount the tale of finding Rona Winter unconscious in the restroom. While she felt sorry for the woman, there were more pressing matters on her mind. One in particular was about their daughter's bizarre request at dinner.

She interrupted Kurt's story. "Do you think it's strange Lorna likes her meat rare?"

"Were you listening to me?" Kurt asked, cocking his head curiously at his wife.

"Yes, sorry, how awful. Hope Rona will be okay, blah, blah, blah. Now listen. Something's bugging me, and it isn't postpartum crap, so don't go there, okay?"

Kurt looked at his wife apprehensively. He knew damn well whatever bee she had in her bonnet wasn't postpartum. Practically the moment she started spiraling after their son's birth, she ran and got a prescription for the pills to control the depression and the crazy mood swings. That was a big part of the reason Kurt wanted to untangle himself from the lovely Ms. Devonshire. Things with Amanda were good.

He grew very uncomfortable whenever his wife said something was bugging her. The last time something truly bugged Amanda, it was Tina Hilliard; a situation which nearly landed him in divorce court, prison, or an early grave. He still wasn't sure which. Moral of the story: never let thy wife be bugged, lest ye be damned.

Oh, shit, she knows! his guilty mind screamed, then amended quickly, *No, no, it's something about Lorna and meat, not you, Bozo.*

Their relationship had evolved into a quiet complacency which suited them both, since surviving an unthinkable experience together—one only a handful of people knew about or would ever believe. It forged a nearly unbreakable bond between them. The volatility, which seemed to be the cornerstone of the first ten years of their marriage, had at last been replaced with harmony. The only thing capable of rocking their world anymore was Kurt's infidelity or Amanda's mood swings, which when she bore children, became violent.

Now she was on the drugs; those miraculous little blue pills that prevented her from such charming behavior as smashing all their dishes against the wall, or kneeling on the bathroom floor whacking her hair off. Both were events which followed the birth of Lorna, a time they would rather forget.

Amanda was living up to her end of the bargain, and Kurt knew damn well if he didn't live up to his there would be hell to pay. Amanda was not enveloped in any postpartum fog that left her insulated from reality anymore. She was fully aware of what time her husband came home at night, as well as every nuance of his speech, his body language and his eye contact.

Since he transferred from the Violent Crime Division to Narcotics, Kurt's hours were longer and his office farther from home. This could account for the increased hours away. He could not, however, outrun his wife's intuition. Not for much longer anyway, and he knew it. When Amanda interrupted his recounting of the day's events with a random question about Lorna, he wondered if he was once again not seeing something clearly because his mind was preoccupied with Ms. Devonshire's glorious breasts. Kurt was well aware that when his dick wandered, his brain followed. He was living proof of the old adage about a man having only enough blood to run one organ at a time.

"What was the question?" he asked.

"Lorna wanted you to cook her steak rare tonight. Why would a child ask for rare meat?"

"When, besides tonight, has she ever requested rare steak?"

"Well, maybe she hasn't. I mean, we don't eat steak that often. I just think it's weird a seven-year-old would ask you to—and I quote—'make it raw, Daddy' while you are manning the grill. Don't you?"

Kurt frowned. "Yeah, I guess it's a little strange." He paused, and then said hesitantly, "Let's face it, Amanda… she is kind of an odd kid."

Amanda's eyes flew open in comic shock. She surprised Kurt by crumpling onto a chair and laughing uncontrollably. "Jesus, Kurt," she sputtered between giggles, "we have never said that out loud before."

"No," he smiled, "we haven't, but isn't it the pink elephant in the living room? Our daughter is a straight A student, she is pretty, charming, has a great sense of humor and everyone loves her—teachers, other kids, babies, dogs, you name it. And I love her more than life itself. But, Mandy, am I wrong or is she like a thirty-year-old running around in a little kid's body?"

Amanda gradually pulled herself under control. She looked at Kurt with a mingled expression of shock and relief. "I know," she nodded, "I see it too. So what do we do about her… ah, eccentricities?"

"Do?" Kurt shrugged. "I don't think we do anything. She is who she is. So we have a unique child who enjoys a rare porterhouse."

"It isn't just the steak, Kurt, and you know it. It's the whole fascination with blood thing. There, I said it."

"Are you talking about when I cut myself? Can't you let that go already?" Kurt scowled.

Amanda's lips thinned to a severe line. "Kind of hard to forget the sight of your little angel sucking on a bloody tissue like it's a freaking Eskimo Pie, Kurt."

"It was years ago! She was only four years old. Little kids do weird things sometimes. I don't think that single incident has anything to do with the fact she requested an undercooked steak tonight. A fascination with blood, this does not make. I think you are over-exaggerating a little… and honestly, I think I know why," he said tentatively.

Amanda's lips disappeared even further. "Oh, don't you dare say I'm making too much of this. Have you forgotten when all the weirdness with her started?"

"Honey, Francis Barclay was a long time ago. It is him you're talking about, isn't it? She wouldn't even remember that. She was far too young for it to have any lasting impact."

The subject of Francis Barclay was rarely brought up between them anymore. His name an unutterable curse, carrying the same weight and connotation of the evil Voledermort in Harry Potter books.

"We don't know what he did to her during those hours she was with him," Amanda replied stubbornly.

Kurt slapped the table in frustration. "God! Not this again. The doc gave her a total checkup. She was completely unharmed. Weirdly enough, she even liked that… whatever he was. She liked him, Mandy! Called him her new friend, remember that? Besides, this is all ancient history. Every time she even bites a cuticle it's like Armageddon with you."

Amanda's voice took on an edge Kurt knew well. He mentally reprimanded himself for treating an already sensitive subject so callously. This was getting ready to turn into a nasty quarrel.

"Tell me, Einstein, have you ever heard of a child developing a taste for bloody Kleenex? One who wasn't kidnapped by a vampire, that is?" Amanda snapped.

Kurt recoiled like she'd just slapped him. He was both irritated and a little scared. He'd found a strong mental lockbox in which to place the events of that long-ago summer, and he intended to keep them there.

Francis Barclay did not harm Lorna, for which Kurt was damned grateful. Amanda was never convinced. Every now and then, if Lorna did something just a little left of center—like asking for her meat to be cooked rare for instance—Amanda regurgitated the whole nightmare and voiced every fear she could never let go of.

Kurt hated it. His wife would never let him forget Francis Barclay.

"Amanda, quit it. You are overreacting about absolutely nothing, and frankly, you're giving me the creeps. So our daughter is a little eccentric. Hell, she's just a kid. Now can we drop it?"

Amanda glared at her husband a moment longer, and then turned her back, returning her attention to the dishes.

While no more was said on the subject, later that evening, when Kurt reached out for her in their bed, she stiffened under his touch, and gently but firmly pushed his hand away.

Lorna Dale sat on her bed looking out the window at the deserted street. She had sensed her maker's presence drawing closer over the last week, and was now tingling with anticipation. There was so much to tell him. Today was the first time she'd fed from a grown-up. She knew she couldn't feed from her baby brother very much because he was so small, and her mother once noticed the marks. Thankfully she thought they were insect bites.

Lorna only fed from Nate when she was really, really hungry. Of course, attempting to feed from her parents was completely out of the question. She shuddered to think what would happen if they woke up in the middle of the night to find her biting them. There wasn't an acceptable explanation on earth for that scenario.

Lorna didn't require much blood yet, but as she grew her needs were changing.

On impulse, when she left rehearsal to use the restroom, and saw Mrs. Winter enter the lavatory before her, she decided to see if she could somehow subdue the woman and render her unconscious so she could feed. Lorna had discovered for a child she possessed eerie strength. Kelly's mother was quite short for an adult and of rather petite stature. Lorna would never have tried this with someone her father's size, but she thought it was worth the risk with Mrs. Winter.

Acting purely on instinct, she pulled the fire extinguisher from the wall beside the bathroom. She quickly slid in behind the woman just as the door was closing. She swung the extinguisher up with all her might and delivered a clean hit to the base of the woman's skull. Mrs. Winter crumpled gracelessly to the floor, like a puppet whose master has dropped its strings. Her purse tumbled from her hand, scattering the contents noisily across the tile floor.

Lorna fed quickly, satisfying the aching hunger for the moment. She stepped over the fallen woman and entered one of the stalls, needing to take care of the business she'd left play rehearsal for in the first place.

Being the very thoughtful child she was, Lorna kicked Mrs. Winter's car keys out from under the stall so she would be able to find them when she woke up. Lorna cleaned some smeared blood from her chin, washed her hands and smoothed her hair.

With a final baleful glance at the prone figure on the floor, Lorna quickly left the bathroom. She replaced the fire extinguisher on the wall and returned to rehearsal, drawing no undue attention.

It was after regular school hours. The only people in the building were those connected with drama rehearsal. The hallway was deserted—or so Lorna thought.

She believed no one would ever find out who knocked out Mrs. Winter. In fact, the woman didn't even know she'd been struck. She thought she had just fainted.

Lorna didn't realize it would be so easy to get blood from grown-ups. This was a pleasant surprise.

I don't have to feel bad either, she reasoned. *It wasn't like I killed anyone. Kelly's mom didn't even have to stay in the hospital or anything.*

There were a few apprehensive moments when the woman failed to come out of the bathroom and collect Kelly from rehearsal. Lorna feared maybe she actually had killed her. Also, it was scary getting blood right in broad daylight like that. If she wasn't so awfully hungry, she never would have done it. She just couldn't feed from Nate anymore. The last time he moaned in his sleep when she sucked from the back of his knee, and it kind of hurt her heart a little. Besides, Mom would figure it out. Her mom was really smart, and sometimes she watched her with this funny look in her eye, like she knew something wasn't quite right. She couldn't risk it anymore. Today Mom might think the marks were bug bites, tomorrow she could realize they were big sister bites. Lorna realized she must find another way to get the blood. You just never knew when the uncanny mom-vision was going to kick in.

Lorna did not develop a taste for blood until she was four years old—two full years after Francis Barclay accidentally turned her.

She recalled going to the park with her mom and playing on the slide. A little boy in front of her went down the slide on his stomach. He landed on the cement face first, lacerating his scalp and spilling a copious amount of blood. The rich smell emanating from the wound made Lorna almost delirious with desire. Her nostrils flared, her eyes dilated, and for the first time, her very small fangs popped free. She felt a rush of adrenaline and ran her tongue hungrily over the razor-sharp points.

Her mother was helping the wounded child's mom tend to him, and they carried the boy away from where he'd fallen. They did not see Lorna's uncontrollable reaction.

She knelt beside the puddle and sucked the boy's blood directly from the ground, as though she was wandering in the desert and found water from an oasis. Inhaling deeply and sighing with desire, she licked the cement clean, all the while enjoying the stinging sharpness of her newfound teeth.

Her eyes, already changing from the same cat-green as her mother's, were becoming a deep and intense aquamarine color. They darkened further, and then sprang aglow like fog lamps in a pitch-black field, as she drank of her first blood.

The whole thing happened in only a matter of seconds. Her fangs retracted automatically and the light in her eyes extinguished a moment later. By the time her mother turned back, Lorna was standing by the slide, looking like the poster child for innocence.

Not long after this incident, one or two days a week Lorna found she felt very hungry for blood. It was not unlike the hunger she felt for food around dinner time, but more intense. And if she couldn't have blood, she grew weak and found it hard to focus. Of course, at the age of four these things didn't really register. She only knew she liked it and felt good after drinking it, so she located it in the oddest places. On her father's discarded tissue from a blotted shaving cut, for instance. Her mother nearly had a fit when she saw her sucking on it. Lorna learned right away, her strange hunger was something she would have to keep from her parents.

She turned to insects in the backyard. Those weren't nearly as soul-satisfying as the blood she drank from the child's head wound, or even her father's cut. In fact, the insect blood tasted foul, and it was disturbing to kill the little creatures trundling around in the backyard. Still, instinct drove her.

Eventually, when Nate came along, she turned to her baby brother. She tried to keep those nocturnal visits to a minimum.

She discovered school provided an adequate source of human blood. She only needed to slip into the nurse's office and forage in the trash after someone fell and skinned their knee during recess.

Sometimes, and she wasn't proud of this, she would cause the fall with a well-timed foot stuck out to trip an unsuspecting schoolmate when no one was watching. If she was lucky, she could get enough blood at the site of the fall, so she wouldn't have to sneak into the health office later. The nurse didn't seem to have the uncanny mom-vision her mother did, but you could never be too careful.

Once in a great while, if the fates were really on her side, she could offer assistance to the wounded child herself, transferring some of the blood fresh from the wound right onto her hands. That was the best.

The opportunity for a recess snack didn't always present itself, however. It wasn't like she could keep tripping other kids on a regular basis without calling attention to herself or getting caught. Hence, Lorna was forced to turn to little Nate more often than she was comfortable with. She was always careful to bite him in the exact same place, so there was never more than a single twin mark from her fangs.

Since turning seven, she found her appetites weren't so easily satiated anymore. This was what emboldened her to attack Mrs. Winter in the bathroom. She knew it was a risky move, and there were about a million things that could have gone wrong. She prepared a cover story in the event she couldn't knock her out cold with the fire extinguisher after all. Lorna would say something about smelling smoke coming from the bathroom. Pretty lame, she supposed, but it would probably fly. She wasn't a child who ever got into trouble, so she didn't think anyone would believe she'd unlimbered the fire extinguisher for nefarious reasons.

In the end she managed to render Mrs. Winter unconscious and escape without being seen by her victim. Fortunately, the stupid cover-story she invented was never needed. The payoff was fresh blood and a renewed burst of energy she never felt before. And she had to admit, the attack was really kind of exhilarating. Who knew it would be so easy?

Besides, the woman was not seriously hurt. What happened was no worse than a skinned knee at recess when you looked at it rationally. It would make a visit to Nate's room tonight while her parents slept unnecessary. That was the important thing.

These were all matters she would discuss with her blood-father when he arrived. He was getting closer now. She could feel him, and his nearness excited and gladdened her heart.

CHAPTER 3

Enrico Vasquez had been a janitor at the Alder Lake Elementary School for nine years. He was a reasonable employee, who did a slightly better than average job, and was ignored by most of the faculty and students. He was in his mid-thirties, with a wife and two young children. Enrico led a quiet life. His wife was a hairdresser in a salon that catered to a largely Hispanic clientele, and their marriage could be classified as civil, if not terribly close anymore.

On the afternoon Lorna Dale made her daring attack on Rona Winter in the girl's bathroom, she'd not escaped unobserved after all. From just inside the janitor's closet, Enrico Vasquez watched with mild amusement as she wrenched the fire extinguisher from the wall. He thought it was pretty funny that a kid, a little girl no less, would commit vandalism on school grounds in broad daylight. He would have figured decorating the bathroom with fire extinguisher foam for more of a boy's prank. He planned to report the incident to the principal's office.

He would have stopped her on the spot, but caution got the better of him. She was a little white girl, and he, a Hispanic janitor.

The last thing he needed was some little white chica screaming rape and ruining his life. He resigned himself to cleaning up the mess from the extinguisher as soon as the kid was done with her folly, and then he would report it.

Enrico stood in a doorway across the hall waiting for the child to emerge from the bathroom. He was musing about how little it would cost the school to get glass covers for the extinguishers. Only a few minutes later, the child stepped out of the restroom, fire extinguisher in hand.

She shot a furtive glance up the deserted hallway and quickly replaced the fire extinguisher on the wall. With a final fleeting look around, she returned to the drama room.

Puzzled, Enrico walked tentatively to the restroom and gently pushed the door open a few inches. He took in the spotless walls and sinks. It didn't take long for him to realize the girl had not vandalized the bathroom after all.

Maybe she got scared and changed her mind, he thought. *Maybe she couldn't figure out how to work the extingui…* He caught sight of the woman on the floor and gasped, his ponderings cut short.

Enrico started toward the fallen woman, and then abruptly stopped. He looked around guiltily. Mopping sweat from his brow, he backed rapidly out of the restroom.

The *second* last thing he needed was some grown white chica screaming rape and ruining his life.

What the hell did that kid do? he wondered. *Did she kill that lady? What for? Did she rob her? Do little girls do things like that? Especially in school bathrooms in the middle of the afternoon? Maybe she just found her in there on the floor and was too scared to report it. She's not the only one.*

He knew the right thing to do would be to tell someone, and try to get aid for the lady. But he didn't. The world was the way it was, and no one would believe him if he told them he suspected a little girl had been the assailant.

The woman's purse was dumped out and the contents scattered everywhere. They would think he was looking for drugs or something. He would be blamed for the assault long before a cute little white girl would be, so he said nothing. If the woman was a parent of one of the children in drama rehearsal—and she certainly must be—they would notice her missing soon enough. He needed this job.

Checking his watch, Enrico saw rehearsal would be over in about fifteen minutes. They would find her soon.

He skulked away, trying his best to forget what he saw. He couldn't forget about the strange little girl, though. She never seemed to leave his mind. Eventually his curiosity about her turned into an obsession, which would one day get the better of him.

The play was a huge success. Lorna performed her lines flawlessly. She looked positively dazzling in her costume, a sparkling blue dress with gossamer fairy wings.

Her parents applauded wildly in the audience, while Kurt caught the whole performance on video. Nate was with a babysitter, so Kurt and Amanda took Lorna out for an Italian dinner to celebrate her success. As always, she was polite and courteous.

Her parents never knew that later that night, well after midnight, Lorna snuck out of bed when she woke up with a ravenous hunger. A hunger so strong, she didn't believe an ocean of blood could slake it. After arranging her pillows into the approximate size and shape of a seven-year-old girl slumbering peacefully beneath the covers, Lorna roamed the darkened streets of the city, desperately in search of satiation. It was finally found with a homeless drunk passed out on a park bench several blocks from their home.

He reeked of sweat and stale booze. Lorna thought his blood tasted funny. Mrs. Winter's was much better. This man's had a coppery aftertaste she didn't much care for. However, blood was blood, and she was very proud of herself because this time no one got hurt. In fact, the man barely stirred when she drove her fangs into his neck. His only reaction was a wheezy moan and a noxious belch. Lorna crinkled her nose in disgust as a stale cloud of whiskey fumes puffed directly into her face.

She fed as quickly as possible, then wiped her lips with the back of her hand. Backing away from the snoring figure, she said softly, "Thank you, sir."

Sprinting back home through the slumbering town, Lorna felt good. Quiet as a cat burglar, she climbed through the open window in the den. She replaced the screen and was asleep in her bed five minutes after brushing her teeth.

With a rosy hue to her cheeks, she awoke fresh and well rested for school the next day.

Emboldened by her success, Lorna took to these late-night outings more and more frequently. Feeding off of drunks in the park was like taking candy from a baby. While she disliked the coppery aftertaste their blood inevitably seemed to leave, it satisfied her bloodlust and made it so she wasn't hungry all the time. More important, she was no longer forced to find less appropriate and far more dangerous sources to quench her thirst. Like her baby brother or her classmates' mothers, for instance.

There were always one or two people passed out in the park, and they were awfully sound sleepers. It made for easy prey.

Until one night when everything changed. And what happened on that fateful night made Lorna very, very angry—and left one homeless person very, very dead.

CHAPTER 4

The previous summer, the newest addition to Alder Lake's commercial district was a cozy little antique store by the name of Curious Curios and Collectibles. The proprietress was Beatrice Sugars, a recent divorcee and Detroit transplant. She chose Alder Lake because she longed for the quiet of a small town; a place where her shop didn't need bars on the windows, and her clerks weren't held up at gunpoint every other weekend. Alder Lake was also geographically desirable because it met the criteria of being just far enough away from her ex-husband, Royce. Beatrice Sugars deemed anything over two-thousand miles from Michigan as *just far enough.*

Unfortunately, she found out almost immediately that Alder Lake was not the idyllic little burg she envisioned. Within days of opening the store for business, she was awakened at two o'clock in the morning by a phone call from the local police. Her shop's first burglary.

The culprits absconded with only a single eighteenth century pocket watch from a display cabinet, before they hastily fled the blaring alarm. They were just young, foolish kids who were caught the following week when they tried to pawn the watch. More upsetting to Beatrice was the damage to her store left in their wake. The repairs would cost more than the value of the single piece they managed to run off with.

The front window was shattered to gain entry into the store, and three glass display cabinets that dominated the center of the shop were also destroyed. There was broken glass everywhere. The dozens of items neatly laid out in the cabinets were now scattered in total disarray amid the jagged shards. Cleanup was not going to be easy.

It was a disheartening welcome to the town she was now forced to call home. Beatrice bought a house and signed a five-year lease for her shop space. The ink was barely dry on either one. Her savings account was completely drained—not only from the move, but the nasty divorce preceding it. Like it or not, she was staying in Alder Lake. *Home sweet home*, she thought bitterly.

Things improved a little the day following the break-in, when Amanda Dale came to call. The shop was closed while Beatrice filed police reports and insurance papers, and tried to schedule the necessary repairs.

It was mid-afternoon on a sweltering July day. Beatrice was ill-tempered and very distraught; no one from Alder Lake's finest had shown up to write the official police report, despite repeated promises they would send someone out. She needed to give the report to the insurance company or she couldn't get all the broken glass fixed.

Beatrice, sweating in a tank top and shorts, was perched precariously on a stepladder. She was nailing up boards to cover the broken front window, when the first friendly voice she'd heard since moving into town broke through her dark reverie.

"Welcome to Alder Lake! I can see the teenage welcome committee beat me here for the official greeting. Guess I can put away my scissors now. Looks like I missed the ribbon-cutting ceremony. Did you get your picture taken with the mayor?"

Beatrice turned around and wiped a sweaty lock of hair from her brow. The woman belonging to that cheerful voice was a pretty redhead, with a gift basket dangling from one arm.

Extending her hand, the woman said, "Hi, I'm Amanda Dale, and I come bearing gifts." She raised the arm with the basket, wagging it back and forth. "Actually, I come bearing wine, and by the looks of things you could probably use some."

Beatrice felt an answering smile on her own lips as she reached down and shook Amanda Dale's hand.

"Beatrice Sugars, nice to meet you. My friends call me Bebe, but I don't have any in town yet."

Amanda surveyed the broken window with sympathetic eyes, and looked speculatively at the woman before her. She was a lovely African-American lady with flawless caramel skin, small elfin features, and luminous light-brown eyes.

"Well, Bebe, you should hire someone to help you get those boards up, you shouldn't be doing that all by yourself. It's too hot to be doing a man's work today."

This earned her a bitter grimace from the other woman. "I called the only handyman listed in your teeny tiny Yellow Pages. He said he can't make it 'til next Tuesday. Hell, I can't even get the cops to come out and take a report so I can give it to the insurance company."

She felt unwelcome tears sting her eyes and swiped at them angrily with the back of her hand. "Sorry, Ms. Dale, I don't mean to pull out the damsel in distress routine. And I'm way too tired to try and play the race card, but clearly I don't rank very high on anyone's priority list in town." Bebe sighed heavily, looking forlornly at the broken window.

"It's that bad?" Amanda asked.

"The inside looks like Armageddon, and I see no one on the horizon with a broom to help me clean up this mess."

Amanda reached up and took Bebe's hand to help her off the stepladder. She nodded toward the shop. "Do you have a phone in there yet, sweetie?"

"I do."

"May I use it?" Amanda handed her the gift basket, adding, "Oh, and see if you can find a pair of wine glasses somewhere in this calamity."

Bebe opened the door and ushered Amanda to the telephone. She surveyed the rubble and hunted for a couple of drinking glasses while Amanda made calls.

Thirty minutes later, both women sat companionably in folding chairs, sipping wine. They watched as two men set to work putting up boards on the broken front window.

Ten minutes later, Detective Medwyn Blazer, Alder Lake's newest violent crime detective, was leaning on the counter and filling out a police report.

Amanda greeted him affectionately when he entered the shop. "Hey, Blaze! Boy are we happy to see you. Miss Sugars and I were just saying we needed a hero right about now."

The detective was the first black man Bebe had seen in Alder Lake besides the mailman. He and the pretty Ms. Sugars appraised one another with surreptitious glances and stolen peeks above the insurance form.

Too bad I had to meet her this way, Blaze thought.

Of course, this was just the kind of violent crime he moved to Alder Lake to battle. Broken glass he was fine with, broken people he'd seen enough of.

While Bebe talked to the detective, Amanda quietly let herself out of the shop. She returned a short time later holding a broom in one hand and a dustpan in the other.

"How about now?" Amanda asked. "See anyone on the horizon with a broom?"

The two women worked side by side, sweeping up broken glass, and carefully removing all the collectibles from the smashed cabinets. By late afternoon they had restored order to the devastated shop. Even the nice detective stuck around for an hour after finishing the report and helped set things to right.

Amanda had been impressed with Blaze since he first moved to town, though they didn't get to know each other until some time later.

They'd found themselves seated side by side at a banquet table at the annual officers' ball a couple of years back. Blaze confided that he left Los Angeles because he started to think all humanity fell into only two categories: crazy or mean. He told Amanda that Alder Lake had restored his faith in mankind.

"Yes," Amanda remembered telling him, "we do have this effect on the weary traveler."

She also remembered thinking, *What a hottie! Whoa, if I were single…* She allowed the thought to evaporate quickly, casting a wistful glance at her husband. From then on, she'd kept a tight rein on any wandering lustful thoughts when she was around the handsome detective. Her husband may have had little restraint when it came to extramarital dalliances, but Amanda was a woman of strong resolve.

Had she been able to read minds, she would have known Detective Blazer thought Amanda Dale was just about the sexiest woman he'd seen in Alder Lake, and were she not married to the man seated directly to her left, he would have been pursuing her attentions with great fervor. But Mama Blazer taught her son at a very young age that prospecting in another man's gold mine—especially one who carried a gun—was a good way to get yourself injured, or worse.

Blaze's mama schooled him on many things in his formative years, but the lesson he remembered best was not to sow his seed in another man's garden. It was advice he always heeded, no matter how pretty the flower. In the case of Kurt Dale's wife, the flower was quite tempting indeed. That's why he couldn't understand Kurt's reputed wanderlust. Amanda not only bore him two beautiful kids, she also stood by his side through circumstances which gave her every justifiable reason to leave, and bleed him dry in a divorce settlement.

She'd been publicly humiliated when he was accused of killing his mistress. Even then she never left. Blaze figured part of it was the kids; Kurt was clearly a very devoted father. His office gave testament to that devotion with numerous photos of his children, plus a few of his wife thrown in for good measure.

While the kids were a compelling motivation to keep the family together, Blaze didn't think they were the entire reason why Amanda never packed her bags.

He appreciated how Amanda helped Bebe in the wake of the vandals looting her shop. She'd given a newcomer a helping hand, while most everyone else in town still treated Bebe like an outsider. Having moved to Alder Lake not so long ago, Blaze knew how far a gesture like that went.

Bebe wasn't the only newcomer Amanda ever made feel welcome. When Blaze joined the department and bought his house, Amanda sent over a chocolate cake with a really nice note welcoming him to Alder Lake. In Blaze's humble opinion, the lady was good people. Given the ration of shit she'd taken from her husband without ever walking out on him, he thought she was probably a pretty good wife too. Not the kind who deserved to be cheated on.

Of course, Blaze realized no one could speculate what went on behind closed doors in any marriage. There were two sides to every story. He supposed it was never just one spouse to blame. However, in his heart, Blaze thought Amanda deserved better. He never really warmed to Kurt. He didn't know if the vague dislike he felt had more to do with the guy's personality, or if it was all the rumors of infidelity travelling the town's busy grapevine.

Maybe Blaze just wasn't the cheating kind, so he didn't care for Kurt on general principle. His mama raised him better than that. He was pretty old-school when it came to relationships, especially the one involving the mother of your children. That one was positively sacred.

Of course, it was easy to climb up on such a high horse, when you had neither child nor wife waiting for you at the end of the day, and the only one you returned home to was the cat. He kept his lofty ideas on the sanctity of the marital union to himself.

Wisely, Blaze never mentioned his feelings about Amanda Dale to anyone. He kept them locked away in his mind where they couldn't get him into trouble. He kept his feelings about Kurt in much the same place.

Over the last couple of years Blaze became a regular fixture at the Dales' house for barbeques or game nights, when there were larger crowds and most of the officers turned out.

Amanda knew Blaze wasn't exactly crazy about Kurt. Not because he'd ever said anything, it was just woman's intuition. The two men were cordial enough to work together and that was all they needed to be.

Amanda's relationship with Blaze was far warmer and friendlier than her husband's. She appreciated how Blaze always asked after little Nate when he came over. He took the time to talk with Lorna as well—and not in that patronizing way people without children often do. He genuinely seemed interested in what she had to say.

Some adults seemed to look right through kids; Blaze was not that way. He would hunker down so he could talk to Lorna at eye level, and it was not uncommon to see her daughter chatting animatedly with the detective at these gatherings. Amanda thought he would make a great father some day.

Amanda oohed and aahed over much of the vintage jewelry Bebe offered for sale in the shop. As they were finishing straightening up, she asked Bebe if she could purchase a rhinestone brooch she'd been eyeing all afternoon.

Bebe insisted she would take no money for the piece and folded it into her new friend's hand.

"It's the least I can do after you rescued me. I'll throw in dinner too, if you don't have a family waiting on you." She looked up hopefully.

Amanda smiled. "I do, but they can fend for themselves tonight. Just let me call my husband and let him know."

Later, seated in a corner booth at La Travisa, the same restaurant they had taken Lorna to the night of her play, and unarguably the best Italian restaurant in Alder Lake, the two women were sharing a bottle of wine. They chatted while waiting for their dinner to arrive, surrounded by the rich aroma of baking bread and simmering Italian spices.

Neither woman knew it yet, but this restaurant would become the site of many shared meals and good bottles of wine between them, amid those same wonderful scents, and the homey checked tablecloths and candles decorating the small bistro.

Bebe laughed when Amanda told her she was married to a local cop. "Well, no wonder they came running when you called," she remarked dryly. "I thought it was just 'cause you were prettier than me."

"Naw, they just know better than to piss me off. My husband has told them how scary I can be when I'm crossed," Amanda joked.

Amanda shared few details of her marriage with her new friend. She did, however, admit the fifteen years she and Kurt had been married were not all happy ones. She spared the other woman the bitter details of his extramarital activities, though the implication was clear: Kurt was a less than ideal spouse.

"I can relate," Bebe said, her eyes downcast. "I moved damn near across the country to get away from my ex-husband. I'm a board certified expert when it comes to being married to an asshole."

Amanda smiled. "You know, I think I'm gonna like you."

When the subject came up about Bebe looking for some good part-time help, Amanda impulsively said she would like to apply for the job. She really liked this woman, and she believed it might be good for her to have something to do away from home one or two afternoons a week. She loved her children, but was a bit starved for some adult companionship. Bebe was delighted and hired her on the spot.

Over the next few months, as the long, hot summer gave way to fall, the two women became close friends. Amanda loved being around all the interesting antiques and unusual finds in the shop. She worked two weekdays and every Sunday afternoon. After they closed the shop on Sundays, the two women would have a drink or a bite to eat. It was a routine they both grew fond of very quickly.

As the women cemented their friendship, Amanda came to realize how lonely Bebe was. Her children were grown and far away. There had been no one special in her life since the divorce. In fact, she admitted she hadn't even been on a date since leaving

Detroit. The night Bebe made this announcement they were halfway through a bottle of Chianti.

"I haven't seen the working parts of a man in over a year," she declared.

This got Amanda thinking about the charming, and very single, Detective Medwyn Blazer. She saw the way Bebe looked at him when he took the police report after the break-in.

"Well… what about Detective Blazer? He's good looking, and such a nice guy. What do you think of him?" Amanda prodded.

Bebe was quiet for a few seconds as she contemplated the question. She took a small sip of wine. "What do I think?" She batted her eyes. "Why, I think I'd like to climb him like a tree."

The musical tinkle of their laughter carried out into the night air from the open door of the restaurant.

CHAPTER 5

Liking Bebe Sugars more and more, Amanda decided to do a little matchmaking. She thought Detective Blazer might be just what her new friend needed. The weather was still holding, with the full chill of autumn still a few weeks away. Weekend barbeques at the Dale residence were not uncommon.

The two women had become fast friends. Amanda was grateful to have a lady friend in her life again. Since the death of Ellen Wyatt five years earlier, there was no one she could confide in. Bebe filled that void very nicely.

Bebe felt comfortable enough to share much of her past with Amanda, including the nasty details of her divorce. She spoke about years of emotional abuse endured before finally finding the courage to leave. Bebe married Royce right out of high school. The union produced two great kids, both now grown. Bebe said they made all the hell she had gone through worth it. One was a law student at Purdue, the other a successful software developer in Silicon Valley. Her son, the software developer, was married and expecting his first child. Bebe laughed about being the youngest woman in North America ever to be called Granny. Amanda could tell she was thrilled at the prospect of becoming a grandparent.

Bebe's first child was born right before her eighteenth birthday. The second followed only a year later. By most standards, she was awfully young to be a grandmother. Fortunately, Bebe adored her daughter-in-law, who called often with updates about the pregnancy. Her son was over the moon about becoming a father.

Amanda had been less forthcoming about her relationship with Kurt. While she admitted to weathering some horrible marital storms, she left out the gory details. Not only did she not like to think about the past—Kurt's former infidelities only served in making her bitter—she also didn't want Bebe to have a low opinion of her husband.

Amanda had filed Kurt's last mistress on a high interior shelf. All the events surrounding that horrid dark time in her life shared space on that shelf with Tina Hilliard. To bring it out now into the harsh light of day, after all the years it remained safely hidden, could only lead to trouble. Besides, if she started talking about Tina Hilliard, what was to stop her from telling the whole story—Francis Barclay included. She wasn't going to put herself in a position where she was even tempted to open that dank vault up for inspection. Amanda liked Bebe—no, actually she adored her—and if her friend learned of the events that took place five years ago, she might just decide her new BFF was crazy.

Forever burned into Amanda's memory was the look on Kurt's face when she was deep in the clutches of the worst of her postpartum depression after Lorna's birth. She'd seen the same horrified expression on the faces of John and Ellen Wyatt. She could not bear to see it on this lovely woman's sweet face ever. Amanda was never going to be that crazy lady again.

When Amanda told Kurt she wanted to have a barbeque the following weekend and invite some people over, she did not mention her romantic motives. Sometimes Kurt didn't approve of what he deemed her *over-involvement* in the affairs of the community. Besides, she figured, this is a girl thing. He wouldn't understand.

"Kurt," Amanda said, "I'd really love to have a barbeque next weekend. Well, more of a barbeque party. We could invite our friends, and it might be nice to ask Carolyn Devonshire and her husband to come. I only met her once at the department Christmas party last year, and you two have worked closely for so long now. I think it would be a nice gesture."

"No," Kurt hastily declined. "Umm, I mean no to inviting Carolyn. I see enough of that woman during the week. I don't need her coming to the house on my days off." He immediately noticed his wife's eyes flash at his fast speech and quick excuse. "The barbecue sounds great though," he threw in to cover himself.

Amanda's eyes narrowed. They lingered on Kurt's face just a beat too long. "Good," she replied harshly and walked away.

Kurt felt a cold stone roll against his heart when he heard the stinging sharpness in her voice. He knew right then the jig was up. His wife was only a few short breaths from discovering his latest infidelity, and he resolved to end it immediately. Before the flicker of mistrust he saw in Amanda's level gaze could ever take hold in her mind. There was still time to extract himself from Carolyn Devonshire before that tiny grain of suspicion in his wife's eyes could grow. He was determined to take care of this little problem as soon as possible.

Kurt found his mind wandering to John Wyatt again. What would John say about his latest indiscretion? Who was he kidding? John, even if he were still here, would never be his confidante again. Not after the events of five years ago. Not after John's wife drugged

Amanda, kidnapped Lorna, and murdered Richie Welch, Alder Lake's own bad boy.

Kurt helped him cover it up. Ellen went mad after Francis Barclay attacked her. Her erratic, and ultimately fatal actions, had been the real death of the friendship between them. Francis Barclay was just a very unpleasant side-effect.

It was a sign of Kurt's desperation when his old friend John was who came to mind for advice in his current circumstances. It was also a good indication that after fifteen years of marriage, two children, and one dead mistress, maybe it was finally time to grow up.

Whatever thrill Kurt once felt from these affairs, the allure never lasted long anymore. The cold fact of how dangerous and stupid these liaisons were weighed heavily on his mind. He really did love Amanda. They had a good marriage and two fantastic kids. If he lost his family because of a senseless fling, he wouldn't be able to live with himself. His wife was a smart woman—too smart, really. And she knew Kurt almost better than he knew himself. He could feel the noose tightening.

So why, Kurt wondered, did trouble always find him in the form of a woman? Why was that damned old pattern so hard to break? He shared a healthy sex life with his wife, so why could he never resist temptation? He could no longer fall back on Amanda's postpartum depression as his scapegoat. That ship had long since sailed.

He supposed he liked the attention and feeling desirable. He loved the rush he got from something new and shiny—and totally forbidden. He wondered why he could never stop at some harmless flirtation. He would have the same attention and none of the risk. He always had to take things too far. Always had to be burned by the same tired old flame.

Kurt marveled that the only thing needed to wake him up was one slightly longer than normal glance from his wife, and a single word spoken a bit too caustically. He resolved this time not to get caught, quite literally, with his pants down. He was bailing out while there was still time. Before he broke his wife's final straw and she turned into an episode of *Snapped*, a show about wives who went psycho and killed their husbands.

This time he wouldn't need Francis Barclay to take out his mistress, he had a feeling Amanda would do it right after she murdered him. Who could blame her? Kurt was aware she'd forgiven his indiscretions far more times than he deserved already. He was a dumbass, he figured, but not a big enough one not to recognize time had just grown painfully short for a Carolyn Devonshire exit strategy.

Sundays were Kurt's days to watch the kids. His wife spent four hours every Sunday working at the antique shop that opened downtown earlier this year. After work, she and Bebe Sugars would usually stop for drinks or dinner somewhere.

He kissed Amanda goodbye and watched her back out of the driveway before checking on the children.

Lorna was in the backyard taking advantage of the unseasonably warm weather. She and a friend were swimming in the pool. Nate was down for a nap. This was the perfect time.

Kurt pulled his cell phone from the charger in the kitchen and texted Carolyn. The text was short: *Call me ASAP.*

He stood at the window watching the two girls in the pool and waiting for the phone to ring. A few moments later, it did.

"Hey, handsome, why the weekend call? Don't you play Mr. Mom on Sundays? Besides, you know I can't possibly meet for a rendezvous with Bill home."

"That's not why I needed to talk to you. Listen, Carolyn, I hate to do this on the phone, I really do, but we have to stop seeing each other."

He was met with stunned silence. "Carolyn, did you hear me?"

Her voice took on the same edge he heard in every woman's voice he ever cheated on his wife with when he tried to end the relationship. He dubbed it "The Universal Mistress Whine." It was the number one leading cause of the Mistress Migraine.

She barked a humorless laugh. "Yeah, I heard you."

"Well… aren't you going to say something?" Kurt closed his eyes against the pregnant silence on the phone.

"We aren't going to talk about this with my husband outside the back door mowing the grass. What's wrong with you, Kurt? Next time you want to have this particular conversation, you can fucking man-up and wait to do it to my face, you prick."

Kurt turned away from the innocent children splashing in the pool. He couldn't bear to have this confrontation while he watched his daughter play.

He walked further into the kitchen, away from the window, and sat down heavily at the kitchen table.

Damn, why didn't I send an email or a text message? he thought miserably. *Could have avoided all this unpleasantness by breaking up with a little help from modern technology.*

"Carolyn, please don't make this harder than it already is. We both knew this day would come. We are both married, and I have a family."

"Oh, right, now all of a sudden you're the devoted family man? What a crock of shit."

Kurt winced like he'd been struck. "Jeez, Carolyn, don't be like this. Please try and understand. We still have to work together. This doesn't need to turn ugly."

"Why is this happening now? Is it someone else? That new blonde twenty-something in the court clerk's office, maybe? If you had any stones you'd tell me the truth."

Kurt sighed. "No. Of course not. It's nothing like that. It's my wife. She's not stupid. She… I don't know. She just isn't an idiot, that's all," he finished lamely.

Carolyn continued to berate him. The more he tried to explain, the angrier she was becoming. The altercation felt like it had lasted a thousand years, and still there was no end in sight. He wondered how long her husband could possibly stay outside mowing their lawn. What did they have? The fuckin' back-forty out there?

Outside, Lorna and her friend were thirsty. She wasn't allowed to drink soda without permission, so she went in search of her dad to ask if they could take a couple of Pepsis from the fridge.

She followed the sound of his raised voice to the partially open kitchen window. He was on the phone, and judging by his tone, clearly not happy.

She extended her hand to open the door and then hesitated. If he was mad at somebody, he might not let her have a soda. Better to wait until he calmed down and was in a better mood before she asked.

Lorna stood outside the open window and listened to her father's side of the heated conversation. He was talking to someone named Carolyn. She'd heard the name before. It was some lady he worked with. Why was she upsetting her daddy like this?

Lorna didn't understand what they were talking about, but she knew that tone of voice, and Daddy only sounded like that when he was really unhappy. Lorna was very protective of her father. She didn't like it when anyone upset him. She didn't like it at all.

CHAPTER 6

At least thirty people spilled from the Dales' kitchen into the backyard. Amanda and one of the other officer's wives were laughing at a rather off-color joke someone had just told.

Kurt was manning the barbeque, wearing a chef's apron emblazoned with the words: Kiss the Cook. He flipped burgers and began piling them on a platter.

His daughter appeared at his side and handed him a fresh can of beer. "From Mommy," she said.

He bent down and kissed her cheek. "Tell Mommy thank you, sweetie." He popped the can open and handed his daughter the platter of burgers to carry back to the kitchen.

Medwyn Blazer walked in. He headed toward the kitchen, where Amanda and a few other wives were crowded around the kitchen island.

He nodded his thanks when Amanda handed him a can of beer, and popped some potato chips into his mouth. He waved out the back door to some fellow officers and excused himself to join them in the yard.

Amanda looked anxiously toward the front door. *Where is Bebe?* she wondered.

The party was in full swing when she excused herself. She plucked Nate from one of the other women's arms to take him upstairs for a diaper change. She dialed Curious Curios and Collectibles from the extension by their bed. Bebe answered on the third ring.

"Where are you?" Amanda asked excitedly. "Detective McHottie is downstairs with no one to play with."

"I'm waiting for that idiot teenager I hired last week to relieve me so I can come over."

"Bebe, I am ordering you to close the shop. I know you like to stay open later on Saturdays, but there is a boy-toy with all the necessary working parts in my backyard, along with twenty or thirty other close personal friends, who I invited just so you two kids can *accidentally* run into each other. Now get your ass down here. You hear me?"

Bebe laughed. "Yes, ma'am. Leaving now."

Twenty minutes later Bebe and Blaze were sitting side by side in lawn chairs, grinning at each other like school kids.

Watching from the kitchen window, Amanda thought, *Damn, I'm good! My work here is done.*

The breakup did not go exactly as Kurt had planned. Of course, they never did. Carolyn convinced him to meet her at the hotel the following week so they could "talk about this like adults." Against his better judgment Kurt went.

Little talking occurred that afternoon, because when Kurt entered the hotel room Carolyn flung herself at him like a rabid junkyard dog.

An hour or so later, Kurt lay gasping and sweating beside her on the bedspread.

Carolyn purred in his ear, "Still wanna break up, hon?"

Kurt barked a humorless laugh. "No, Car. We're good." The Mistress Migraine was back, and caustic acid began churning in his stomach.

He had a disquieting moment of bitter déjà vu. He saw with vivid clarity the ghost of his former girlfriend, Tina Hilliard. Even the scent of Tina's perfume seemed to linger in the air before him.

The events of this afternoon had been like running a videotape of the first time he tried to break things off with Tina all those years ago. The situations were identical.

Kurt hoped with all his heart when he and Carolyn did finally end things, it wouldn't be under equally horrible circumstances.

An involuntary shudder raked his body as he began getting dressed. From the moment he entered the hotel room and Carolyn jumped on him, he felt a suffocating premonition of doom.

Kurt tried very hard to dismiss the overwhelming foreboding that had wrapped him in its rigid embrace. He rationalized the cause, telling himself the feelings were brought on by nothing more than the eerie similarities the two events shared.

It must have stirred up an old and ancient memory, like dust in an attic, of poor Tina and the sad fate which had befallen her. No amount of justifying could unwrap that miserable cloying feeling from his heart. It clung to him like a wet sheet for the rest of the day.

Bebe and Blaze went on their first official date the same day Kurt rendezvoused with Carolyn at the hotel intending to end their relationship. The restaurant Blaze selected was, in fact, right across the street from that very inn.

They were seated at a table by the window and enjoyed a lovely meal. They discussed many things over dinner, not the least of which was their age difference—Bebe was nine years older than the detective. She swore she would not tolerate being called a "cougar" should their relationship flourish.

On that amusing note, they walked out of the restaurant. Blaze took his date's hand to usher her across the street to where the car was parked.

Bebe abruptly let go of his hand and cried, "That bastard!"

Blaze started to ask what was wrong, and then saw for himself. "Oh, you have to be kidding me," he groaned. "Just what the hell is he doing with her?"

"If you have dolls, I can show you," Bebe spat with pure venom.

They watched with grim horror as Kurt Dale, and a woman who was not his wife, emerged from the hotel across the street.

The lady was smiling. She looked nearly triumphant. Her joyful countenance was in direct conflict with the pained expression on Kurt's face. He looked rather morose. They were arm in arm, the woman clinging to Kurt's side.

The pair walked to a white Lexus sedan, and Kurt opened the driver side door for the woman.

They embraced for a moment, before she peeled herself from Kurt's arms and slid smoothly behind the wheel.

Folding her shapely legs into the car, she reached up briefly to stroke Kurt's face. He walked to the curb and watched her drive away.

Bebe and Blaze observed Kurt's shoulders sag as he turned and walked up the block to his own vehicle.

They stood in horrified silence watching these events play out. They looked at each other with equally troubled expressions when Kurt drove away.

Bebe spoke first. “Please tell me we did not just see that.”

“Can’t put the toothpaste back in the tube, darlin’.”

Bebe uttered only one word: “Shit.”

“Yes,” Blaze nodded, “that just about covers it.”

“You don’t seem surprised.”

“It’s a small town. You hear things. I don’t think this is his first rodeo. Do you know who the blonde is he’s apparently shagging?” The disgust was evident in Blaze’s voice.

“Not a clue.” Bebe shook her head.

“She’s the Deputy District Attorney for Alder Lake. The *married* deputy DA.”

Bebe replied again, “Shit.”

CHAPTER 7

The real trouble started when Posy McManus found herself kicked out of the Westpark Mission for stealing. She was forced to find shelter for the night in the park. It was just a few dollars and an old threadbare sweater, but she had been warned before by the minister who ran the shelter.

"*Dammit, Reverund,*" Posy muttered, shifting uncomfortably on the bench she'd managed to squeeze her bulk onto. She clutched her bottle of Blue Nun tighter to her chest and began to doze off.

Some indeterminate amount of time later, Posy was awakened from troubled sleep by a stinging sensation on the inside of her left arm.

A child of the streets, Posy was no stranger to protecting herself. Especially if she thought someone was trying to steal her Blue Nun.

With a squawk of rage, she reached out blindly and smacked. Her hand connected with something or *someone* hard enough to send them sailing backward. She didn't know what she hit because it was awfully dark and she couldn't see very well.

It turned out to not only be a someone, but a little someone, judging by the yelp Posy heard as her assailant clattered to the ground a few feet away.

Posy scrambled off the bench and stood in a mock karate stance, waving her hands before her. She was disoriented, squinting into the gloom.

"Who the fuck is there?" she growled into the shadows.

A child's voice, dripping with the purest rage Posy ever heard, responded, "You hit me! You knocked me down! You can't do that, I'm just a little girl and my daddy is a policeman."

The pure menace of the child's voice, coupled with the absurdity of the words spoken, left Posy completely rattled. She had encountered many things in her years on the streets, but this experience was new. A little kid with the voice of Satan, saying things which made no sense whatsoever.

"I'm s… s… sorry," Posy stammered. "What do you want?"

"I want to finish. I was not done yet," the weird kid replied in that chilling voice.

"F… finish w… w… what?"

"Drinking. I want to finish drinking you." With eerie speed, the child closed the gap between them.

Posy felt the child's warm breath against her neck. She gasped, jerking her head back to look down into a pair of the most murderous and piercing blue eyes she had ever seen. They glowed in the dark night like two perfect orbs of radiant horror.

The bottle of wine slipped from Posy's grasp. It landed with a clatter on the bench. She tried to back away from this pint-sized nightmare, but the bench was right behind her. Posy smacked into it and landed heavily on her backside.

The child leapt at her with malignant purpose, her mouth a yawning chasm of doom. Posy screamed and kicked out with both legs. They connected squarely with the child's hip, and once again the girl was thrown backward.

Posy tried to scramble up and over the bench to run, but the child moved with the oily speed of a serpent. She uttered a furious growl and launched herself on top of the woman.

They tumbled to the ground together in an untidy heap behind the bench. With strength Lorna did not know she possessed, she pinned the woman down and drove her fangs into the front of her neck.

Still the woman struggled, so Lorna bit harder. She shook her head back and forth like a dog with a rope toy. Finally, a fountain of hot blood spurted into Lorna's face. She drank greedily from the jetting stream.

Moments later, with the woman lying motionless beneath her, Lorna rose from the ground and stood unsteadily on her feet. She looked down into the glazed eyes of the woman she had just fed from and gasped.

"Lady, hey lady, wake up." A wave of terror washed over her as she shook the woman's limp arm.

Oh no, she thought dreamily, *I think I killed this one.*

"Why did you fight me?" Lorna asked the prone figure on the ground. "Why didn't you just let me drink? I didn't want to hurt you. It was an accident… I… I was just hungry. Honest, I was just hungry. I didn't want to do this. You made me!"

Lorna backed slowly away from those staring, lifeless eyes and raced out of the park towards home.

Dawn was breaking as Lorna climbed through the window in the den. When she reached the downstairs bathroom, she was horrified to see she was drenched in blood. Her hair was stuck to her face in red, sticky streaks, her clothing spattered and clinging to her small frame.

In that strangely adult voice she could adopt, she looked down at herself and muttered, "Dang it, I loved this blouse." She shrugged the blood-soaked shirt over her head.

Looking angrily at the ruined blouse, she thought, *Stupid lady. Wrecked my top AND made me hurt her.* A voice in her head corrected, *No… not hurt. Killed. You killed this one.*

"ACCIDENTALLY," she cried into the slumbering house, and then quickly clapped a hand over her mouth.

Lorna tiptoed upstairs and opened her parents' bedroom door a crack. She peeked at the two sleeping forms on the bed and slowly shut the door.

She walked down the hall to her bathroom and stripped out of the rest of her soiled clothing.

She showered and washed her hair. She felt a little sick when she brushed her teeth and saw her spit tinged faintly red.

The stained clothing, she placed in a plastic garbage bag. She toyed with the idea of putting the ruined clothing in between her mattress and box spring, but what if her mother changed the sheets before she could dispose of it? She started to drag her small desk chair over to the closet, intending to throw the bag to the back of the top shelf. She changed her mind abruptly, realizing she was not tall enough to retrieve it, even standing on the chair.

Finally, after careful consideration, Lorna descended the stairs and entered the garage through the door in the kitchen.

She dug some old clothes out of a box her mother intended to drop off at the Goodwill. She put the bag with the soiled clothes at the bottom of the box and covered it up with the clothing intended for donation. She knew she would have to dispose of the bag before her mom got around to dropping the box of clothes off, but figured there was time. The box had been sitting out here for over three weeks already. Apparently her mother was in no hurry to run that errand.

After her night's activities, Lorna thought she would be tired, but strangely she was quite energized. Instead of going to sleep, she spent the next hour working on adding beads to a purse she and her mom were making from a craft kit.

Finally, with an untroubled heart, Lorna fell soundly asleep until she needed to get ready for school.

While Lorna was killing Posy McManus in the park, Francis Barclay woke with a start in a barn. He was still over sixty miles outside of Alder Lake.

"Oh no," he sighed miserably, "she has killed."

The horse in the stall next to him sensed his disquiet. She neighed softly.

Francis lay awake with a troubled heart, wondering if his child would be caught and put to death like his family. He was too late to avoid this tragedy. All he could do now was to remove Lorna from Alder Lake before they found and executed her. Hopefully he could take her before anyone found out what she had done. He would not let them kill his progeny.

Where do I take her? he wondered. He would only have a limited time back on this earth before he would, hopefully, return to his permanent slumber. Whose care should Lorna be left in once she was taken out of her parental home?

The obvious answer was another vampire. One who was still alive, unlike him. *Yes,* he decided. *I will find her a suitable place to live with someone of our kind. It's not safe for her in Alder Lake anymore.*

He sat up in the gloom and put his fingers to his mouth. He whistled once, and called, "Samantha! Here, dog." He patted his leg.

A beautiful golden light appeared in the dark and gradually took shape. It became a lovely Golden Retriever with glowing amber eyes. She shimmered in the darkness before solidifying. Samantha wagged her tail and ran anxiously to her master.

"Samantha, my faithful pet, you must help me find someone." He reached out to pat the dog's head and rub between her ears.

The horse neighed again, this time louder. Francis peeked between the barn's wooden slats, concerned the horse's agitated sounds might have awakened someone. He saw light in an upstairs window.

The farmer in the house a few yards away was unsure what had intruded upon his dreams. He went to the window and pulled aside the curtain to peer out into the darkness. When he saw the golden radiance spilling from beneath the barn door, he hastily pulled the drape shut and extinguished the light. He returned to bed, convinced he was still dreaming.

The dog looked thoughtfully at her master, as if to say, *I'm listening. What do you need?*

"You must find a family," Francis told her. "A vampire family for the child, Lorna."

The dog barked one soft *woof.* She understood.

"You must find them and bring them to us once I have acquired the girl."

The dog licked her master's face. She barked once more, *Woof, I'm on it.*

Samantha began to shimmer and grow opaque. She winked out of sight, leaving only a fading golden outline in her wake. The horse turned and faced the wall. She thought perhaps she was dreaming too.

"I'm coming, child," Francis Barclay whispered as he fell back into fitful sleep.

CHAPTER 8

Detective Medwyn Blazer entered the police precinct with a troubled heart. The night before, he and Bebe sat on her couch drinking tea until late into the night. They were trying to decide what to do about the scene they stumbled upon after their first date.

There really was no answer. Neither wanted to be responsible for breaking up a family with small children, yet both cared a great deal for Amanda Dale.

Reaching no conclusions, they agreed to meet again the following night to discuss it some more. They also wanted to see one another again. Kurt Dale's infidelity was as a good a reason as any to spend time together.

Compounding Blaze's angst, the moment he arrived at work Captain Fitzgerald grabbed his arm and began herding him back toward the door. "We have a homicide in the park. Let's go."

A seasoned police officer, Blaze immediately put his worry about the Dales' marriage aside and left the building with his captain.

Fitz recited the few facts he knew about the crime on the short drive over: female, mid-forties, known to be homeless, discovered by a dog walker about twenty minutes ago. Uniformed officers were already securing the scene when they arrived.

After performing a dismal canvass of the neighborhood and a local homeless shelter which yielded nothing, Blaze returned to the precinct. He sat at his desk in the Violent Crimes Unit of the Alder Lake police department and thought about the detective he had replaced.

Though all the belongings of the desk's previous occupant had long since been cleaned out, every once in a while, Detective Blazer would come across a ghost of John Wyatt's past. He would stumble on something shoved back in a drawer or cabinet, and overlooked during the former detective's hasty exit from Alder Lake.

One of these little gems from the past was a file folder retrieved by a laborer. It was discovered behind the desk, lying abandoned and forgotten for five years, until the floors were refinished and the desk moved.

Inside the folder were photographs of a murder victim from long ago. Her name was Tina Hilliard. Blaze thought little about the photos until this morning.

While Detective Blazer transferred to Alder Lake four years before, strange stories still circulated about the rash of murders that plagued the town during the year preceding his transfer. Some speculation about the serial killer, which few people would talk about—except in hushed tones at Smokey's Tavern after tipping back a few drinks—was that the perp had not been human.

The word vampire surfaced more than once. Blaze always laughed it off as small town lore.

He wasn't laughing now. The neck punctures on Tina Hilliard's neck were identical to one wound found on the lady in the park. It was on the inside of her left arm.

The victim today also displayed a bloody and gruesome neck wound. That one was no neat puncture. It was a jagged tear, leaving shredded and flapping skin in its wake.

Whatever had been at the woman's throat, quite literally, ripped her apart. She looked like a wild animal had been at her. The park housed nothing more threatening than a squirrel, and Alder Lake had no roaming beasties. An animal attack was extremely unlikely.

At least, not a four-legged one, Detective Blazer amended.

After four years of the tranquility of small town life, and a delightful shortage of truly violent crime, Blaze was both exhilarated and deeply troubled at the same time. He wouldn't say he was exactly bored with the cases constituting violent crime out here in *the sticks*, as he still thought of Alder Lake. After all, wasn't that why he put in for a transfer from the mean streets of Los Angeles in the first place? He did not want to bear witness to the sheer horror human beings were capable of delivering upon one another. All that ugliness left him jaded. He came to Alder Lake to rejuvenate his belief in mankind, and so far the town had not disappointed. He'd found good friends and a pleasant community to become involved with. Now, he may have found a good woman as well. Yet, if he was to be completely honest, he did long for a little more excitement than the position provided. He hated to admit this, but there was a welcome adrenaline rush now that one of those nasty and bloody cases had been thrust into his capable hands.

It was not often Blaze wished for a partner. The caseload was really too small to warrant one. He knew with recent budget cuts, there was only enough money in the payroll to allow for one violent crime detective. He really wished there was someone to bounce this investigation off of.

Blaze knew there used to be two such detectives in this role. John Wyatt—he who had fled after the serial killings. From what Blaze understood, the man's wife apparently suffered a nervous breakdown and was killed chasing the suspect on her own. Blaze supposed if his woman had done that, he would have run away under cover of darkness too.

The other detective, Kurt Dale—he who was quite possibly the last human being on earth Blaze wanted to talk to today.

He had never warmed to the man, and couldn't quite put his finger on why until last night. There were stories on the town's busy grapevine about Dale's wandering eye. Blaze heard tell that one of those dalliances landed him in serious hot water. Apparently Dale's mistress was the serial killer's first victim, and for a while the whole town thought Dale might have done the deed.

What Detective Blazer did not know was that the photographs pulled from under his desk—photos he was now studying with such a keen eye—were those of that very mistress.

Blaze found it very hard to believe any man could endure such an ordeal and come out of it unscathed. By some miracle, Dale was lucky enough to keep his marriage intact, his career afloat, and not land in jail for murder. How could he turn around and start cheating on his wife again a few short years later?

He must have a death wish, Blaze thought, shaking his head. With a weary sigh he picked up the phone.

Kurt was just finishing sending a text message to Carolyn. They'd been sexting all day and he was now quite het-up and anxious to see her. He was firming up their afternoon plans when his desk phone rang.

"Dale," he answered automatically.

"Detective, this is Medwyn Blazer," the caller announced with odd formality.

Kurt was unconcerned initially to hear from Blaze, though he did notice the man's greeting seemed a tad official.

They worked together on occasion, when a narcotics crime also fell under the violent crime unit's scrutiny. The two divisions were not mutually exclusive.

While most of their interaction these days was social in nature, and usually took place at Kurt's home, from time to time the need arose for work-related contact.

Kurt suspected the other detective's appearance at the social functions was due more to his wife's presence than his own. He knew Blaze liked Amanda very much. Then again, she was pretty popular with most of his co-workers. She always had been. Given Kurt's history with women, it was quite a mystery why he didn't seem to have a jealous bone in his body when it came to all the attention his wife received.

"How you doin', Blaze?" Kurt asked, his mind still half on the afternoon ahead with the insatiable Ms. Devonshire.

"Well, not so good, actually. We had a murder last night. I wondered if you might be able to meet me later to help sort it out."

"Today?" Kurt asked, not hiding his disappointment very well. He really wanted to see Carolyn. Due to her last several texts, visions of her lovely lips sliding down his penis danced through his mind. Yesterday's troubling déjà vu was already fading. He had to give her credit; the lady sure knew how to get a guy's attention.

"Yeah, it's kind of important," Blaze responded coolly.

"Is it drug related?"

"I don't know what it is. That's the problem. I think it may have something to do with the serial killer you dealt with five or six years back."

With that, all the spit dried up in Kurt's mouth. His hands started shaking violently. Suddenly Carolyn Devonshire's lips, and her superior blowjob skills, were the furthest thing from his mind.

Blaze waited patiently as a hush fell over the phone line.

Kurt suddenly sounded weary. "What time?"

"How about now? My office?"

"No! Not at the department."

"Why not?" Blaze asked curiously.

"Meet me at Smokey's tonight, say about seven. We should have a beer if we're going to dig up this old grave," Kurt responded miserably. He shuddered at his own poor choice of words.

A beer? Blaze wondered. *Why would he want to have a beer to discuss a case?*

"You want to have a beer?" Blaze asked incredulously.

"I don't want to talk about this anywhere near the department, Blaze. Truthfully, I am probably going to need something a lot stronger than just beer if your murder has anything at all to do with… with before," he finished lamely.

Blaze thought, *He must have seen us last night. He's going to try and offer some lame excuse about what he was doing with the DA. There's no other explanation for why he'd want to meet for a beer.*

Blaze had no idea what awaited him at that meeting.

After his strange phone call with Kurt Dale, he drove to Curious Curios and Collectibles. The shop was quiet. Upon seeing Bebe, his heart felt lighter than it had since spotting Kurt emerge from the hotel with the prosecutor the night before. Bebe's face lit up in a radiant smile when he walked in.

He gave her a chaste kiss on the cheek. Since Kurt Dale's untimely appearance at the end of their date, all romance was suspended by unspoken agreement. They needed to decide what to do with the unwanted knowledge they both shared. They were both, however, enjoying the feel of the sizzle in the air between them.

"Detective, what brings you here?" Bebe looked at him curiously.

He didn't mince words. "I think Kurt saw us last night."

"No, he never even looked our way, Blaze."

"Well, he must have. I called him to discuss police business, and he asked me to meet him tonight for a beer."

"A beer? Really?" Bebe's eyebrows arched in surprise.

"Yeah. He said it was about the case I called him on, but it doesn't make much sense. I've discussed dozens of cases with him before. He never wanted to meet me at a bar to talk about them. We aren't really friends, you know."

"You're right, that is awfully weird."

"I'll come over tonight after the palaver, okay?" Blaze asked.

"Sure, but what are you going to say to him? About last night, I mean," Bebe wondered.

"I have no idea. Guess I'll wait and see what he has to say first."

Blaze was quite unprepared for the strange conversation he and Kurt would share later that night. He was equally unprepared for how troubled his heart would be after that meeting. And it would have nothing whatsoever to do with the state of Kurt and Amanda's marriage.

Kurt muttered, “Shit, not again,” to the empty office. He texted Carolyn, explaining something had come up and he couldn’t meet her.

She rang his extension almost immediately. He let the call go to voicemail. He couldn’t deal with her right now. He couldn’t deal with anything right now. He told the department secretary he was not feeling well and left the office five minutes later.

What should he do? Call John in Florida? No, John was the last person he should call. Who, then? Leroy? Another bad choice. Was there anyone from that whole sickening nightmare who hadn’t lost a loved one to that fucking monster? Anyone but him?

Kurt was still blissfully unaware that in reality, he too had lost someone very dear to his heart to Francis Barclay. That revelation was still a ways off. For now there was no one he could turn to. He would not—no, he COULD not tell Amanda about this.

About what? his internal voice inquired. *You haven’t even spoken to Blaze yet. You have no idea what this is about. You are just assuming the worst because someone got killed, and Blaze has a theory it might be tied to the previous murders. But you don’t know. This could be anything.*

But in his heart, Kurt did know. He always knew. Someday Francis Barclay would return.

CHAPTER 9

Lily and Benjamin Jarvis appeared to the outside world, a successful, upwardly mobile middle-aged couple. Two incomes, no kids, one dog, and a nice house in an affluent neighborhood in the suburbs.

Little did anyone know the Jarvises were not nearly as normal as they appeared. They were, in fact, not entirely human. They were vampire. They met in college, where Ben turned Lily with her full consent after they'd been together for two years and were officially engaged.

Ben graduated medical school three years after they were married. He now ran a successful practice, specializing in internal medicine in a small town fifty miles north of Alder Lake.

He funded a blood bank located at the hospital where he worked, so he had access to all the blood he and his wife could ever need. There was no need for either of them to ever feed on live humans. Lily preferred AB negative.

Benjamin came from a long line of vampires, and a long line of doctors. The Jarvis clan never killed for their blood. For generations, the family turned to the field of medicine to ensure their needs were met. No one outside of relatives, and the select few they chose to share it with, ever knew they were anything other than a successful family, with rather a lot of members whose chosen career path was medicine.

Benjamin was a board member at the hospital. Lily worked as an art appraiser for an upscale gallery. She was also a gourmet cook, who enjoyed teaching an occasional class at a local culinary school. They gave generously to charity, attended numerous fundraisers, and were often seen gracing the society pages of the local newspaper. The Jarvises enjoyed a wide social network and threw legendary dinner parties. Few people ever turned down an invitation to the Jarvises. They were highly regarded in the community, their standing among the town's elite impeccable. No one ever suspected anything about them was any different from their peers. Nothing appeared amiss.

They had a freezer in the basement where the blood was stored.

The first one in the house to sense Samantha's arrival was their dog, Lionel, named after musician Lionel Hampton. Ben really liked jazz.

Lionel was working with great gusto on a rawhide bone on the rug in front of the television, while his owners watched a movie with French subtitles on the large plasma screen TV.

He suddenly jumped to his feet and cocked his head sideways, à la the RCA Victor dog, Nipper. Lionel focused his attention on the French doors that opened on to the backyard. They had been left open, allowing in the pleasant evening breeze on this warm summer evening.

His bone completely forgotten, Lionel offered one puzzled and strangely quiet bark.

"What is it, baby?" Lily asked the dog. "Who's out there?"

Her husband picked up the remote control and paused the film. Just then, a radiant and beautiful golden light appeared on their back patio. It momentarily blinded them with its brilliance.

Lionel ran anxiously toward the back door, barking excitedly and wagging his tail. Benjamin and Lily exchanged a startled look and cautiously followed their dog to the door.

As Samantha emerged from the light, Lily gasped and grabbed her husband's arm. "Is that one of your relative's dogs?"

Ben shook his head. "Not that I know of."

"Ummm... well, it didn't come from *here*, if you know what I mean," Lily replied, looking nervously toward their neighbor's window.

"I can see that."

"We'd better get her inside before someone sees." Lily reached to usher the visiting canine inside.

Since time immemorial, the ritual of all adult dogs at their first meeting, is a slow and cautious circling about one another, complete with a cursory sniff of hindquarters. This ritual is performed to decide if the new arrival is friend or foe. Samantha and Lionel were no exception to this time-honored tradition.

Lily and Benjamin watched nonplussed as the dogs became acquainted.

"Who is she? She is a she, right? She's too pretty to be a boy dog," Lily whispered to her husband.

Once the ritual between the two dogs was complete and they each deemed the other acceptable, Benjamin hunkered down next to Samantha and confirmed her gender.

With a puzzled frown, he looked into the dog's eyes and uttered a startled laugh. "She's vampire, Lily."

"A vampire dog? Do we have those?"

"I've never actually seen one. Why would someone turn a dog? But this one is of our kind. Look at her eyes, they glow prettier than mine."

Lily joined her husband on the floor and stroked the newcomer's head. "Yes, I see. She is quite beautiful. Perhaps her master is gone and she needs a home?"

"Maybe, but where did she come from? Honey, grab the stethoscope from my bag, will you?"

Rising to get the medical bag, Lily looked at him curiously. When she returned, Ben placed the stethoscope in his ears.

He listened first to Samantha's chest, then her neck, and finally her back. He pulled the stethoscope from his ears and sighed. "No heartbeat. She's not missing her master. She isn't even alive anymore. She's here for a reason. Someone sent her to us. A messenger, maybe."

"If she was sent with a message, then why is there no note or some explanation of why she's here?" Lily looked troubled.

"I don't know, dear. I can't even imagine what anyone would want from us."

"What do we do about her?" Lily asked, scratching the dog between the ears.

"We keep her here and care for her until we hear from the one who sent her."

"You're sure someone will contact us?"

"Quite sure. It was no accident she materialized on our patio. We are needed. Perhaps by someone on the other side—the spirit world. In the meantime, I suggest we get another rawhide chew from the pantry. Ghost dog or not, she's eyeing Lionel's treat with naked lust."

Lily offered a nervous smile and went to get the newcomer a bone.

CHAPTER 10

Smokey's was crowded when Blaze arrived for his meeting with Kurt Dale. The loud bass from the sound system vibrated under his feet. He could even feel it in his fillings. He was unfamiliar with the band; five scraggly young men and one skinny girl, with the charming name of Candy and the Canines. They must have been quite popular to have pulled in a crowd like this.

He inched his way through the dense horde of people and spotted Kurt Dale at a booth in the back of the bar. He slid in opposite the detective and took in his pale, haggard face. Kurt nursed a drink held in one trembling hand. It looked like whiskey.

"I can't hear myself think in here, Kurt," Blaze shouted over the thundering music blasting through the speakers. "And I sure as hell can't hear anything you might have to say. This is no place to discuss police business." He eyed the drink in Kurt's hand with disapproval. "And that's not conducive to good police work either. How many have you had?"

"Not enough," Kurt replied, draining the glass. He rose from the booth and motioned for Blaze to follow him outside.

Once they reached the alley behind the bar, where the music was muted enough to carry on a conversation, Kurt began with no preamble, "Blaze, how much do you know about the murders that happened here the year before you moved to town?"

"Not a great deal. I've heard some things. Weird things. Stuff that sounds like ghost stories, more than the tale of a serial killer."

"Do you have any crime scene photos of the victim you wanted to talk to me about?"

Blaze held up a folder he'd carried into the bar with him. He handed it to the other detective.

Kurt took one look at the arm wound of the victim and paled even further. He placed one hand against the cinderblock wall for support. When he got to the photo of Posy McManus's neck wound, he muttered something under his breath. It sounded to Blaze like, "She must have fought like hell to get ripped up like that."

Looking around the alley, Kurt said, "We can't talk about this here. Can we go for a drive?"

Blaze raised his eyebrows. "Kurt, what's this about? Why can't we just talk about it at the station?"

The other man exploded, "Because we just can't. We can't talk about it where anyone might overhear us. It's bad shit, Blaze. Very bad!" He rubbed one shaking hand through his hair, and looked at Blaze with desperate eyes. "You don't know how bad this is. Please, let's just get in your car, okay?"

Blaze shrugged and produced his car keys. Once settled behind the wheel, he scrutinized Kurt in the passenger seat. He realized for the first time that the man was truly frightened out of his mind. He wondered again if this might have something to do with what he and Bebe witnessed last night. It was possible Dale knew the affair had been discovered. Yet, somehow Blaze doubted the man's strange behavior was because he'd been caught playing grab-ass with Carolyn Devonshire. This appeared to be about something even more troubling to Kurt.

After they pulled out of the crowded parking lot, leaving the delightful strains of Candy and the Canines behind, Kurt opened the window and began to talk.

"I had a…" his voice cracked. He cleared his throat and started again, "I had a girl on the side back then. Did anyone ever tell you about that, Blaze? It's a small town, people talk. You probably heard about it."

Blaze nodded, saying nothing.

"So," Kurt went on hesitantly, "this girl on the side. Well, she got… She got killed. You probably heard about that too." Now he started speaking faster and faster until his voice was speeding up like a 75rpm record. "The person who killed her was actually targeting me. He was targeting me and John Wyatt. Wyatt was my best friend, and the other detective working the case at the time."

"I know about Wyatt. He left because of that case, right? His wife went crazy and drove a car into your house or something."

"Yeah, she did. Here's the thing, Blaze… The murderer… What have you heard? Have you heard maybe he wasn't a man at all? That he was something else… Something really bizarre?"

Blaze pulled the car off the road and into the parking lot of an office building. He turned off the engine and faced the distraught man beside him.

"Kurt, whatever you are trying to tell me, why don't you just say it? It's going to be a long night if you keep asking me questions about the rumors circulating through town about something that happened five years ago."

Kurt's shoulders sagged. "Because what I have to tell you is going to sound like the biggest load of crap you ever heard spew from a guilty man's mouth. That's why."

"Guilty of what, exactly? Cheating on his wife or something far worse?"

"You heard I killed the perp right? Killed the *serial killer?*" He made air quotes around the words.

Blaze nodded.

"I didn't kill him. He was... He was already dead when he arrived in town. He'd been dead for a long time. He came back to get revenge for the murder of his family. He ran out of steam and died again before he was through. I think he might be back again now to finish what he started." Kurt watched the other man carefully to see how he was accepting this story.

Blaze looked at him neutrally and said nothing. His face betrayed nothing he might have been thinking.

Kurt continued, "I think the woman in the park, well, she was just collateral damage until he hunts down who he really wants... Until he hunts me down. You saw the wounds on her arm and you know they match the wounds on the pictures you found of Tina Hilliard, right? Isn't that the reason you believe this new murder might have something to do with the old ones? The pictures you found were of the woman I was involved with. Tina was Francis Barclay's first victim."

Blaze looked at the other man expressionless. When he didn't answer and the silence stretched out like an eternity between them, Kurt sputtered, "Blaze, he was a vampire."

Kurt held up a hand as though Blaze had raised an objection to this declaration. "Believe me, I know how this sounds. But it's true, Blaze. I had ancestors who were lawmen and so did Wyatt. Our people killed his family, and he returned to get revenge. He didn't succeed. His body, or what was left of it, gave out on him before he could finish the job. Your perp for the woman in the park is him. Francis Barclay is back. For the life of me, I don't know how the hell he managed to come back again. We cremated him and planted the ashes a hundred miles from here." He thrust his face into his hands.

Once he pulled himself together again, Kurt talked for another twenty minutes, rehashing a story he hoped never to have to tell—hoped never to even have to think about again. He fished a napkin from Smokey's Tavern out of his pocket and handed it to Detective Blazer. John Wyatt's phone number in Florida was scribbled on it.

"Call him," Kurt nodded at the napkin. "You won't believe me until you do, and probably not even then. But call him. Then go visit Leroy Clovis, the mailman. They won't want to do it, but they will both tell you the same crazy story I just did. And you will probably wonder when crazy became catching."

When Blaze could unstick his tongue from the roof of his mouth, he asked, "How did you plan to catch a vampire, Kurt?"

He thought, *Am I really having this conversation with another detective? Did I really just ask that question?*

"I didn't know how to catch him five years ago, and I still don't."

"I'm not sure how I'm supposed to respond to this. You said yourself, you know how it sounds."

"You don't have to respond. Just talk to John and Leroy." Kurt opened the passenger door and climbed out of the car. He walked away without looking back.

It was almost 8:30 by the time Blaze pulled up to Bebe's house. The delectable aroma of home cooking filled his senses when he walked in the door, and his stomach rumbled appreciatively. He had forgotten all about dinner in the wake of his very creepy discussion with Kurt Dale.

Bebe kissed him deeply on the lips and said, "Dinner first. Kurt Dale later." She led him by the hand to a candlelit table and a waiting glass of wine.

It was during the meal when Blaze decided to share with Bebe his very jarring conversation with Kurt Dale. It wasn't exactly breaching protocol by talking about a case. This was more about Kurt Dale's mental state than it was about the murder in the park.

"He said what?" Bebe looked at Blaze with dawning alarm as he recounted the conversation. They were settled on the couch, having just finished eating.

"I'd say the guy was insane, but he actually told me to call his former partner and the town mailman to get verification of this story."

"Honey, did he say anything to you about last night? Maybe you were right and he did see us there. Maybe this is some elaborate plot to make people think you are the one that's crazy, so his wife doesn't figure out he's banging the blonde. If you go asking questions about a vampire, what are people going to think about your mental state?"

"He didn't say anything about last night. I think you were right, he never even saw us. This wasn't about that. He's scared. In fact, I think he's terrified. Maybe the guy is completely off his rocker, but something has him afraid of a great deal more than just getting caught playing around with the deputy DA."

"So, what are you going to do? It's not going to get you any closer to solving the case you are working on by talking to that former detective or Leroy Clovis, is it?"

"Maybe not. I just have nowhere else to start on this one. Besides, I am honestly curious to hear what they have to say about this vampire nonsense. Aren't you?"

"I can't imagine they are going to back up his claim. Not unless, as Kurt said, crazy is catching."

CHAPTER 11

When Blaze arrived at the precinct the morning after talking to Kurt, he asked the secretary to have Leroy Clovis come see him when he delivered the mail. She gave him a puzzled look, waiting for him to elaborate on his request. When he didn't, the secretary said she would send Leroy back when he showed up.

Once settled at his desk with a cup of coffee, Blaze pulled out the napkin from Smokey's with Kurt's former partner's phone number written on it.

The phone rang four times before an automated voice instructed him to leave a message after the beep. He did so.

He was surprised, when an hour later his phone rang and the caller announced she was Jan Wyatt, John's wife.

"Can I ask what this is about, Detective Blazer?"

"Well, I really need to talk to your husband, ma'am. It's police business."

"Yes, well, John isn't police anymore. And he has nothing to do with Alder Lake anymore either. Nor does he want to. It holds nothing but very painful memories for him, so I am going to ask you to please leave him alone."

"Are you going to give him the message I called, Mrs. Wyatt?"

"Unless you give me a very good reason to rip open old wounds, then no I am not. He only started sleeping through the night without having nightmares about that place these past few months. It's not good for him to think about anything to do with Alder Lake. Why did you call? Why now, so many years after all the tragedy he suffered there?"

Jan Wyatt sounded as if she was about to cry. This just made everything Kurt had told him even stranger. The case of the dead woman in the park was growing more curious by the minute.

It was evident that if he didn't tell this woman the purpose for his call, there would be no chance of ever getting through her to Kurt's former partner. She was a fortress, hell-bent on standing guard at the edge of her husband's life.

"Okay, Mrs. Wyatt. Here's the thing. I don't want to upset him, and I sure don't want to take him on any unpleasant trips down memory lane. I have a homicide here, and I was told your husband might be able to help me figure out who committed it. I'm sorry to say it may have something to do with all that business five years ago when he left. Maybe it's just a copycat killer or something like that. I don't know exactly what I'm dealing with here, and your husband knows that case like no one else. He's the only person who can help me."

Jan Wyatt sat thinking for a minute. "What about Dale? He knows all about it too. Can't you ask him?"

"I did. He's the one who told me to call John."

"Well, of course he did," she snapped. "When did Kurt Dale ever care about anyone but himself?"

Another member of the Kurt Dale fan club, Blaze thought.

"Please, Mrs. Wyatt, I only need a couple of minutes to talk to him, and you have my word I will try not to upset him. You aren't going to want it on your conscience if whoever did this strikes again, and I could have caught him with one conversation with John, now are you?"

Blaze winced when she retorted, "Well, you aren't going to want it on your conscience if my husband commits suicide because of one conversation with you, now are you, Detective?" She slammed the receiver down, disconnecting the call.

Blaze was pretty sure she was going to give John Wyatt the message. He'd found a good guilt trip was usually effective in these situations.

In the reception area of the precinct, Leroy Clovis looked blankly at the police station secretary when she told him Detective Blazer would like to have a word with him. The few pieces of outgoing mail slipped from his fingers and fluttered noiselessly to the floor. He bent to retrieve them.

The last time a cop wanted to have a chat with him, he ended up stealing holy water from a church, carving out a stake meant for a vampire's heart in the garage, and unintentionally getting his stepson killed.

Leroy's wife, a recovering alcoholic like himself, inevitably fell off the wagon every year at the anniversary of her son's death. Leroy still carried tremendous guilt over Richie Welch's demise, so the last thing he wanted was to have a conversation with any cop about anything.

With heavy footsteps, Leroy approached the detective's office and tapped lightly at the half-open door.

Blaze stood up from his desk and offered Leroy his hand to shake. He waved him to a chair. "Hey, Leroy, thanks for stopping in."

The two men did not know one another at all. While they had seen each other when Leroy delivered the mail, they had never conversed. Leroy had taken great pains to keep it that way. He'd lost his taste for having friends on the force after what happened to Richie and John Wyatt's first wife.

"No problem, Detective. What can I do for you?"

"Well, first you can call me Blaze."

Leroy offered a small nod. "Blaze, then. What's this about?"

"I wondered what you could tell me about the serial killings in Alder Lake about five years ago. I am told you know some things about the person who committed the crimes."

Leroy involuntarily bit his lip. His face closed up tighter than a bank vault and his eyes narrowed to slits. His formerly pleasant demeanor completely vanished. "Why?" he asked.

"I need to find out if a recent murder might have anything to do with those killings."

"Shit, he's back? Who did he kill this time? Did he get Kurt?" Leroy cried, alarmed.

Blaze was thunderstruck by the other man's reaction. He chose his words carefully. "My understanding was the suspect in those homicides was killed. Why would you think he might be back and gunning for Kurt? Who is fine, by the way. What would make you think anything happened to him?"

Leroy looked uncomfortably down at his shoes. "Have you spoken to Kurt, Detective?"

The fact that the man returned to calling him by his title rather than his nickname spoke volumes to Blaze. Leroy didn't want to answer these questions or help him with this investigation, and he sure as hell didn't want to be friends. To Leroy Clovis, he was always going to be Detective Blazer—never Blaze.

"Yes, I have spoken to Kurt. I'm sorry if this is making you uncomfortable, Leroy. I have a murderer out on the streets who I would like to catch before he kills anyone else. I can't help wonder why I'm told 'ask someone else' every time I ask a question about that rash of murders. What gives?"

"What exactly did Kurt tell you about who the murderer was? Answer that one question, and I will tell you what I can. If the little son of a bitch is back, I don't envy you being the one elected to bring him down."

"Leroy, was the murderer human?"

Leroy exhaled loudly and scrubbed a hand across his forehead. There it was. He looked across the desk at the other man for a long moment before finally replying, "No. Not like you and me."

"Then what was he?"

Leroy appreciated Blaze asking the question in a straightforward manner, with no hint of the tone, or bemused look in his eye people reserve for dealing with folks they deem unstable. However, nor did Leroy kid himself into thinking this detective—this Johnny Come Lately to their town—a man who did not see the carnage Francis Barclay had wrought or the fear he inspired, would for one minute believe him when he answered that question.

"He was exactly what I suspect Kurt Dale told you he was. A vampire."

Blaze did not understand how an entire town could adopt the same insane notion. He'd been here for four years, and while the murders preceding his relocation weren't spoken of often, inevitably every time the subject did come up, the word *vampire* always accompanied the dialogue. It was like some kind of Jim Jones let's-all-drink-the-poison-Kool-Aid group mindset. And it was starting to seriously freak him out.

"Leroy, I have been a cop for a long time. I have investigated hundreds of homicides, and I can honestly tell you I have never seen a real life vampire or a murder victim of one."

"Oh, I'm sure you haven't. No one here ever did either. Until five years ago. How exactly did this current victim die? Little puncture holes to the neck?"

Before the detective could answer, Leroy held up a hand. "Never mind. I know you ain't gonna tell me that, and honestly, man, I don't want to know. The only thing I will tell you is this: I am not crazy and neither is Kurt Dale. He may not win any husband of the year awards, but he's not a mental case, and if he told you the killer was a vampire, he was telling the truth. I hope like hell Francis Barclay isn't back. But if he is, heaven help us all. Good luck to you, Detective."

"Francis Barclay? That was the suspect's name?"

"Tell you what, Detective. Go to the library and ask for a book called *Alder Lake; Its History; Its Ghosts.* There is a story in there about the Barclay family and their murder. Francis was their son, and he returned to Alder Lake to avenge their deaths. Kurt and his partner back then, a man named Wyatt, had family here who participated in murdering the Barclays. A long time ago, this was. It was those two detectives Francis Barclay was hunting when he came back to Alder Lake five years ago. There were other families involved too—last names were Hilliard and Ash. Look up the records about the deaths of people with those last names about five years ago. The descendants were Barclay's victims. He died again before he could get the detectives. If Barclay is back, it's them he's after. Someone should probably let John Wyatt know."

Blaze jotted down the names Leroy just gave him. His story was a mirror image of the one told to him by Kurt Dale, only with quite a few more details. What the hell happened here five years ago? It either made everyone lose their minds, or could it have really been something supernatural?

Blaze had seen some strange shit in his career over the last fifteen years, but this was completely unchartered territory for him. He felt like he had just been deposited right between the pages of an Algernon Blackwood novel. He dealt with human creepiness, not the creepiness of characters out of a weird tale.

Blaze firmly believed there was evil in the world, he'd seen it firsthand. He also knew beyond a shadow of a doubt, the origin of all the world's evil could be traced back to a single source: humanity. Monsters existed, but they were all of the human variety. The only vampires he'd ever been acquainted with were the ones in movies or on television.

To Blaze, the newest generation of TV vampires all seemed to have six-pack abs and million dollar smiles. *Thank you, Stephanie Meyer,* he thought wryly. And while he would never admit this to his peers, he loved vampires. While the *Twilight* saga was too juvenile for his tastes, he was a closet junkie for the show *True Blood.*

Unlike his neighbors, he had the sense to know it wasn't real. So how could so many people, in a town full of seemingly rational residents, believe a real live vampire came to visit on that long-ago summer? Who was this Francis Barclay, and was he dead or not?

CHAPTER 12

The Dale household had grown into a quiet and tense abode over the last few days.

Amanda knew something was wrong with Kurt, but he wouldn't talk about it. In fact, he wouldn't talk at all. She asked him what the problem was numerous times and received nothing but short answers, brusque nods of the head, and fingers run nervously through hair. She finally gave up. When he was ready to tell her he would. What surprised her, was when Lorna cornered her while she changed Nate's diaper and asked what was wrong with Daddy. The child's insights never ceased to amaze Amanda—nor frighten her just a little.

She thought about spewing some grownup bullshit to placate her daughter, and then decided against it. Why lie to Lorna when she had no idea what was wrong with Kurt herself?

"I don't know, honey. He hasn't told me."

"I'm right, aren't I? Daddy is upset about something."

"Well," she replied hesitantly, not liking the troubled look she saw come into her little girl's eyes, "he does seem a little more preoccupied than usual. It might just be work. He doesn't like to talk about his cases too much."

What Amanda did not know was that when she mentioned Kurt's work, Lorna was immediately reminded of hearing her daddy on the phone not long ago, sounding very upset when he was talking to that woman, Carolyn. After overhearing her father's heated conversation, Lorna looked on Google for the names of the city employees. There was only one Carolyn listed. Lorna surmised she must be the woman Daddy had been talking to. Her last name was Devonshire, and she was a District Attorney. Lorna also wrote down the address of the District Attorney's office. Now Daddy was upset again, and Mommy thinks it's because of his work.

Lorna was sure the lady named Carolyn was the source of her father's angst. She didn't mention that overheard conversation to her mother. Mostly because she did not want her to know she'd been eavesdropping on a private conversation. Also, Daddy had not told Mommy what was bugging him, so he probably didn't want her to know this Carolyn lady made him mad. But Lorna knew, and she was starting not to like this Carolyn woman one bit.

The week drew to a close with no progress in the investigation into Posy McManus's murder, and no leads, vampire or otherwise. The only progress had been in Blaze's relationship with the lovely Bebe Sugars. Even that didn't help his troubled mind. He sat at his desk thinking many unpleasant thoughts, most of which circled around Kurt Dale. His affair with the Deputy DA, for one. His vampire killer, for the other.

It was late Friday afternoon, and he was just about ready to call it a day and go pick up Bebe from her shop. He was just shrugging into his jacket when the phone on his desk rang.

"Detective Blazer," he answered officially. He was greeted with nothing but an extended silence, and knew at once John Wyatt was on the other end of the line.

Blaze had pretty much given up on hearing from John. He wasn't sure his worried wife would give him the message, or just sweep the whole sordid affair under the rug and forget about it.

"John, is that you?" He did his best to sound friendly and nonthreatening.

There was a sigh, and then, "Hello, Detective. How did you know it was me?" He quickly added, "Never mind, I was on the job long enough. I know. Sometimes I still miss those hunches. Don't get to use my cop instincts much these days."

Blaze smiled. He liked the man instantly. "It's like riding a horse. They never leave you. And please, call me Blaze. Thanks for calling me back, man. I wasn't sure if you would. Your wife wasn't overjoyed to hear from me."

"Truthfully, neither am I. I will try and answer your questions though, as long as you are prepared for the answers. You may not like them… Or believe them, for that matter."

"Well, I've been getting a lot of practice in stretching my imagination just lately. Let's start with Francis Barclay. Who was he?"

"I think a better question is, 'What was he?' I imagine by now you've heard the word vampire floated out a few times. Am I right?"

"Yes indeed. And just like that, huh? Not even going to try and sugarcoat it, are you? So tell me, was he really a vampire?" Blaze worked very hard to keep any judgment or disbelief from his voice. The last thing he needed was this man getting defensive with him. John Wyatt might be his only remaining hope of cracking the case of the lady in the park. It would not serve him well to alienate the man. It troubled Blaze a little bit that he was starting to bend his mind just enough to entertain this weird possibility.

"Thank you for not asking, if myself, and a large portion of the population in Alder Lake are all insane. I'm sure that's what you're thinking. It's decent of you not to say so," John replied.

"Well, was he a vampire? I'm honestly interested in the truthful answer to that question."

John Wyatt exhaled noisily. "Yep, he was indeed. Not the *Twilight* brand, with the pretty candy coating. Don't be picturing that. Francis Barclay is scary, and he has a longstanding grudge against a lot of people in Alder Lake. If he's back, you've got problems, Blaze—big ones. That boy has good reason to be very pissed off."

Blaze was momentarily stunned. He felt like John Wyatt had read his mind with that *Twilight* comment. "Okay, John, what problems do I have, apart from solving the murder of a dead lady in the park?"

"Well, for one, the murders most likely aren't going to stop with just your lady in the park. I'm quite sure she was just collateral damage. We had one or two of those five years ago. A big gal named Norma Krueger ran afoul of Barclay and paid with her life, so did an FBI agent we had on loan. Barclay will kill anyone who gets in his way. For another, Kurt Dale better watch his back. He's probably the reason why young Mr. Barclay's returned… and me, of course. He may not know I blew town. I think he wiped out everyone else he was after. At least if all the family names of those responsible for killing his people were listed in the book. Who knows if they missed one or two."

That book again. Leroy mentioned it too. "You mean some history book about Alder Lake? Leroy Clovis mentioned it."

"I was going to ask if you spoke to him. How is Leroy handling this? We both suffered some pretty bad collateral damage of our own as a result of Francis Barclay."

"I heard about that. I am very sorry about your wife," Blaze offered uncomfortably.

John was quiet for a long moment. Finally, he asked, "Is there anything else, Blaze?"

The detective offered a rueful laugh. "You mean do I have anymore questions? Sure—like maybe a hundred or so. You see, I have never investigated a murder by vampire before, so I'm not sure what the protocol is here. Maybe you can enlighten me as to what you think I should be asking… And who, for that matter."

John surprised him by replying, "The most important thing is believing it's true. Then you won't waste as much time as we did trying to wrap our heads around the whole freak show. Start with the history book. That's what finally turned the corner for me. It's at the library, and it's the only book ever written about Alder Lake. Read that and I'm sure we will talk again soon," John said, his voice tinged with regret. "And one more thing…"

"What's that?"

"Tell Kurt to come clean with Amanda. If he doesn't tell her Barclay might be back, she won't be as careful as she needs to be now. And, well, she'll probably think he's cheating on her again because he will be acting weird. He doesn't give that woman enough credit for being able to read him."

Now Blaze was the one who remained silent. This man clearly knew the Dale family dynamics extremely well. He answered cautiously, "Maybe you ought to tell him yourself, John. Kurt and I, well, we aren't really friends."

John sighed again. "I understand. As much as I don't want to make that call, I will. For Amanda and the kids, if not for him."

Blaze thought to himself, *I wish you would tell the asshole to stop cheating on the lady, too. That'd be real helpful just about now.* He wisely didn't say that out loud.

The Kurt Dale fan club just kept on growing.

CHAPTER 13

No seven-year-old child should be troubled by sleepless nights. Then again, Lorna Dale was no ordinary child. She was disturbed by not only an aching hunger, which never stayed satiated for long, but also by worry over both of her fathers: the human one and the one who made her vampire.

She wished she could make her human father—her daddy, feel better. And she felt bad because she knew her blood-father was troubled too. The worst part was, she herself, was the source of his grief. It was unbearable.

Tonight at dinner Daddy barely ate anything, and his face looked pale. The meal was oddly quiet and subdued, with her mother having not just the usual one, but two glasses of wine. Lorna noticed her mother shooting worried glances at her father.

Lorna's mind turned to the woman, Carolyn. Her inner voice spat the name like a foul oath. She was convinced Carolyn was the reason for her daddy's somber and troubled mood.

Since her disastrous experience the last time she found someone to feed on, Lorna hadn't returned to the park to find prey. She knew not to go there again. She wasn't worried about getting caught. Who in the world would suspect a little kid of killing anybody? That wasn't why she couldn't go back to the park. She could not use it as a feeding ground anymore for just one reason: Her blood father had very clearly sent the message not to. It was that simple. She was forbidden to do so and she would not disobey. What his message neglected to impart was just where she should go to feed now. The hunger was getting overwhelming, and she was going to have to find somebody to take blood from soon. When she tried to mentally send this message to her blood-father, the only thing she ever seemed to hear back via their strange psychic link was that he was on his way and would be with her again soon. In the meantime, her appetites were a constant agony like a rotting tooth, and her daddy was upset. Both situations needed remedies at once.

When the long distance line connected and Kurt's cell phone rang, he had to smile when he saw who the caller was. "John! Hey man, how are you?"

John Wyatt heard the genuine warmth in his old friend and partner's voice. For just a moment the last five years dissolved and it felt like their friendship had not died with his first wife, Ellen, on that miserable night she drove through the picture window of Kurt and Amanda's house.

"Hi, Kurt. I'm doing okay, but I hear you may have some trouble out your way again."

Kurt sighed miserably. "Yeah. I guess we might," he hastily added, "But, despite what I told Blaze, it doesn't mean it's…" he left the sentence unfinished.

"Well, maybe it isn't," John said gently, "but if there is even the slightest possibility it could be Barclay, Amanda has to be told."

John heard another miserable sigh. He waited patiently for Kurt to reply.

"John, it can't be him. It just can't be! We cremated him. It's impossible."

"See, that's the kind of thinking that can get you into a lot of trouble. It was impossible when he rose from the ground the first time too. Doesn't mean it didn't happen. If he found some way to spin up out of those ashes, then your entire family is at risk. Now isn't the time for denial. Amanda has to know."

"How can I tell her? She's never gotten over what happened. She might have been able to put this behind her if that…that monster hadn't kidnapped Lorna. Even though the kid is fine, Amanda has spent the last five years believing he damaged her in some way. If Amanda thinks Barclay is back she is going to completely freak out."

"Yes, she will probably be upset. But at least she will watch her back, which is exactly what she needs to do."

"It's not that simple. Frankly, I think Amanda blamed me for that whole fiasco. She still does. All of it."

John chose his words carefully. "Come on, Kurt. It's not Barclay she blamed you for and you know it."

Kurt's voice betrayed his guilt when he answered in a small voice, "No, I guess it's not."

"Tina Hilliard is in the past. As long as you aren't running around on her again, Mandy won't blame you for warning her, that however slight the possibility, Barclay may have come back for an encore performance."

Kurt's silence spoke volumes. John exploded, "Oh, Kurt! Shit, you aren't…"

Kurt sputtered, "I swear, I never meant for this to happen. I am trying to break it off, I am trying!"

"Listen to me, and listen good. You get the fuck out of whatever mess you are in now. No long drawn out goodbyes, no tearful farewells. Just walk the fuck away. I don't care who she is, or what the situation is, just get out of it, and get out now."

"It's very complicated."

"With you it always is." John sighed wearily. "Give me the cliff notes version of the complication."

"I work with her."

John was speechless. He did not know any man could be as stupid and reckless as Kurt Dale. He reminded himself that he no longer had to follow after his old partner with a mop trying to clean up his messes.

"Yeah, that's bad, but it doesn't change the fact that you have to stop seeing her now. Because I have news for you; If Mandy finds out you are doing this again, her wrath is going to make that dead vampire's look like child's play."

Amanda Dale was not the only one to notice her husband's tension. On his friend's advice, Kurt had been avoiding his lover like the plague. He ignored Carolyn's phone calls, her emails and her text messages. He locked himself in his office with the door closed and blinds drawn, refusing to speak to her. She wasn't currently prosecuting an active case requiring Kurt's attention, so there was nothing forcing him to speak to her. She was feeling very much like woman-scorned, and the sensation was not one she cared for in the least.

Carolyn planned to confront Kurt tonight and force him to tell her what the hell she had done to piss him off so badly. The last time they communicated was to plan an afternoon rendezvous. Kurt seemed to be looking forward to the meeting, yet he cancelled it only minutes after firming up their plans. What followed was the stone-cold silent treatment she'd been suffering through ever since.

How were they supposed to work together with hostility like this between them?

She knew he wasn't terribly happy with the affair anymore. Not since she'd thwarted his last attempt at breaking up. She wondered if she should have just let him go then.

The truth was, it was partly her pride—being the one doing the breaking up was always so much more satisfying. Also, she wasn't ready for this little ride to be over yet. He was just so damn good in the sack. She didn't confide in Kurt that her husband had suffered from erectile dysfunction for years. Sex was virtually nonexistent between them. There were pills for the problem, but he didn't like to take them because they made his heart race. Where did that leave her? A heartless bitch if she left, she supposed. A divorce would be messy and expensive. Besides, in her way she loved the man, and didn't want to leave anyway. She just wanted to get laid once in a while. Kurt fit the bill so nicely. Why did he have to go and mess things up? It's not like she was asking him to leave his wife or anything, she just wanted things to stay status quo.

She sat watching the clock and listening for Kurt to arrive. He hadn't spent much time in the office this week since their mysterious falling out. She looked on the interdepartmental website at his calendar, and the most pressing bit of business he had booked was speaking to the kids at the local high school about the new drug prevention program.

God, this really is a sleepy, boring little town, she thought. *We put away three drug dealers who were trafficking here in the past year, and now no one gets up to any mischief anymore. It's a wonder we even have jobs.*

If there was no reason for Kurt to come in to the office, how the hell was she supposed to get this miserable confrontation over with? She was determined to deal with it today. He would have to put in an appearance at some point, wouldn't he?

Detective Medwyn Blazer carried the complete case files for the murder of Tina Hilliard, Norma Krueger, and the triple homicide of the Ash family in a box. He tried to obtain the file on Greta Fike, the FBI agent who was Barclay's last casualty, but by then the feds had taken over the case. They took the file with them when they vacated Alder Lake and refused Blaze's request for a copy. On top of the files lay the book, *Alder Lake; Its History; Its Ghosts*.

He had pulled the case files before leaving the office. The book, he obtained from the library on his way to pick up Bebe. This was his homework for the evening. He placed everything in the trunk of his car, out of sight.

He waited for Bebe at the curb while she locked up. They had dinner at the Italian restaurant she and Amanda frequented regularly. Their first girls-night-out dinner felt like a lifetime ago to Bebe now.

She was enjoying getting to know the handsome detective, and happy about how quickly their feelings for each other had grown, but there was already trouble in paradise. Its name was Kurt Dale. And the distracting shadow he cast over their relationship seemed to grow larger with each passing day. She suspected Kurt and his many secrets were the sole reason why their relationship had not moved into the bedroom yet. A direction she was most anxious for it to travel.

"I don't know how much longer I can stay hushed about Kurt's misdeeds. Amanda already knows something is bothering me. She's a very perceptive lady," Bebe said around a mouthful of ravioli.

Blaze nodded thoughtfully, working his way through a large meatball hero. "I know, baby. It doesn't seem right to keep it from her. I'm just not sure which is worse, staying silent, or wreaking havoc in a household with two little kids. Besides, Kurt has bigger problems right now. I think the affair will burn itself out. It might have done so already."

Bebe looked at him curiously. When he didn't elaborate on exactly what Kurt's bigger problems might be, she didn't push the issue. She wondered how Blaze could just dismiss Kurt's blatant infidelity like this. Blaze had grown very evasive on the subject of vampires and Kurt Dale's mental health since bringing that very odd subject up initially.

Since Blaze clearly didn't want to talk about it anymore, Bebe stopped asking. He told her it tied into the case of the poor woman found dead in the park, and he wasn't comfortable discussing an open investigation. She respected it was police business and confidential, so she let the subject drop.

Though, she did have to wonder why he ever brought it up in the first place, if he was just going to leave her hanging in mid-air like this. She was still very curious, she just wasn't about to pry into things he didn't want her to.

When he drove her home, Bebe invited him in for a nightcap. He demurred, explaining he had homework to do. Once again, there was no elaboration on just what the homework might be. She gave him a long and somewhat frustrated kiss goodnight.

Blaze offered a final wave and drove away, blissfully unaware of Bebe's gaze following him, the embers of unfulfilled passion still smoldering in her eyes.

She liked the good detective very much, but a seed of disquiet began to bloom when he grew silent on the subject of Kurt Dale. Amanda was very dear to her, and the only truly close friend she'd made in this town. Bebe hoped she and Blaze would figure out together how to handle the discovery of Kurt's affair. Preferably after they had fulfilled their own desires. She could see now, Blaze was not going to help her with either quandary. She did not like harboring this dirty little secret. It made her feel like a traitor.

She desperately wished she could share these feelings with Blaze, but his mind was on something else now. It still had to do with Kurt Dale apparently, only now the fact that he was cheating on her best friend seemed to take a backseat to whatever this mysterious new issue was. Sadly, Bebe thought the detective's attraction to her had also taken a backseat to Kurt Dale, and she didn't like it one bit.

She would have to figure out what to do about the lying son of a bitch on her own. She hated the tiny grain of resentment for Blaze which had taken root in her heart because of this. *Damn Kurt Dale anyway!* she thought bitterly.

Detective Blazer opened the library book chronicling Alder Lake's history. He turned to the well dog-eared page where the story of the Barclay family murder began and started reading.

> *February, 1801*
>
> *The grisly murders of six local residents plunged the peaceful town into a state of terror never before experienced in this quiet rural community. The pressure rested solely on Sheriff Sebastian Dale's shoulders to solve the gruesome slayings, bring the killer to justice, and restore tranquility once again to his quiet town.*
>
> *When the fourth body was discovered in a shallow grave by the river the sheriff had his own private thoughts regarding who was behind the savage killings, but with no proof other than a shred of torn cloth found clutched in the hand of one of the victims, and the suspect being a local man of good standing, he wisely kept his*

suspicions to himself and worked diligently to bring the bestial killer to justice.

When two more victims of this blood-crazed fiend were discovered, Dale was convinced the murderer was Matthew Barclay, and that Barclay's wife and son were also involved in this satanic triad. His findings were so startling and so disturbing that Sheriff Dale shared them with only a few of his most trusted confidants.

Acceptance of the sheriff's accusations was difficult, but being a well-respected and fair man, eventually the men he had taken into his confidence accepted his unthinkable revelation. With little evidence to tie the Barclay family to the murders, they were unable to take them into custody.

With the discovery of the fifth body, a seventeen-year-old girl who was to have been married the following month, the sheriff held a secret meeting. Those in attendance decided on a drastic plan of action they felt was their only recourse.

With no tangible evidence to prove the Barclays' dark secret, they believed they had no choice but to eliminate them. It was the only way to ensure the killings would stop. As their plan was being discussed, a sixth corpse was found in a grove of trees at the edge of town.

On a chilly, overcast night, Sheriff Dale and Deputies Garson Hilliard, Joshua Wyatt and William Ash saddled their horses and headed for the Barclay place. They were determined to put an end to the reign of terror in their community.

In the early hours of the morning, the ashen-faced lawmen returned to town, firmly convinced that their removal of this inhuman family was the right and only solution to end the bloody slayings that held Alder Lake in a grip of fear.

When Matthew Barclay attempted to attack Deputy Hilliard, they were certain Sheriff Dale's suspicions, as shocking and unbelievable as they seemed, were entirely true. The members of this well-regarded family were the worst kinds of fiends from hell.

Barclay and his wife were executed swiftly and without mercy, their house burned to the ground. Their son, seventeen-year-old Francis, hearing the men storming up the porch steps, ran out the back door. He was soon found crouching and cowering in a shallow gully. As the men approached, Francis, as if possessed by Satan himself, stood up, glaring at them with a look of demonic evil twisting his features into a mask of eldritch horror. In a voice choking with hatred, he swore he would bring death and ruin to his killers and their families for revenge of the ruthless murder of his parents. A bullet through the brain cut short his maniacal ravings.

They buried him unceremoniously in an unmarked grave in the town cemetery. Some months passed before a charitable soul paid to have a headstone engraved for the boy and placed it on the mound of earth that was Francis Barclay's final resting place. It read simply:

Francis R. Barclay
September 21, 1784 - February 22, 1801.

Eventually the fate of the Barclay family was made known. There were some among the townspeople who wondered silently if Sheriff Dale made a mistake. What if the killings continued? No one ever gave voice to such fears. Their town leaders and lawmakers were implicitly trusted and respected. Eventually all fears were put to rest because the killings did indeed stop.

Yeah, Blaze thought, *they stopped for over two-hundred years. Then they began again. But I am just not convinced it's the same guy, no matter how many people tell me it is. Kind of a long time to hold a grudge, isn't it?* He chuckled softly.

He then read the gruesome details of the murder of Tina Hilliard. He stared for a long time at Kurt Dale's name on the short list of suspects. Another name on the list was Richie Welch.

He logged into the police database from his home computer and discovered Richie Welch was now deceased. A drug deal gone bad, during the same time as those serial killings, five years ago. Something about the story didn't sit well with Blaze. While his disquiet had something to do with the dubious timing—a dead drug dealer at the same time as four unrelated murders—it was more than that.

He printed out the case file for further scrutiny. He couldn't put his finger on what bothered him. It was something about the mirror-image statements of the detectives who found the Welch kid's body that raised his hackles. His breath caught in his throat when he saw the names of the two detectives: Wyatt and Dale. Their statements were identical twins. Just a little bit too perfect.

They lied, a small inner voice whispered in his ear. He didn't know how he knew that, but he learned early in his career to pay attention to that voice. Why would they fabricate a statement about a small-time hood's death? Welch had a rap sheet as long as his arm, but none of it was drug related, and he hadn't been in any trouble for at least two years before he met his untimely demise.

When Blaze cracked open the case file on the triple homicide of the Ash family, his eyes went immediately to the suspect list. There was the name of Richie Welch again. A minister, his wife and teenage daughter murdered. Welch was the daughter's boyfriend. Blaze thought it very unlikely that a kid who had never done anything worse than rob a liquor store would graduate to murdering his girlfriend and her parents. What connection to the Hilliard woman he possibly could have had was even more baffling. Why was he a suspect in her murder as well?

The Krueger woman, whose body was found in a motel room, was "presumed to be a victim of the unknown assailant" terrorizing the town during that long ago summer according to her case file.

Blaze noted that while the crimes all had many similarities, the victims did not. In the case of most serial criminals, the victims usually share many of the same traits. Their age and appearance are generally alike, as are their lifestyles. None of these crimes fit that profile. From the outside they appeared to be far too random to be the work of a serial murderer.

Yo' FBI, you were barking up the wrong tree, boys. Blaze thought. They really should have known better than to think their perp was a serial killer. There wasn't a single earmark that pointed in that direction. The late Greta Fike would have agreed.

The truth was, all six murders, including the unfortunate FBI agent sent to find the killer, remained technically unsolved to this day. Unsolved, unless of course, you factor in a vampire. Then they were all explained with a neat little bow around the entire package. Blaze shuddered. He was deeply unnerved by what perfect sense that scenario made.

Equally unnerving was how much he still needed to learn about this town and its residents; both the living and the dead. Alder Lake's secrets were very well guarded and not easy to unearth.

CHAPTER 14

Francis Barclay was getting closer to his blood-child each day, however his progress was slow. Samantha found him two days earlier with news of the home she had located for his Lorna. This was a huge relief.

He realized since being cremated, his body would never fully solidify again. He'd learned to deal with small parts of his extremities disintegrating; fingers, toes, and sometimes an entire hand would dissolve into sand and simply blow away like dust when the wind picked up. What troubled him now, was that the limb in question was taking longer and longer to reform when it disintegrated. He feared it was only a matter of time before he would lose an arm or a foot permanently.

His dog travelled with him for two days as he drew closer to Alder Lake.

In a Walmart store where he and Samantha stayed for the night, he found clean clothing and shoes that offered his fragile skin protection from the wind. His latest ensemble included a hooded sweatshirt, jeans and lace-up work boots. Francis was also pleased to have found a wealth of food in the vast store. While he wasn't exactly hungry anymore, for either food or blood, his taste for junk food and sweets had not deserted him since his last visit. He made a feast of doughnuts, cinnamon rolls and chocolate ice cream, washing it all down with a quart of milk. His lips and fingers left both soot and chocolate marks on the carton.

For Samantha he found a package of salami and beef jerky, before eventually wandering into the dog food aisle and laying open a bag of kibble for her.

The only way he knew it was dog food was by the large color photograph of the collie on the bag. In his day the dogs ate table scraps. They did not have their own special fare.

He was also absolutely delighted to have found a gift for his child in the gigantic metropolis he had stumbled upon for shelter. He hoped Lorna would find some comfort in his present.

Walmart seemed more like an entire village to Francis Barclay than it did a mere store. He hoped to find accommodations equally as luxurious again. To date, the best place he'd found to sleep was an out-of-business laundromat.

Strangely, neither dog nor master tripped any motion sensors or showed up on the Walmart surveillance cameras. The following day when the store employees discovered the crumpled heap of beach clothing and the obvious signs of vandalism to the grocery aisles, they immediately pulled surveillance footage from the previous night.

Finding no intruders visible on the tape, they simply threw the discarded beachwear into the dumpster out back and cleaned up the very minimal mess left behind in the grocery aisles.

There was less than fifty dollars in merchandise missing, it didn't even warrant a call to the police. However, the store manager and the security personnel were both quite troubled that the responsible party somehow managed to escape their state-of-the-art cameras.

Francis knew Lorna was suffering and needed to feed, but he could not allow her to ever put herself at risk and kill someone again. He would see her into her new home as quickly as he could make the arrangements. Before then, he felt he must meet with her and instruct her on her new life, her new family and her new home.

Samantha had brought him a photograph of the couple who would adopt Lorna. They appeared very suitable. They had taken exemplary care of his dog, who was now even wearing a collar and tag with the couple's name and address. The animal was well fed and looked nearly mortal again. This pleased Francis greatly.

After wandering into the office supply department of his night's lodging, Francis located an envelope and some paper. He found a writing instrument, and after wasting a futile twenty minutes in search of an inkwell, he discovered the quill possessed writing fluid already inside of it. He marveled at this bit of technology, just as he had so many others on his last visit to this noisy and frightening new world.

Mindful of his loosely knitted hand, he wrote a note to Lorna's new parents. When he finished he blew off the few particles of soot which had rained down on the paper. He placed his child's gift and the note into the envelope. After finding some string, he carefully secured the envelope to his dog's collar for her to deliver to the couple the next day.

The previous night someone appeared to Francis in a dream. He was pleased to discover he would soon have allies in his quest to save Lorna. Though the woman from last night's dream did not yet know she was to help him, Francis Barclay's heart was much lighter as he bid his dog farewell and began the rest of his journey the following day.

Lily Jarvis arrived home from work on a Friday afternoon to find the beautiful yellow Labrador asleep on the dog bed. She was delighted to see her. The dog disappeared a few days before and Lily wasn't sure if she would ever return.

Lily and Ben still did not know why the dog had shown up in the first place. They'd received no word from anyone to explain the dog's sudden appearance in their lives. By now, they were quite fond of the Lab and hoped she would stay.

Lily immediately texted her husband: *she's back!*

She took two leashes from the hall closet. When the dogs heard their metallic music, they both came running.

Not long after Samantha's arrival, the Jarvises purchased another leash so the new dog could accompany them on their walks. The leash was really just for show, since the dog could vanish into thin air any time she chose. They also purchased an additional food bowl, a dog collar, and another dog bed.

Being dead certainly hadn't hurt Samantha's appetite any, though, strangely, she never needed to relieve herself. Lily wondered how Lionel felt about that. To her, he had always seemed a little embarrassed when he needed to move his bowels.

Also unnecessary, the identification tag they ordered. Since Samantha was a ghost, she really didn't need one. Like Lionel's, it bore their address and phone number in case she ever got lost. She was part of the family now, and received all the same perks as their Lionel.

When she vanished into thin air three days ago, both she and Ben missed the dog a great deal. However, it was Lionel who took it hardest of all.

He sat at the door whining and would eat very little. Even his toys were of no solace. Lily was greatly relieved to see their new ward back home, and Lionel's food bowl sitting empty.

When Lily bent to affix Samantha's leash, she saw the envelope attached to her collar. It was a bulky thing and she was instantly curious what it held. She rummaged in a drawer for a pair of scissors in order to cut the envelope free. It was tied with string, and someone had taken great pains to make sure it stayed secure. When she tore it open a vaguely charred smell assaulted her nostrils and a figurine slid into her palm. Accompanying the item was a small scatter of what appeared to be ashes. With a slight mew of disgust, Lily wiped them off with a paper towel before examining the figure. It was a cheaply made thing, but lovely in its own right, as it was a likeness of their ghost dog. A Yellow Labrador.

Lily looked into the envelope. She shook the folded piece of paper into her hand and blew off a thin mist of more ashes, before donning a pair of reading glasses. The short note read:

> *Please deliver the statue to Beatrice Sugars, c/o Curious Curios and Collectibles in Alder Lake. Tell Madam Sugars to deliver it to the girl, Lorna. Advise her not to speak of the gift to the child's parents. Thank you for taking care of my dog, Samantha. Yours will be a most suitable home for the child.*
>
> *I remain in your debt,*
> *Francis Barclay*

Lily read the odd note again. She felt like she was reading a foreign language. *Child? What child?* she thought with growing alarm. With numb fingers she grabbed her cell phone from the counter and dialed Ben's office phone.

When his nurse informed her Ben was with a patient, Lily insisted he be told to call home right away. She hung up the phone in frustration.

The dogs had grown restless. Lionel clearly needed to relieve himself, so she stuffed her cell phone in her pocket and took them out for a short walk. Ben called just as they returned and she was putting their supper down on the floor.

"You need to come home right now!" Lily cried.

"What's wrong, honey? Is it the dog? Is she alright?" Ben's voice was tight with concern.

"She's fine, but I think I know why she was sent to us now. There's a note, Ben. It's about a child. You have to come home right now."

"A child?"

"Yes! It says something about us being a suitable home. Please, just hurry."

"I'll be there as soon as I can. I have one more patient waiting in an exam room. Once I see to her I will leave. Try and calm down, we knew we would find out sooner or later what the dog's appearance was about."

"I know, but I didn't think anyone would want us to take in a child. Whose child could it be?"

"What else did the note say?"

"It gave the dog's name. Samantha."

"Oh, really?" He sounded oddly disappointed. "I was thinking we should call her Solara because she looks like the sun when she appears. You know, the gold light? But Samantha's pretty. Suits her, doesn't it?"

Through clenched teeth, Lily responded, "Yes, lovely. Ben, come home. We have important things to discuss."

Hanging up, Lily turned to Samantha. "Someone sends a note telling us we are to adopt a child, and what does Ben want to talk about? Your name!" She rolled her eyes at the dog. "Aren't you glad he has his priorities straight?"

CHAPTER 15

Curious Curios and Collectibles was nearly as quiet and tense as Amanda's house had been over the last week.

Amanda was frankly growing quite tired of everyone and their sulky moods. After ushering a customer out the door and looking around to ensure they were alone, Amanda marched to the back of the shop where Bebe had spent most of the afternoon cataloging inventory from an estate sale.

She demanded, "Okay, lady. Enough! Tell me what's bothering you."

Bebe began, "Nothing is…"

Amanda cut her off. She growled, "It's bad enough having to deal with a husband who acts like the world just blew up, I don't need it here too. Here is where I come for sanity, not this bullshit. Now, either talk to me, or you can hire another one of the teenage morons to work my shifts. It's up to you."

Bebe took in Amanda's arched eyebrows, her arms crossed haughtily over her chest. From her stern stance, Bebe knew she meant business.

Not exactly lying, she replied, "Fine. I don't want you to quit. It's Blaze, okay?"

"No, not okay. What about Blaze?"

Bebe sighed. "He's all preoccupied with a case or something. He's more interested in it than he is my lady parts."

Amanda nodded knowingly. "Dead lady in the park. He still hasn't solved it. Doesn't even have any leads, is what I hear from my babysitter's dad."

Bebe forgot how plugged into everything in this town Amanda was. She could probably find out everything she needed to know about the investigation from her friend, without ever having to ask Blaze a thing.

Bebe wondered how it was Amanda didn't know her husband was banging the DA.

"Who is your babysitter's dad, hon?"

"Oh, he's a cop, of course. A sergeant. Works out of the same precinct as your McHottie."

Bebe asked, "He told you all that? Blaze refuses to talk about anything to do with the job or his case."

Amanda shrugged. "He's kind of the by-the-book type, isn't he? Don't worry about it. Once he puts this case to bed, I'm sure you and your lady parts will have his undivided attention again."

"I hope you're right. My overactive libido is not enjoying his lack of interest one bit."

Amanda smiled. "You mean you guys haven't hit the sheets yet?"

"No. Not for lack of trying, mind you. I have done everything but hang a sign from my boobs, and give him a map and a flashlight."

Amanda laughed and hugged her. "He'll come around. Maybe he's just trying to take things slow. I know he really likes you. Just let him get through this case. I hear it's bothering him."

"I hope you're right."

"All cops are like that. They live the damn job. Take it from someone who's been married to one for a long time. I'm highly qualified to dispense sage advice on the subject. I have a doctorate in being ignored."

Bebe looked at her friend and felt such a sense of profound sadness. The full weight of the secret she was keeping weighed on her chest like a piece of furniture. She looked away quickly, hiding tears that had sprung unbidden to her eyes.

"So, what's wrong with Kurt? You said we're both acting weird."

Amanda shrugged. "No clue. Probably work related."

The thought that floated quickly through Amanda's mind was, *Or other woman related. He gets like this when he's cheating too.*

She didn't say that out loud. She wasn't even sure why such an unwelcome notion flew into her head like an irate bird just then. Of course, knowing Kurt, it was a possibility. She would examine those thoughts later… or maybe not.

Amanda strong-armed the notion away. "I finally got him to agree to dinner and cards tonight at our neighbors. I'm tired of him moping around the house."

"The cop's daughter babysitting for you?"

"Yeah. You and McHottie doing anything tonight?"

"Nope," Bebe frowned, "I have an exciting evening planned cataloging the rest of the stuff from that estate sale and getting it out on the sales floor. I'll be working pretty late."

"Sorry, Bebe. I feel like I should help with that. I didn't know you were doing it tonight or I wouldn't have made plans."

"It's okay, sugar. Anything from that booty you want to pilfer before I turn it loose on an unsuspecting public?"

Amanda grinned. "As a matter of fact there was a little boudoir lamp with a feathered shade I was salivating over."

Carolyn Devonshire glanced longingly at the clock. The brief she'd been working on was not even half done, and it was due tomorrow. One of the dealers she convicted last year was appealing. She needed to write the standard brief; a hundred and one reasons why the conviction should stand, and the accused not be granted a new trial.

The hour was late, and Ms. Devonshire was tired and quite annoyed. Most of her irritation could be pinned at the breast of detective Kurt Dale. The bastard never even bothered to grace the office with his presence today. Carolyn put off writing the brief all day in hopes of waylaying him the minute he sat down at his desk.

It was rather difficult to dictate a legal brief when you were jumping out of your chair every time you heard a door close.

Carolyn was armed for battle and determined to have the long overdue confrontation about Kurt's tsunami-like moods. However, due to his inexplicable absence, the moment never presented itself. The lady had spent an entire day working herself into quite a frenzy.

While they'd been having some difficulties since Kurt tried to end their relationship by phone, in the last three days he'd turned into someone she didn't even know. Not only irritated, but jumpy and nervous like he was scared of something. Probably his wife finding out about them, Carolyn figured. But why couldn't he just tell her that? Because manning up was not Kurt Dale's strong suit, that's why.

Carolyn was shaken from her dark reverie by the squeak of her office door opening. She looked up, and was startled to see a beautiful little girl with auburn hair standing in the doorway. The child looked vaguely familiar, but she could not place where she'd seen her before.

"Are you lost?" Carolyn asked, rising from her desk.

"No." The little girl shook her head. "I have to talk to Carolyn. Are you Carolyn?"

The DA walked around the front of her desk to appraise the youngster more closely. She looked harmless enough, but for some reason this child gave her the creeps. She offered a nervous smile and put out her right hand to shake. "I'm Carolyn. Who might you be, young lady?"

The girl proffered her hand and allowed the older woman to shake it briefly before pulling it from her grasp. "I don't want you to upset my daddy anymore."

It was then Carolyn remembered where she'd seen this pretty little angelic face before. It was smiling out from a frame placed squarely in the center of Kurt Dale's desk.

This was Kurt's daughter, standing in her office at almost ten o'clock at night, and telling her not to upset her father. Could things be any stranger? Her mouth formed a small, startled o, as she struggled to unstick her tongue from the roof of her mouth.

"I see," Carolyn responded. She perched one hip on the corner of her desk. "And does your daddy know you're here? Is he in his office now?"

The only explanation Carolyn could fathom that would explain the child's presence in the building at this hour was if Kurt were here and he'd brought his daughter with him.

The little girl rolled her eyes comically. "Of course not. Daddy doesn't work at night. I didn't think you did either. I was just going to leave a note. He and Mommy are playing cards with Darlene and Russell."

For just the briefest moment Carolyn's puzzlement gave way to a white-hot, blinding and all-encompassing rage.

She thought, *All day I'm sitting here waiting for that asshole to put in an appearance, and he's acting like the perfect suburban husband, out with the little wifey. Just who does he think he's trifling with here? If he keeps this crap up, I swear I will be wearing his balls for earrings.*

She choked back the venom and asked, "How did you get here?"

"I took the bus. Once my babysitter puts us to bed and gets on Facebook, she totally forgets about me and Nate. She won't even notice I'm not there."

It took only a moment for the gravity of the current situation to reassert its dominance in Carolyn's mind. At once, her anger dissolved into alarm. Was the child deranged? She certainly didn't look crazy. In fact, she looked like a mini-me of the other picture gracing the good detective's desk—the one of his wife. Only the daughter had quite dazzling blue-green eyes, Carolyn observed. They were very unique, unlike any eye color she had ever seen before.

Carolyn raised her eyebrows. "You snuck out of your house and took a bus here? A driver let you on by yourself at this hour?"

"Oh, no. He never knew I was even on the bus. I got on in the back and hid behind the seats."

Carolyn was both worried and impressed with this child's cunning. "And you got into the building how?"

"What do you mean, how? I just walked in."

"The doors are locked after five o'clock," Carolyn said. "You couldn't have just walked in."

"I did," Lorna insisted. "Then I took the stairs up because the elevator buttons didn't work."

"No, they wouldn't. You need a keycard to run the elevators after hours. So, let me get this straight. You snuck out of your house, concealed yourself on a bus, and came all the way down here just to tell me not to upset your daddy? Is that right?

The little girl nodded, her curls bobbing up and down. "Yes, ma'am. He's been very upset lately, and I heard him talking to you on the phone. I don't know if it was a work fight or something, but I need you to stop upsetting him. I don't like when he gets like this, and… And well, you don't want to do that anymore, or I will have to make you stop."

Carolyn's eyes flew open in shock. *A not-so-veiled threat from this Shirley Temple look-alike? Really?* Carolyn thought incredulously.

"Well, how do you know I'm the one who upset him? Maybe he's mad at your mommy, huh? Ever think of that?"

Carolyn realized in that moment she had just sunk to a new low. Was she really trying to milk information about the state of Kurt's marriage from this strange child? A kid who should have been home in bed, but was somehow magically standing in her office in the middle of the night?

As impossible as this situation seemed, Carolyn realized she better start acting like the grown-up. And fast. What the hell was she going to do with this kid?

She wished she had just let the bastard off the hook when he tried to sever things. This crap she did not need.

Lorna responded, "No, he isn't mad at Mommy. She can tell he's upset too. Only she calls it *preoccupied.*"

"I see." Carolyn actually thought the word rather accurate for Kurt's current state of mind.

"Will you promise to stop making Daddy mad? Because I really have to go. I can't stay out much longer. I have to feed before I go home, and I'm not even sure where I can do that now." The little girl sighed miserably and tears filled her brilliant blue-green eyes. "I'm not even sure which bus I have to take to get back home now."

What the fuck did she just say? Carolyn thought. *Feed?*

"Um… Okay, listen, kid, you can't take the bus anywhere at this hour. You shouldn't even be out. It's very nice that you want to protect your dad and all, but it's dangerous to be out all by yourself at night. So, why don't you just take a seat and I will give your folks a call. I can get you something from the vending machines in the cafeteria if you're hungry. Alright?"

At the mention of calling her parents, all the color drained from the child's face. Her eyes darkened like smoke.

"Call Daddy?" Lorna cried in alarm. She began whipping her head wildly back and forth. "No, no, no. You can't!"

For the first time since this bizarre encounter began, Carolyn started to feel truly afraid. She hurried back behind her desk to put some space between her and the weird kid who had stormed her office. She plucked the receiver from her desk phone, her eyes never leaving the child's suddenly menacing face.

As she began dialing Kurt's cell phone number, the little girl launched herself like a projectile over the desk. She knocked the telephone from Carolyn's grasp, and sent several items on her desk clattering to the floor. A stapler flipped in the air and Lorna swatted it aside like a pesky insect.

In disbelief, Carolyn watched the airborne stapler fly across the room. She could not understand how things had spiraled out of control so quickly. She could distinctly remember Kurt telling her what a little doll his daughter was.

Oh, yeah, Carolyn thought. *She's a doll, alright. Just like Chuckie from the Child's Play movies.*

One ankle buckled beneath her and she lost her balance. Lorna took advantage of this setback and tackled the DA to the floor.

Carolyn rapped her head sharply against the corner of her desk. She cried out as she felt warm blood run into her eye.

At the sight of the prosecutor's blood, Lorna's fangs popped free without warning. She gasped, and immediately raised a hand to cover her mouth. However, there was no hiding the pure, naked lust now shining in her eyes once she looked upon that most coveted of treats.

Carolyn observed these developments with a dawning horror, unlike anything she had ever experienced.

"What the fuck are you?" she spat at the child with revulsion. "You're some kind of monster." She fought valiantly to wrestle herself out of the narrow space where she was pinned beneath the freakishly strong little girl.

Amazingly, tears sprang to Lorna's eyes again. She sobbed in a wounded child's treble, "I am not a monster. You take that back."

Carolyn managed to get her legs out from between her desk and the wall.

As she was scrambling to her feet, the child started pummeling her with clenched fists, repeating, "Take it back, take it back, take it back."

Carolyn thought she must be witnessing a temper tantrum straight out of the devil's dreams. She could not tear her eyes from those two dagger-sharp fangs jutting from the girl's mouth. She managed to work one of her high-heel pumps off, and brandished it like a weapon.

"Get the fuck off me," she yelled, backing away from her diminutive assailant.

Lorna pulled in a hitching breath, screwed her fists into her eyes and bawled.

Carolyn actually started to feel sorry for the child for a split second, before reminding herself that the little fiend just attacked her.

When Lorna removed her hands from her eyes, the look of pure murderous hate reflected in them pressed a cold knife of fear into the prosecutor's breast.

Suddenly her office was bathed in an eerie blue light. When she realized the child's eyes were glowing—not just bright, but literally glowing with their own interior iridescence—and responsible for the office's sudden transformation, she descended into complete and utter hysteria. She turned screaming and fled the office.

Carolyn made it as far as the hallway before the little girl caught up with her.

The DA got in one good shot with her raised high-heel shoe, gashing Lorna's scalp. It wasn't a deep wound, but it was enough to make her bleed. In the moment Carolyn relished that small victory, and allowed herself a glimmer of hope she might have slowed the child down, she felt a sharp sting at her throat. She wondered how this little pipsqueak had ever gotten the best of her.

Her last thought was, *Because she isn't human. Kurt Dale spawned the devil.*

Like so many women before her, Carolyn Devonshire profoundly regretted the day she ever laid eyes on Detective Kurt Dale. The room went gray and she lost consciousness.

Besides the shallow gouge on her head, a deeper scratch had been carved into Lorna's cheek by Carolyn's fingernail. Blood merged from the two lacerations and ran down the little girl's face, comingling with the blood of her victim.

With a moan of pure ecstasy, Lorna drank greedily from the Deputy District Attorney's gushing throat.

The problem of where she would feed had been solved.

CHAPTER 16

Once Lorna finished her attack on Carolyn Devonshire, she lay panting on the blood-stained carpet in the city's municipal building.

Now that it was all over, she was fighting hysteria of her own. Her head ached miserably. The DA's blood no longer flowed, but Lorna was frightened to discover her own still pattering down her face at an alarming rate.

This hadn't been like killing the homeless woman in the park. That had been an accident.

Carolyn Devonshire called her a monster and hurt her feelings. Then she hit her over the head with a shoe. When Lorna took her down that final time it was with the intent to kill.

Lorna didn't think she had ever felt such pure murderous hate in her heart for anyone her entire life as she did for that woman. She wasn't sorry she was dead.

Being able to feed wasn't her goal during the vicious attack, it was just a byproduct that she was quite grateful for. She didn't think she could have lasted another day without blood.

Now she'd better get out of here. She was unsure how much time had passed, or if her parents were home yet. They would probably check on her when they returned from Darlene and Russell's. If she wasn't in bed, she would be in unimaginable trouble. Lorna knew there was no way on earth she could talk her way out of this one. Coming here had been a big mistake—quite possibly, the worst of her whole life.

When Lorna finally managed to push herself up from the floor, blood ran into her eyes. She felt a moment of heart-stopping vertigo. She closed her eyes against the nausea and waited for the room to turn upright again.

When the wave of dizziness passed she stood up, wiping blood from her eyes and smearing it down her face. Lorna was mortified to see her clothes were covered in blood too. In fact, she realized with increasing horror, there was blood everywhere. On the walls, the floor, matted into her hair, and endlessly flowing down her face and neck.

She was a cop's little girl and she didn't want her fingerprints left in blood anywhere. Lorna had known about fingerprinting since she was old enough to crawl. While she had to get out of the building immediately, she also knew she'd better wipe down everything she could remember touching first. She pulled a wad of tissues from a box on the Devonshire woman's desk and carefully set to work erasing the evidence.

Once she was satisfied her tracks were covered as well as they could be, Lorna wiped her hands with more tissue and stuffed all the soiled pieces into the pocket of her blood-sodden jeans. Finally she pulled a few fresh pieces of tissue from the box to use on the door handle when she exited the building.

Lorna cast a final glance around the office to make sure she was leaving nothing incriminating behind, apart from an ocean of spilled blood. She ran for the stairwell.

Lorna did not spare the prone body of the prosecutor even a fleeting glimpse before hurrying down the stairs.

The moment the door opened out onto the street, a shrill and ear-shattering alarm began wailing right beside her head. Lorna's heart leapt into her throat. She ran blindly into the street, fleeing that auditory assault.

Once she was a block away, and the sound of that shrieking and somehow accusatory alarm was far enough behind her to be only a distant echo, she stopped running.

She sagged against a wall and fought to catch her breath. The blood from her head wound was flowing again. She slid down the wall and sat down.

Lorna knew if she panicked, she was dead. She fought off the paralyzing fear struggling to overwhelm her entire body. In a few minutes the fresh air began to calm her.

She could not go home in the state she was in now. She was drenched in blood and needed medical attention.

It was then that the voice of her blood-father spoke clearly in her head. *Go to Ms. Sugars, she will help you.*

Lorna knew the antique shop was down here somewhere. It was probably close by, but she didn't know the address. She also doubted Bebe would be there this late at night.

She was just about to speak these objections out loud when the voice of her maker spoke again. *All will be well. Just start walking and I will guide you.*

Lorna rose unsteadily from the sidewalk. She felt an invisible hand grasp her arm just above the elbow and begin leading her down the street. She stayed close to the buildings, trying to avoid passing directly under streetlamps.

There was no one on the street at this hour and she avoided being seen. In downtown Alder Lake, the streets rolled up early.

At the corner, the invisible pressure on her elbow turned her left. She travelled two more blocks before being pulled across the street and deposited into an alley.

When the pressure disappeared from her arm she was standing directly in front of the delivery entrance to Curious Curios and Collectibles.

CHAPTER 17

Francis Barclay was just thinking of where he might find lodging for the night. All his limbs were intact, and he was enjoying the absence of a breeze on this mild evening. Suddenly he was overtaken by a mind-numbing panic. The sound of his blood-child's scream exploded in his head. All the strength ran out of his legs. Collapsing against a van parked at the side of the road, he closed his eyes. At once, he knew Lorna had killed again.

Using the psychic link he had discovered in his mind, he reached out to her in the dark and tried to calm her. He could not get through. She was too distraught to hear him. He squeezed his eyes shut tight and continued trying to call out and soothe his child.

Finally, what seemed like a long time later, he made contact. It was several more minutes before she simmered down enough to listen to him with her inner ear.

After he safely negotiated her through the slumbering town and deposited her at the Sugars woman's shop, Francis sat at the curb exhausted. He pondered what to do next.

No more than ten minutes passed before his eyes flew open wide in alarm. He reached out to Lorna again. This time to scold her.

Francis needed to get to Alder Lake and get the girl out of there now. She was sure to get caught this time.

Judging by the child's sheer terror, this victim had been no homeless person in the park. He was out of time, and no longer had the luxury to continue his journey on foot.

It was time to meet Lorna's new parents. They would need to help him save his child, and it would have to be soon.

The game was Hearts, and Darlene had just shot the moon, winning the game.

"Hah!" she cried triumphantly, raising her hands in a victory salute.

Amanda laughed, "Well, that's it for me. I have been humbled enough for one evening."

Kurt looked relieved to see the night coming to a close. He'd brought his melancholy mood with him to the neighbors and spent the whole evening preoccupied.

It was obvious to everyone his mind wasn't on the game, or the conversation that flowed easily around him.

When Russell suggested they sit outside and have a nightcap; ginger ale for him and brandy for Kurt, he began to decline.

Amanda cut him off. "What a lovely idea. Darlene and I can have some girl talk."

She shooed Kurt from his chair. Amanda was in no hurry to return home and deal with more of the same from her strangely somber husband. She would rather prolong the evening by helping Darlene with the dishes.

If she had been honest with herself, she would have known what she was really trying to avoid was ruminating on this afternoon's unwelcome thought about Kurt having yet another affair. Her own contemplations bothered her much more than Kurt's dark mood.

With a resigned sigh, Kurt followed Russell Coombs out to the back porch. For one melancholy moment, when they first stepped outside, both men looked toward the field behind the house and unknowingly shared an unspoken memory of Francis Barclay.

Kurt was startled when Russell, seeming to read his mind, asked, "You ever think about him? The vam… well, you know." Kurt choked on his brandy.

"Sorry, didn't mean to hit a nerve." Russell clapped him on the back.

Kurt waved a hand. He caught his breath and replied, "Funny you should ask. I think about him all the time lately. You?"

Russell, looking solemn, nodded. "Mostly I think about my dog. How she changed."

Since having Samantha put to sleep, Russell had often spoken of his belief that Barclay turned her into a vampire. Kurt could never quite believe that. He thought it far more likely that twenty years of boozing and untold bottles of Jack Daniels had seeped into Russell's head and rearranged the furniture. He wouldn't go so far as to say his neighbor was delusional, but sometimes he wondered.

Russell, having been sober for some time, read Kurt's thoughts in his eyes. He didn't care what his neighbor believed, Russell knew his dog had died a vampire.

The two men sat in silence for a few moments. Finally Russ asked, "Is that what's bugging you? That debacle? It was a long time ago, Kurt."

Having never considered Russell Coombs a confidante, Kurt wasn't anxious to start now. The problem was he desperately needed someone to talk to. He recognized what a dismal job he was doing of hiding his anxiety from anyone around him. Even the neighbor seemed to know something was eating him.

The *debacle,* as Russell called it, was at least an experience both men had shared. Not in the same way, but they both understood that Francis Barclay wasn't human.

Russell acknowledged being stone drunk on the night Lorna was kidnapped and his dog turned. Still, he never believed that his sketchy recollection of those events was brought on by booze playing tricks with his mind. Samantha was living proof that it wasn't. Besides, there was not enough alcohol in the western hemisphere to ever make him forget Francis Barclay's eyes.

Kurt asked, "Russ, how much of what happened the night Francis Barclay kidnapped Lorna do you remember?"

Russ looked down, embarrassed. "Well… Frankly, not a lot. I remember some of it, but the details are pretty hazy. I'm sure you know I was tanked most of the time back then. Why do you ask?"

Kurt shook his head. "Never mind."

"What is it, Kurt? Maybe I can help. I'm not drunk now, you know."

Kurt hung his head. He wouldn't meet the other man's eyes. "I worry he's going to come back."

Russ felt a nasty shiver of fright crawl up his back. He clapped a reassuring hand on Kurt's shoulder. "He won't."

Russell had tried to sound confident, but it rang hollow, so he repeated it with more conviction than he felt. "He won't."

Neither man believed it any more the second time.

Bebe was muscling an armoire into a corner in an effort to clear some floor space for a 1930's hat and jewelry display she was going to set up.

A loud and insistent rapping exploded at the back door of her shop. Bebe jumped, uttering a startled squawk, and banged her shoulder against the armoire.

"Who the hell can that be at this hour?" she mumbled, rubbing her aching shoulder.

Bebe made her way to the back room and cautiously pushed aside the window shade. For the briefest moment she hoped it was Blaze, knowing at the same time it wouldn't be. Blaze would have called first. He wouldn't just show up pounding on the back door in the middle of the night, scaring her half to death like that.

When she looked outside her heart leapt into her throat. There was a little girl, covered head to toe in blood, standing on the porch. Under the harsh fluorescent light it looked nearly purple, but Bebe could tell it was blood. She placed a hand to her chest in hopes of slowing her pounding heart.

The girl looked back at her with glowing eyes.

Bebe gasped, her heart taking off at full-gallop again. She spun around to run for the telephone. If ever there was a 911 moment, this was it.

Her visitor spoke, halting Bebe in her tracks. "Bebe, help! It's me, Lorna. Please don't leave me out here."

Bebe rushed back to the door. "Lorna!" she cried, throwing the bolt so hard she ripped a fingernail half off.

The child rushed inside, throwing herself against Bebe with such force she nearly knocked her over backward. Lorna wrapped her arms around her waist in a death grip and began sobbing uncontrollably.

Bebe held on to her for a few moments, stroking her back with a soothing hand. Slowly, she pried the girl off and held her at arm's length.

Taking in the blood, Bebe exclaimed, "Christ, child! What happened to you? How badly are you hurt?"

"I don't know. I don't think it's too bad. I'm still bleeding some from where she hit me with the shoe though, and it hu… hurts," Lorna sobbed. She inhaled a watery breath and began to cry even harder.

"So much blood," Bebe moaned. "We have to get you to the hospital."

Lorna grabbed her arm and dug her fingers painfully into Bebe's flesh. "Wait! Please just give me a second to catch my breath. The blood isn't mine—At least, not all of it. I have to get home. No hospital!" She sounded scared to death, and was adamant about not seeking medical attention.

"But, honey…" Bebe started to say.

Lorna pulled in another shaky breath. She was starting to cry even harder. "No hospital!" She shook her head violently. "You don't understand, Bebe. I can't. I have to go home right now. I just… I can't go like this. I have to clean up. Please, just help me clean up. I really messed it up this time."

Bebe stopped trying to maneuver the child toward the door and pulled her to a chair instead. She sat her down and kneeled in front of her.

"Lorna, sweetie, I need you to calm down and get it together, okay? What did you mess up? If this isn't your blood, then whose is it?"

Lorna's eyes shot sideways. "I can't tell you that. Please, Bebe, my parents are going to kill me if they get back from Russ and Darlene's and I'm not home. My father said to come to you. I don't know what to do," she wailed.

The desperation in the child's voice nearly broke Bebe's heart, but she had to find out what was going on. The more Lorna spoke, the less sense she was making.

"Your father sent you here?" Bebe asked, her voice incredulous.

"Ye... No! Not that one. The other one."

Lorna sounded anguished. She once again wrapped her arms around Bebe with panicky tightness. Then suddenly, with no warning, Lorna's voice took on an oddly whiney tone that was completely unlike her.

She moaned miserably, "Yes, Father. I know that. I wasn't going to tell her... I... Alright, yes."

"Lorna, who one earth are you talking t...?" Bebe began.

Lorna screeched in an ear-splitting decibel, "I SAID OKAY!"

The child abruptly disentangled from Bebe's embrace. The queerest light Bebe ever saw flooded the little girl's eyes. They shone with a preternatural radiance that was nearly hypnotic. All at once an odd blue cast filled the whole room.

Bebe froze. When she'd first witnessed that glow upon Lorna showing up at the back of her shop, Bebe believed it to be a trick of the unnatural fluorescent lighting outside. She saw now that wasn't the case. Bebe suffered a moment of the purest terror she had ever felt.

Lorna looked at her with a calm she never would have believed possible following her previous hysteria. Her tears gone, Lorna's voice turned suddenly flat and menacing. It was a voice straight out of a horror movie, and it was unlike anything Bebe would have dreamed could possibly issue from any child's mouth.

Through clenched teeth, Lorna growled, "I love you, Bebe. So does my mother, so I don't want to hurt you. I need you to listen to me now. My mom and dad can't know I was here. They can't even know I was out tonight. I am out of time, so you have to stop asking me questions. Just clean me up and get me home. Do you understand what I am telling you?"

Bebe's first reaction was to protest and keep firing off questions. The light emanating from the child's demon-like eyes stopped her. She was a woman with a well-honed survival instinct. An instinct long-tested and refined to near perfection during the two decades she lived with Royce. She listened when her self-preservation voice spoke up. It started yelling at the top of its lungs when that strangely flat voice suddenly issued from Lorna's lips.

Bebe rose from the floor and took the little girl's hand. In a tone so nonchalant it surprised even her, she replied, "Okay, honey." She led her into the bathroom without another word.

Once she had Lorna stripped out of the soiled clothing, she went to work on her with a wet washcloth, using gentle strokes. She washed her hair in the sink using liquid soap from the dispenser kept there. Bebe apologized when the child winced in pain when she rubbed too hard on her injured scalp.

After Lorna was clean, Bebe assessed the injuries. She assured the girl none were life threatening. She retrieved a first aid kit from a cabinet and applied ointment to the scalp wound and the laceration on her face.

All business now, Bebe told her, "Your hair will hide the wound on your head, but that one on your cheek is going to show. Your parents will see it if you don't cover it with something." Then she snapped her fingers and said, "Wait here. I'll be right back."

She disappeared into the shop, returning only a few seconds later, holding an ancient looking trunk with rusted latches.

Bebe placed the case on the closed toilet seat and popped the clasps.

Rummaging around inside, she told Lorna, "I just took this in. It's an old makeup kit from a movie production company. There must be something in here."

She was grateful to see the bizarre light in Lorna's eyes had extinguished while she was bathing her.

Lorna yawned. She sat patiently on the edge of the sink wrapped in a bath towel. It all but swallowed up her small frame.

Bebe marveled at how helpless and fragile she looked. She pulled several jars from the trunk. She tried and rejected two different tones of industrial strength cover-up, before finally settling on a shade she thought would appropriately camouflage the cut on Lorna's cheek.

Once Bebe covered it to her satisfaction, she replaced the lid.

Handing the jar to Lorna, along with a sponge that had seen better days, Bebe told her to use the concealer until the scrape healed.

She took Lorna's hand and helped her off the sink. "No guarantees your mom isn't going to see that, even with the makeup, so you best have a story ready in case she does."

Lorna nodded. "I've had to make up things before."

When Bebe looked at her questioningly, the little girl just shrugged. Bebe did not ask any questions.

She tightened the towel around Lorna's narrow shoulders. "Come on, let's find you something to wear and get you home."

Bebe looked at the clock. It was five minutes to eleven. If Kurt and Amanda weren't home already, they most certainly would be soon.

Quickly thumbing through a rack of vintage clothing, she selected a dress. It was a little too big for the girl, but would suffice under the circumstances.

"I don't have any shoes that will work, and your tennies are covered in blood," Bebe commented.

Lorna looked downtrodden. "It's okay. I will just go barefoot."

Bebe pulled a pair of athletic socks from her gym bag and handed them to the child. "Put these on."

Once Lorna looked as presentable as was possible, Bebe instructed, "You better hide that dress when you take it off tonight. If your mom sees it, she will recognize it. She hung up all those clothes out there. And hide the socks too. I'll try and wash your clothes. If I can't get the stains out, I will dispose of them for you. Blood isn't easy to get off."

Lorna looked at Bebe with tears shining in her eyes, and a voice filled with such gratitude it was heart-wrenching. She murmured, "Thank you, Bebe. Thank you for helping me. I am not very good at… I haven't learned how… Oh, never mind. Just thank you."

Bebe nodded and pulled her purse from a hook behind the door. She wasn't sure which scared her more, Lorna showing up in the middle of the night drenched in blood, or her sudden and total mood swings, coupled with the completely nonsensical things she was saying. She seemed to switch from helpless child to menacing terrorist within seconds. The glowing eyes and demon-voice… Well, those Bebe refused to even think about.

"I don't know what you have gotten yourself into, child." She pulled Lorna to her and gave her a brief hug.

"I don't know either, Bebe." Lorna replied sadly.

"Come on. Let's get you home."

They drove in silence for the short ride to Lorna's neighborhood. Bebe doused the headlights before turning onto the peaceful residential street.

Kurt and Amanda Dale were finishing their nightcaps when Bebe stopped the car a few houses down the block from their home.

Lorna gave Bebe a final hug and stepped out of the car. Bebe watched with frightened eyes as the little girl waved to her. She disappeared through a partially open window at the corner of the house.

Bebe left the headlights off until she was completely clear of the neighborhood. After about five minutes, she realized she was shaking uncontrollably and had to pull over. With Lorna out of the car, the full weight of the evening's events bore down on her like an avalanche. Bebe opened the window and pulled in deep breaths of cooling air.

The immeasurable relief she felt at being shut of the child was mingled with an almost crippling terror.

She picked up her cell phone, intending to call Blaze. Her mind replayed Lorna's strange transformation from *little-girl-lost* to *demon-child,* complete with Halloween-glowing eyes. Abruptly, Bebe dropped the phone like it was hot. She knew she couldn't tell anyone. Especially not Blaze.

Her mind replayed all of the strange things Lorna said in a series of broken sentences: *I really messed it up this time. I'm not good at it. I don't know how yet. She hit me with a shoe. I love you and I don't want to hurt you. My father said to come to you.*

Just who the hell was she talking to when she started whining like that? *Father,* she had said. If it wasn't Kurt Dale the little girl was speaking of, then who?

There was something very, very wrong with her best friend's daughter. Bebe's overtaxed mind could not even begin to try to figure out what it was.

Her thoughts turned to the blood. There were many questions racing through Bebe's mind pertaining to it: What happened to result in all that blood? Whose blood was it? Lorna told her it wasn't all hers. Was Lorna responsible for spilling the blood? Where was the person the blood issued from now? Did they need help?

Bebe wondered if she was now an accessory to some unknown crime committed by her best friend's daughter. Was she doing something illegal by washing the girl's clothes? Maybe destroying evidence?

Bebe would not have to wait long for the answer to those burning questions.

CHAPTER 18

Bebe arrived home, her body exhausted, her mind deeply troubled. She glanced at the blinking light on the answering machine and knew immediately the message was from Blaze. She hesitated, her finger poised over the machine.

Instead of playing the message, Bebe walked into the kitchen and poured herself a healthy belt of scotch. She drained the glass and then refilled it. Plopping down onto a kitchen chair, she nursed the second drink more slowly.

"So many secrets," she said to the empty house. She wondered how, in only a few short months, she had become embroiled in so much drama and the keeper of so many unwanted secrets.

Upon moving to Alder Lake, Bebe believed Amanda Dale had been the best thing that happened to her. Now she felt like the lady was the worst.

Kurt's affair was a painful enough secret to keep. Lorna's was far worse.

While Bebe had no idea what the child's secret actually was, it was obviously malevolent. She wondered how on earth a seven-year-old could possibly be harboring a secret as sinister and dangerous as the one Lorna appeared to be.

Bebe wished like hell she could turn back time and close the shop early. She would give anything to erase the last two hours.

She found herself feeling the now familiar bitter resentment toward Blaze. Had he not been so preoccupied with his precious case, or Kurt Dale, or whatever the hell was eating him, she would have been out with him tonight. Or better yet, in with him.

She wished she could have been anywhere besides her shop. How did she get sucked into a seven-year-old child's nasty and bloody predicament like this?

Her mind, sufficiently numbed by the scotch, turned toward the more mind-boggling events of the evening. Exactly what was Lorna Dale, anyway? She was certainly no average little grade-schooler. All you had to do was behold the light show in the kid's eyes, and you knew damn well she was not.

Bebe wondered if Kurt and Amanda knew about the sheer wrongness of their child. Had they ever bore witness to their daughter's strange eyes when they lit up like that? Ever heard the voice of a demon issue from her pretty little mouth?

The phone rang, startling Bebe into spilling her drink, and out of the game of twenty questions she was engaged in. She muttered an expletive as she rose to answer it.

She stopped just before picking up the receiver. She was in no condition to talk to anyone right now. She needed time to think. Allowing the machine to answer the call, she stood dejectedly with her hand resting on the phone as Blaze's voice filled the room.

"Hey, pretty lady. Where are you? I tried your shop, your cell, and the house. You aren't picking up anywhere. Did you forget I'm a cop? My mind is programmed to assume the worst. Call me when you are home safe and sound or I am going to have to put out an APB on you."

"Shit," Bebe muttered. She sighed bitterly and drained the rest of her drink.

She picked up the phone and began to dial Blaze's number, before inspiration struck. She hung up and began rummaging through her purse in search of her cell phone. A text message would be the safest method of communication right now.

Bebe pled exhaustion as her excuse for not calling. She assured him she was safely in her house, doors locked and windows bolted against the outside world.

Sweet dreams. Sleep well, pretty lady, he wrote back.

Fat fucking chance, Bebe thought bitterly and poured another scotch.

Bebe was roused from fitful sleep by the ringing of her telephone at just after six the next morning. She thought she must still be asleep and dreaming when she fumbled the phone to her ear.

Blaze exclaimed, "You are never going to believe who got killed last night!"

"Huh?" Bebe grunted, trying to claw her way out of a thick cobweb of slumber.

"Bebe, wake up!" Blaze complained.

Bebe sat up and kicked the covers off. Suddenly the room felt stifling. "Okay, okay. I'm awake." She yawned and rubbed her eyes. "What's going on?"

"Deputy DA, Carolyn Devonshire was just found murdered in the municipal building. Kurt's lover is dead."

"Oh God, Blaze! No! Did Kurt…" she left the rest of the question unspoken.

"I don't know. I just got the call. Haven't even started the investigation yet. You know what this means?"

"Yeah," Bebe sighed, "it means Amanda is going to find out he's been cheating."

"And Kurt is going to be a suspect in yet another murder," Blaze muttered angrily.

"What do you mean *another* murder?"

"Jeez, Bebe, don't you ever talk to anyone in this town? Don't any of the locals ever come in and gossip in your shop?" Blaze wondered. "I heard this story the first week I moved here." He proceeded to fill Bebe in on the last murder in which Kurt Dale had been a suspect.

Bebe wasn't surprised Amanda had never shared this particular piece of history with her over wine at La Travisa. She marveled at how chatty the good detective had become all of a sudden. Apparently, all it took to get him talking was one dead DA.

Bebe did not put Lorna's bloody appearance at her shop the previous night together with the news Blaze had just shared. It never even entered her mind that Lorna might have had something to do with Carolyn Devonshire's demise. Regardless of Lorna's unexplained peculiarities or her strange and erratic behavior, she was still her best friend's kid. Bebe never even contemplated the child might be a murderer.

Bebe did not know that on the other side of town, Amanda Dale was in a similar form of denial about her husband having yet another extramarital affair. Some things were simply too painful to entertain.

Bebe wondered what Blaze's latest piece of news was going to mean for Amanda. She asked Blaze, "So are we supposed to tell Amanda about Kurt and the dearly departed DA, or do we let her find out when this thing hits the newspapers and you start investigating her husband?"

"Hell, I don't know. We've been sitting on this for over a week. She's gonna hate us both."

Bebe couldn't help but speculate about how Amanda would feel if she knew the other secret Bebe was keeping from her. The far worse one about her little girl's blood-filled outing the night before.

She told Blaze, "I can't tell her. I just can't do it now. I suppose in hindsight maybe we should have told her when we found out, but we didn't."

"Well, I have to talk to Kurt. He has to be told I am aware of his relationship with the DA. He'll know he's automatically a suspect. Maybe we just leave it up to him to tell her, and Amanda never needs to know we knew about the affair."

All Bebe could think about was how her life was becoming one lie on top of another, one secret on top of another. She wondered how high a house of cards could reach before it all came crashing down.

The murder of Carolyn Devonshire was all over the news just a few short hours after Blaze's early morning phone call to Bebe.

The municipal building was a sea of reporters, news vans and curious onlookers. Crime scene tape was stretched end to end, keeping the steps clear of the gathering mob. The front doors were locked and no one was admitted inside. Even most of the staff was sent away after a cleaning crew discovered the body.

Blaze arrived shortly after the coroner and crime scene technicians. He was no stranger to the commotion he witnessed before him, as he surveyed the news caravan and jostling crowd outside the courthouse. He'd been with the LAPD for over ten years, where crime was a routine occurrence, and scenes like this commonplace. It was, however, both disturbing and surreal to watch it play out on a peaceful, tree-lined street in Alder Lake.

When Blaze saw Caroline Devonshire's lifeless corpse, he knew immediately she had been murdered by the same person responsible for the death of Posy McManus. Carolyn's neck was ripped apart in the same grisly manner.

He immediately went to the security office and told the officer on duty to pull the surveillance tapes for the building. He wanted every one of them, from the time the building closed to the public at five o'clock the night before, all the way through this morning when the DA's body was found. He didn't know what time the murder occurred, but he wasn't going to take any chances on losing even one minute of footage.

While the security guard saw to procuring the tapes, Blaze made a most dreaded phone call to Detective Kurt Dale.

He sat heavily in a chair and dialed the Dales' home phone number. Amanda answered.

Blaze fought the urge to simply hang up when he heard her voice. She said hello twice before he was finally able to find his voice.

"Amanda, hey. It's Blaze. I'm looking for Kurt."

"Well, good morning, sweetness. I'm fine thanks, and how are you?" she laughed.

"Sorry," he muttered, "I'm calling in an official capacity, I'm afraid. We have a rather, uh, well, high-profile homicide here, and I need to talk to Kurt about it."

Amanda immediately switched to being the wife of a police officer. The good humor left her voice at once. "Do you have his cell phone number, Blaze? He's on his way in to work now. You can reach him in his car."

"Thank you, hon," Blaze replied gratefully. "I've got it." He disconnected, thankful not to have been asked the myriad of questions he knew Amanda must have wanted to fire at him.

He dialed Kurt's cell phone number next. The man answered on the first ring.

Blaze wasted no time. He identified himself and said, "Kurt, I have some bad news about Deputy DA, Devonshire. I'm going to need to speak with you privately as soon as you get to the municipal building."

There was silence on the line as he waited for Kurt to digest what he'd just told him. Kurt finally let out an anguished wail. "Jesus, Blaze! Carolyn? Is she… is she…"

"Yes, Kurt. I'm sorry, she's dead. She was murdered in the municipal building some time last night or early this morning. You and I need to have a talk."

More silence. Finally Kurt pulled in a shaking breath. "Is this a talk we need to have in an interrogation room, or can we take another drive?"

"Your car is fine for now. I'll wait for you in the back. Trust me, you don't want to go anywhere near the front of the courthouse right now. It's a zoo."

Five minutes later Kurt pulled to the curb and Blaze climbed into the passenger seat of his vehicle.

Blaze waited until they were a block or so away, and waiting at a traffic light, before he turned to the other detective. He asked simply, "How long was it going on with you two?"

The color drained from Kurt's face and he hung his head in shame. "How long have you known?"

Blaze shrugged. "Not long. Bebe and I saw you with her last week. Neither one of us has said anything to your wife. I felt like solving the murder in the park was more important for the time being." He observed Kurt's hands begin to shake.

"Bebe knows?" Kurt sobbed. "I am so fucked."

Blaze looked at Kurt with a mixture of dismay and surprise. "You do realize you may have bigger problems than just your wife finding out you were cheating, right? Where were you last night?"

Kurt snapped his head sideways and glared at Blaze with alarm. "Nowhere near the municipal building, if that's what you're thinking. I have an alibi! Not just Amanda either. My neighbors. We were at their house all evening. I did not do this, Blaze. You must know that."

Blaze said nothing. He looked at the other detective with barely masked contempt.

Seeing the look in Blaze's eyes, Kurt turned back to face the road. "Oh, come on! I'm assuming you pulled the surveillance tapes for the hours in question, right?"

Blaze conceded, "Of course, but I haven't viewed them yet. You won't be on any of them, I trust?"

"No! Hell, I didn't even go into work yesterday. Check my keycard and watch the fucking tapes, Blaze. They won't lie, even if you think I am," Kurt fumed.

He was appalled to even be under scrutiny for this. Then he reminded himself Blaze knew about the affair and his anger dissolved. Of course he was a suspect, he was sleeping with her.

Kurt's thoughts turned to Carolyn. He asked, "What happened to her? Was it… was it him?" he finished lamely.

Blaze nodded, "If by *him*, you mean the perp who did the homeless lady in the park, then yeah, I think so. The wounds look the same."

They rode in silence for a few minutes. Kurt finally asked in a tentative voice, "About Mandy, um, is this all going to come out? I will probably lose my career, as well as my family if it does."

Blaze thought of a hundred different things to say. Most having something to do with reminding him he should have thought about that before he started cheating on his wife again. In the end he decided to keep his moral judgment to himself.

He replied simply, "I don't know, Kurt."

Kurt cleared his throat. "Blaze, if I am truly not a suspect—and once you see the surveillance tapes and talk to my neighbors, I won't be, then why would it…"

Blaze cut him off. "If you're asking if I am going to make it public, the answer is no. I have no control over who else knows about it, though. You weren't exactly discreet. As far as Amanda goes, that's another story. This has been eating Bebe up. I can't promise she won't tell her."

"Will you?" Kurt asked miserably.

"You know, you are putting everyone in an awful position, Kurt. Why the hell should we lie for you or protect you?"

"Look, I know you don't like me very much—especially now. But if you care about Amanda, you must see that no good can come of her finding out. I was trying to end things. I doubt you will believe that, but it's true. I'm not going to beg you not to tell my wife, I realize I have no right to ask that of you. But for the sake of my children, and for the sake of Amanda's feelings, I hope you won't."

They were quiet again for several minutes before Blaze asked, "Kurt, how do I catch this perp? This *vampire* or whatever the fuck he is? Will you be able to ID him from the surveillance tapes if it's the same guy you took down five years ago?"

Kurt gave a grim nod. "Yeah, if it's Barclay, I can ID him. But I don't know how to catch him any more now than I did back then. If he's like he was before, he won't last long anyway. He'll die all on his own."

"Does Amanda know your suspicions about all this?"

Kurt shot his eyes sideways. "I don't want to scare her. She has never really gotten over what happened. If I tell her there's a possibility Barclay is back she might…"

Blaze thundered, "What about her safety? What about your kids? If this psychopath is out to get you, don't you think you better warn your wife so she can watch out for him?"

Kurt would not meet the other man's eyes. John Wyatt had told him much the same thing.

"I will tell her today. I was hoping he'd burn out and die again before she ever had to know. Can I view the surveillance tapes with you? I need to be sure."

Blaze promptly shook his head. "No. You're still a suspect until I clear you. I will let you know when I'm ready for you to see them."

"Can you convince Bebe not to tell Amanda?"

"Kurt, shut the fuck up. Just drive me back to the municipal building, okay? I have more on my mind than your marital problems. If you don't want Bebe to say anything to Amanda about your tomcatting around, then tell her yourself. I've got two homicides I need to solve."

Kurt visibly paled at being so sternly chastised. He said no more as he returned to the courthouse.

Blaze didn't mean to blow up at Kurt that way, but he couldn't stand to be in the car with him for another minute. He could not recall ever feeling such disgust or abject loathing for another human being as he did for Kurt Dale in that moment. The guy couldn't care less that Carolyn Devonshire might be dead only because of her relationship with him. If she was murdered by someone seeking revenge against Kurt, his whole family was in danger. All he cared about was saving his own skin. No one else mattered.

Blaze had never felt sorrier for anyone in his life than he did for Amanda Dale. That vague dislike he'd felt for her husband since the day they'd met four years ago, had just turned the corner. It was now full-blown contempt.

Kurt was an even bigger fool than Blaze ever dreamed if he really thought his wife wasn't going to find out about the affair.

When the well-dressed woman entered Curious Curios and Collectibles, Bebe offered her a warm smile. "Hello there. Is there something special I can help you find?"

The woman approached the counter and extracted an envelope from an oversized handbag.

"Good morning. Are you Ms. Sugars?" she asked politely. The woman appeared a bit nervous.

All at once Bebe's hackles went up. She thought Royce was suing her for more money, and this woman was a process server or something.

She replied flatly, "Yep. What can I do for you?"

"Do you know a girl by the name of Lorna?" the stranger asked.

Bebe was taken aback. Her first instinct was to lie and claim she knew no one by that name. But she could see the woman was uncomfortable, and frankly Bebe was curious. Maybe this lady could shed some light on what her friend's daughter had gotten herself mixed up in.

"Yes, I know a girl named Lorna. Why do you ask?"

The woman breathed a harsh sigh of relief. She laughed nervously, "I thought for sure you were going to tell me you didn't know anyone by that name."

Bebe asked kindly, "Now that you know I do, what is it you want?"

"I know this is going to sound rather strange, but someone gave me something for her. I was told you could deliver it. Can you do that?"

"What is it?"

The woman slid a figurine of a Golden Retriever from the envelope and handed it to Bebe.

Bebe eyed the figurine with misgiving. "What is this? Why can't you give it to her yourself?"

"Because I don't know Lorna personally. Please, just deliver it, and, and… well…"

"Well, what?" Bebe looked at the woman like she was a pedophile. She was getting ready to call the police.

"Please don't tell her parents."

Bebe shook her head violently from side to side and tried to hand the dog figurine back. The woman retreated a few steps, refusing to take it.

"I'm not giving this to Lorna. Who the hell are you, and who put you up to this?" Bebe shouted.

The woman's eyes darkened. They began to burn with the same eerie glow she had seen in Lorna's during her late-night visit.

She watched in horror as the woman's previously mild brown eyes began to shift and lighten to a disturbing, yet somehow beautiful shade of gold. Bebe gasped and instinctively backed up.

"Please give Lorna the dog, Ms. Sugars, and do not tell her parents. I don't have the answers you're seeking. I am just the messenger." With that, she turned and hastily fled the shop.

Bebe stood where she was for a long moment, staring at the figurine and wondering exactly when she had fallen down the rabbit hole.

She was having a hard time believing any of the events of the last twenty-four hours were even real. She hoped it was all a product of her fevered imagination. The figurine in her hand belied that notion.

Her only remaining hope was a bizarre, spicy-food-induced nightmare she would eventually wake up from.

The nightmare continued when the phone rang. Bebe held the receiver loosely to her ear, not really listening to what the caller was saying.

When she finally realized it was Blaze, the feeling of unreality that had washed over her last night, deepened further still. In an oddly strangled voice, nothing at all like his normally deep timbre, he asked her to close the shop and meet him at the precinct right away. There was something he needed to show her.

CHAPTER 19

Lily Jarvis was shaking as she jumped into a newer model luxury SUV, and fled downtown Alder Lake. She felt like an actress in a Hitchcock movie while delivering the dog figurine, per the instructions they had been given.

She barked shrill, nervous laughter and called home to let Ben know the mission had been accomplished. She told him that she had gotten so nervous her fangs nearly popped free.

"Oh no, Lily. Did she see them?" Ben wondered.

"No, I managed to keep them up, but my eyes changed, and she did see that. I think it scared the poor lady half to death."

Ben was immediately concerned. "She didn't see your car, did she? What if she calls the police?"

Lily did her best to allay her husband's fears. She had parked a block away from the shop, and they lived fifty miles from Alder Lake. She doubted they were in any imminent danger of being discovered. She wasn't altogether sure the woman would give the dog figure to the girl however, or that she would not call the authorities. She had clearly been very frightened.

Lily was rather frightened herself, having no idea whose dangerous errand she had just run.

She told her husband, "Maybe I shouldn't have delivered that package. We have no idea who we're even dealing with."

Ben surprised her by replying, "Well, we might soon find out." He explained that Samantha had pulled one of her vanishing acts while Lily was out. She reappeared in their living room thirty minutes later with a sticky note folded into her collar. On it was written a location and the words *please hurry.*

Lily stepped on the gas.

Nearly in a daze, Bebe closed the shop and drove to the police department. She had not even begun to recover from her strange visitor, before Blaze's urgent phone call knocked her sideways again. When she arrived, Blaze was standing in front of the precinct waiting for her.

She was barely out her car, before he took hold of her elbow and hustled her inside. He stopped briefly at the front desk, plucking a visitor badge from a basket next to the receptionist. He hurriedly clipped it to Bebe's blouse, where it hung precariously askew.

When Bebe tried to ask him what this was all about, he held a finger to his lips and shook his head.

"Not now," Blaze whispered, propelling her rapidly down a dismal gray hallway.

She could barely keep up with him, and she was beginning to feel terribly afraid that she was in some kind of trouble. She had all but convinced herself this had something to do with Lorna coming to her for help last night. Maybe even something to do with the strange lady who left that odd dog figure for her.

Blaze opened a locked door with a key produced from his shirt pocket. He ushered her inside a small and stuffy room, smelling vaguely of cigarettes and sweat. He immediately closed the door behind them and yanked a chair out with a clatter. He practically pushed Bebe into it.

She looked around at the cramped space. The room was sparsely furnished with only a single desk and chair. The only other items in the dismal room were a small television set, a portable DVD player and a remote control on the desk.

Bebe thought it was the most depressing place she'd ever seen. If someone tried to interrogate her in a place like this, she was pretty sure she would confess to anything just so they would let her out. She thought even a jail cell would be preferable to this depressing little airless room.

Wordlessly, Blaze picked up the remote and pushed a button.

"Blaze, what…" Bebe began.

"Just watch this." His voice was barely above a whisper.

Bebe pulled her eyes from him and focused on the screen before her. A grainy image emerged. It showed a large glass panel door. A man carrying a briefcase was seen exiting what appeared to be an office building of some sort.

His cell phone must have rung just then because he let go of the door with his free hand, perching it open with one foot as he wrestled a phone from his coat pocket.

While the man was preoccupied with finding his phone, a small girl stepped into the frame. She hurried inside the building behind him unnoticed.

There was a date and time stamp in the lower right corner of the screen. Numbers moved rapidly as the seconds ticked by.

A new image appeared now. It was the same girl, only this time she was standing before a bank of elevators and repeatedly pushing the buttons. The time had advanced from the previous image by only a minute or so.

Bebe felt slowly dawning horror as the next image appeared. The little girl was seen from the rear, opening the door on a stairwell. She wore jeans, a pink blouse, and mint green tennis shoes. Her auburn hair was held back with a coordinating scrunchie. The pockets on the back of her jeans displayed an ornate spray of colored rhinestones.

While the tape was too blurry to make out the child's features, the jeans were unmistakable. Bebe recognized them. They were currently soaking in her washing machine at home.

Bebe began to tremble. Her mouth suddenly tasted sour, and her stomach began to roll. She stifled an acid belch behind one shaking hand.

She no longer looked to Blaze for answers. She could not have spoken now even if she wanted to. Her entire being was riveted on the screen before her. She held the scratched and worn desk with one clenched hand, fearing she would simply fall over if she so much as loosened that grip.

The next scene appeared. The girl emerged from the stairwell. There was a long corridor of offices before her, each one displaying a nameplate on the door. The girl began walking down the hall and reading each one. She stopped at the one clearly marked *Carolyn Devonshire.*

There were no surveillance cameras inside the individual offices, so when the girl disappeared inside the office, the hallway remained deserted on the screen.

The screen changed again. It showed the same empty hallway for only a moment before a blond woman appeared stumbling from the office. She hobbled down the hallway wearing only a single shoe. While the image was just as grainy as the ones of the little girl, she could see the woman held her other high-heel in one raised fist. There was blood running down her face.

Bebe gasped. The unwelcome voice of Lorna leapt into her buzzing mind with, "*She hit me with a shoe.*"

Bebe clutched the table even tighter. She glanced at the counter in the bottom corner of the screen. No more than ten minutes had passed since the child was seen entering the building. Bebe was desperately afraid she knew what the rest of this movie would show, and she did not want to see the finale.

Resolutely, the tape played on. The next scene showed the same hallway, same players. In this clip, the little girl was running out of the open office door as she chased after the woman. She launched herself into mid-air from only a foot or so behind her, knocking her to the floor.

Bebe wanted to close her eyes when the woman raised the shoe. She watched in horror as the very act Lorna had spoken of occurred before her.

The woman hit the child over the head with her shoe in a desperate effort to defend herself.

While the little girl was temporarily distracted by her head wound, the woman tried to crawl away. She pushed open another office door and attempted to escape to safety there, but she was not fast enough.

The child crawled crab-like up the woman's legs and straddled her back. She grabbed the woman's blouse in one hand, pulling it free from her skirt. Tangling her other hand in the woman's hair, the child yanked her head back. Somehow she managed to flip the woman over onto her back.

How can she possibly be that strong? Bebe wondered with awe.

The woman was bucking and thrashing, trying to throw her assailant off. She managed to slide partway into the office with the girl still on top of her. She was now only visible from the chest down. The rest of her was inside the office, mercifully out of view of the surveillance camera. Of her attacker, only her small legs in their rhinestone-studded jeans could be seen.

The woman was violently fighting to free herself, her arms flailing, her legs kicking. She was clearly losing the vicious struggle for her life.

The image jumped again; the counter had advanced only three minutes from when the last image ended. It was the same scene in the hallway, with the same partial view of both people. Only now, the woman had stopped moving. Her arms and legs lay still beneath the small girl.

The previously clean hallway was now bathed in blood. It was everywhere. Splashed on the walls, soaking into the carpet, even spattered on the ceiling. The woman's skirt, her torn blouse, and exposed stomach were sodden with it. So were the young child's fancy jeans.

The next image appeared and Bebe moaned. She didn't even look at the counter in the corner to see how much time had passed this time. She didn't care.

The child had moved away from the body of the woman she had just murdered. She sat a few feet away, looking like she had been dipped in a lake of blood. Her hair and face were streaked with it. Blood was pattering down her neck and pooling onto the collar of her blouse. The blouse now clung to her in a sticky, red glob.

The next frame emerged with a dizzying jolt. The girl was seen staggering back into the woman's office. Within seconds she emerged again into the deserted hallway, carrying a handful of what looked like tissues.

She wiped the blood on the walls and the doorknob of Carolyn Devonshire's office, only succeeding in smearing it even more. She stuffed the wadded tissue into the pocket of her bloody jeans and stumbled over the body of the district attorney as she ran toward the stairs. The girl paused at the stairwell to look back over the carnage, then disappeared inside the door.

The screen went dark for only a moment. The next image was a view of the side of the building. A door opened and the girl staggered through it. Something had obviously frightened her. Her eyes flew open in shock, her hands reached to cover her ears. She practically fell into the street and out of view of the camera as she fled.

At last the screen went blessedly dark. Bebe looked briefly into Blaze's haunted eyes.

In that same oddly strangled voice she had heard when he called to summon her here, he asked, "Was that…"

Bebe began to retch. Her stomach had been churning more violently with each passing loop of the horror film she just witnessed. She reached blindly for the wastebasket on the floor. Her stomach gave one final heave before she started throwing up in a violent jet.

Blaze rushed to her side. He placed a reassuring hand on her shoulder. When he reached for her hand, Bebe pulled it away.

When it was finally over, Bebe ran a shaking hand across her mouth and laid her head on the table.

Blaze still had his hand resting lightly on her shoulder. He whispered, "I'm so sorry. I should have prepared you for that."

Bebe managed, "Water, please."

Blaze sounded miserable. He tried to take her hand again. "I spliced that together about an hour ago. I went through dozens of tapes and put it together in chronological order. I have seen it a dozen times already, but I just couldn't show it to anyone. Bebe, please tell me that isn't who I think it is."

She pulled away from his grasp again. Through clenched teeth, she spat, "Get me some water right now, Blaze."

He recoiled like she had just slapped him and mumbled another useless apology.

She watched him disappear down the hallway. As soon as he was out of sight, she immediately grabbed her purse off the floor.

Checking to be sure the hallway was empty, Bebe ran blindly for the nearest exit. As she reached the reception area, the woman behind the desk cried, “Ma’am, your visitor badge!”

Bebe never slowed. She tripped as she approached the parking lot, barely managing to stay on her feet.

As she reached her car, she experienced one heart-stopping moment when she could not locate her key ring. After what felt like an eternity, her frantically searching fingers finally made purchase. She stabbed at the wrong button on the little plastic remote and only succeeded in setting off the car alarm.

Bebe willed herself to calm down. She forced her shaking hand under control and focused her eyes on the remote. Exhaling a shuddering breath, Bebe finally managed to turn off the alarm and unlock the car.

Just as she was backing out of the parking space, she saw Blaze running full speed to catch her. Bebe floored the gas pedal and peeled from the parking lot of the police department. She was traveling far above the recognized speed limit in order to get away from him. She heard the screech of angry brakes, but had no idea who she’d almost run into.

Bebe was furious. *How could he do this to me?* she wondered bitterly. *Mr. By-The-Book Policeman, who dares not share one crumb of information about a case, and he drags me down there and makes me watch my best friend’s kid kill a woman? Is he crazy?*

How could he even think of involving her? He knew damn well who the child in those grainy images was. He was lying to himself if he truly believed that he had summoned her there and showed her that horrible movie because he needed her to confirm it for him.

He had spliced the whole thing together and viewed it numerous times. He said so himself. He didn't need her to tell him it was Lorna Dale. He knew, dammit! He knew! He just didn't want to carry the burden of this alone.

"What a fucking coward!" Bebe screamed.

She drove home and pulled her car into the garage. Her cell phone had been ringing nonstop since she escaped the police department. Once she was safely inside her house, Bebe reached into her handbag and silenced it. She then unplugged every telephone in the house and closed every blind. If that bastard knew what was good for him, he would not show up here.

The secrets end now, Bebe thought bitterly.

She stripped off her clothes and ran the shower as hot as she could stand it. She felt filthy. That room and that miserable video left her feeling intolerably violated. Bebe imagined the aftermath of a rape would feel much the same way. Once the water washed over her, she let it take the tension from her body with it down the drain. She was suddenly exhausted and in need of a nap. When she woke, she planned to call her best friend. They needed to have a long overdue conversation.

She had no idea what Blaze was going to do with the grisly discovery he had unearthed on those surveillance tapes, but Bebe knew exactly what she was going to do with it.

CHAPTER 20

Amanda sat on the sofa sipping a cup of coffee and watching the special news report about the murder of Carolyn Devonshire. Her curiosity was piqued this morning when Blaze called and said something about a *high profile* murder. There was not much in Alder Lake that could be classified as high profile. She had tried to call Kurt to find out what happened, but he wasn't answering his cell phone, so she was resigned to getting information the old-fashioned way.

The day had started off strangely, and it wasn't improving. There were a number of things on Amanda Dale's mind, and she was growing more troubled by the minute.

Her morning began with Lorna coming downstairs for breakfast wearing her hair in a completely different style than how she normally wore it. Amanda was vaguely reminded of Cousin Itt from the Addams Family as she observed one brilliant blue eye peeking out from behind a curtain of Lorna's hair. She had somehow arranged it so it fell over one eye and covered half her face.

When Amanda asked her about this exotic new look, her daughter mumbled something about wanting to try something different. She would not elaborate, nor would she meet her mother's eyes. Amanda asked if it didn't bother her hanging in her eye like that. Lorna shook her head but said nothing more. Amanda let it drop, but she didn't like it. Lorna had worn her hair back and off of her face since she was old enough to start thinking about such things. Why would she make such a dramatic change?

Kurt was fond of saying *kids are weird,* but Amanda thought this fell a little outside the pale of standard strange kid behavior, and she planned to ask Lorna about it again after school.

After that, the strangeness of the day continued with Blaze's urgent phone call for Kurt. And, it persisted still, when she called Bebe at the shop and there was no answer. Why wouldn't Bebe answer the phone during business hours? Amanda grew even more concerned when she could not be reached on her cell phone either. She planned on driving to the shop as soon as Nate woke up from his nap to make sure everything was alright.

The strangeness reached epic proportions when Amanda turned on the news and heard who the high profile murder victim had been. She was shocked to learn it was Kurt's boss. Why wouldn't Kurt have called and told her about this?

Why indeed? asked the voice inside her head. That irritating voice had become increasingly difficult to ignore in the last few weeks.

Amanda had a vivid recollection of the day she planned the barbeque to set up Bebe and Blaze. That brief few seconds of conversation when she told Kurt he should invite the DA, and Kurt's hasty refusal because, he'd said, "I see too much of her during the week."

Amanda put her coffee cup down and muted the television. *Just how much of her were you seeing, Kurt?* she wondered.

All at once, an unwanted and disturbing image of Tina Hilliard leapt into her mind, and she knew. A small moan escaped her lips.

If she had been honest with herself, she would have realized it some time ago. Something had been amiss with Kurt for quite a while now. She had sensed it for weeks and simply ignored it. She ran from the voice in her head, even though she knew it never lied. Her intuition about her husband operated with one hundred percent accuracy. She just didn't want to believe Kurt could do something like this again. Not after the hell he'd put her through with Tina Hilliard. Not after he had publicly humiliated them both.

Kurt was a narcissist. For his own sake, Amanda couldn't believe he would have put himself in this position again. He had so much to lose. His reputation had been all but destroyed when he was named a suspect in his last mistress's murder. How could he possibly take up with someone again?

She thought the marriage was finally on firm footing. They were good. At least she thought they were, until just recently when he'd started acting strangely again. He had been distant and moody. Amanda knew something was wrong, she just never dreamed it would turn out to be this again.

Oh, sure you did, hon. Just the other day in Bebe's shop, in fact. Remember?

"Shut the fuck up," she told that condescending and smug voice inside her head.

She wondered if her husband had finally snapped and actually did kill one of his lovers.

Her reaction to this revelation was eerily calm. She thought she should be feeling angry and hurt. All the tired old resentment that Kurt's dalliances always inspired should be present and accounted for, yet there was none of that. She figured she must be in shock. In the history of their marriage, she could not ever recall reacting to such a discovery with this weird composure. This was not like her. She should be throwing things, screaming, calling Kurt on the phone and leaving hateful voicemail messages. What the hell was going on here?

Now more than ever, she wanted to talk to Bebe. She wondered again why she wasn't answering the phone. Amanda glanced at the clock and saw Nate would be up in about fifteen minutes. She would feed him, drop him off at daycare, and be at Curious Curios and Collectibles in less than an hour.

As she rose to go upstairs and fix her makeup the doorbell rang. When she saw who it was, she expected to feel a nasty shiver of fright.

This is it, she thought benignly, *Blaze is here to arrest Kurt for Carolyn Devonshire's murder.*

Amanda was vaguely aware that the fear such a revelation should have inspired was absent. She opened the door, and with that same inexplicable calm, invited Blaze inside.

He looked terrible and was clearly very upset. She had never seen him like this before. His clothes were disheveled, dark circles were smudged beneath his eyes, and he looked positively haggard.

Would arresting Kurt really upset him this badly? Amanda wondered. *He doesn't even like him all that much.*

She had never seen such a haunted look in Blaze's eyes before. Once he was standing in the foyer, she asked him what was wrong.

He surprised her by saying, "I was just going to ask you the same thing."

Amanda didn't realize she wasn't looking so good herself, after learning of the DA's death, and coming to a very nasty conclusion about the woman's relationship to her husband.

"What's wrong with me? Nothing really. Unless of course you count that my husband was probably screwing the dead DA."

Blaze's eyes widened. "He told you?"

Amanda's jaw tightened. Blaze had just confirmed her suspicions. "He didn't have to."

What Amanda had mistaken for composure upon figuring out Kurt cheated on her again was really only the calm before a violent storm.

When Blaze showed up, presumably to arrest him for Carolyn Devonshire's murder, that eerie cool façade began to crack. When she gave voice to her suspicions and Blaze confirmed them, it fractured even further. Once their eyes met it crumbled entirely and Amanda began to cry. In seconds she was sobbing uncontrollably.

Blaze, not being an emotional tower of strength this morning either, reached out for her. He folded her into his arms and held her. The embrace was awkward at first, but soon he was holding her tight and stroking her back.

Before either of them was fully aware of where things were headed, Blaze lifted her off the ground and Amanda wrapped her legs around his waist. He backed her hard against the wall, kissing her neck and caressing her breasts.

Once their lips met, three years of unspoken and suppressed passion between them erupted with volcanic force.

Amanda reached down and unbuckled Blaze's belt. He unzipped his pants and rubbed himself against her. His pants slid down and pooled around his ankles. He yanked open her blouse with enough force to send the buttons flying. When Amanda moaned it sounded like a mixture of both sorrow and passion.

With her body suspended in mid-air and her legs tangled around the detective's waist, there was no easy way to consummate the situation; Amanda was wearing jeans. Once they reached the point of no return, Blaze struggled to remove her jeans without putting her down or disengaging from their embrace. He must have sensed what would happen if they stopped for even a moment.

When Blaze began fighting with her pants, Amanda realized it wasn't going to work, and those brief few seconds of overpowering lust evaporated as quickly as they had begun. She let Blaze battle with her jeans for another few seconds, before snorting laughter and clumsily unwrapping her legs from around his waist.

Blaze backed up a few steps to put Amanda down and promptly tripped over his pants. He smiled sheepishly as he bent to pull them up. They both collapsed to the stairs laughing.

Once the humor began to subside, Blaze looked at Amanda sitting on the step beside him.

"You know," he remarked, "I have seen a lot of movies with scenes like that, and I swear the guy is always able to get the lady's pants off."

"Exactly what kind of movies are you watching, Detective?" Amanda asked. This started them off giggling again.

When the laughter had finally exhausted itself, they both said "I'm sorry" at the same time.

They were naturally very embarrassed as the reality of the situation washed over them. The air between them was suddenly uncomfortably thick.

Blaze rose from the steps and reached out a hand to help Amanda up. They couldn't meet each other's eyes. Blaze wondered if he would ever be able to look this woman or her husband in the eye again—not to mention Bebe.

He suddenly felt far less judgmental of Kurt's actions. Blaze realized he had made more bad decisions in a single morning than Kurt had probably made all year. He was deeply humbled.

Amanda asked Blaze why he had come over in the first place. "Surely it wasn't to get in my pants," she remarked dryly.

He could no longer tell her the reason for his visit. Not after what had just transpired between them. The full weight of this terrible mistake struck Blaze with blunt force.

Amanda was Lorna's mother, and she needed to be told what was on those surveillance tapes. That's why he'd come over. How the hell had he ended up practically having sex with the lady on her staircase?

Blaze lied. He told her he was looking for Kurt.

"Yeah, I just bet you were," she spat bitterly. Amanda turned away and savagely tugged her blouse closed, covering her breasts. "Is he going to be arrested?"

Blaze was stunned. He realized what she had been thinking from the first moment she saw him standing outside her door, and the irony cut him like a knife.

Amanda believed her husband killed Carolyn Devonshire. When she found out it was actually her daughter who committed that horrible crime, Blaze knew she would wish with all her heart that Kurt had been the guilty party. He needed to get out of her house or he just might scream.

As he was backing out the door, he stammered, "No, Amanda, Kurt isn't going to be arrested. He didn't kill her."

Amanda was already closing the door, as she remarked more to herself than Blaze, "Pity. I could have finally gotten rid of the bastard."

Blaze wondered how the hell he was ever going to be able to tell Amanda about Lorna now. How do you tell someone their seven-year-old daughter ripped a woman's throat out? How do you arrest a little girl for first degree murder for that matter?

The situation was completely unimaginable. It could never be an easy one to handle, but Blaze had to admit, it probably would have been a little less complicated had he not dry-humped the child's mother against the wall inside her front door.

What the hell just happened? he asked himself.

He knew what his mother would think. He could hear her voice, and see the disapproving shake of her head. *Really, Medwyn?* Mama would say. *Now, I know I raised you better than that.*

This was by far the stupidest thing he had ever done, both professionally and personally.

Today was certainly a landmark day for making lousy choices. First, he showed Bebe that spliced together footage from the surveillance cameras, without even warning her about what she was going to be viewing.

He realized how badly he messed up, as he watched Bebe burn rubber out of the police department parking lot, nearly slamming into a minivan. If she went to his captain, he would probably lose his job.

It dawned on Blaze that he really didn't know Bebe all that well. He still wasn't sure what possessed him to pull her into that room and push play.

The truth was he hadn't been thinking clearly since he'd seen that footage himself. He had just been reacting to the horror of what he'd watched play out on those tapes.

And now, he'd gone and reacted again when Amanda started crying. He could lie to himself and say he was just trying to comfort her, but he knew it wasn't true. He was the one looking for comfort when he pulled her into his arms.

Blaze understood on an intellectual level, watching seven-year-old Lorna Dale murder the DA had rattled him to his soul. He just didn't believe that would excuse the lack of judgment he had displayed since making that horrifying discovery.

He couldn't show that gruesome footage to anyone else, so he'd called Bebe because he just didn't want to bear the burden of such dreadful knowledge alone.

It was the height of indiscretion, not to mention shoddy police work. He was starting to scare himself. What happened with Amanda just now was an even worse indiscretion. He had been a cop for way too long to allow himself to be ruled by emotions. What had gotten into him today? Had he really allowed one little girl—one improbable crime, to be his undoing?

He had no idea what to do about any of this, and there was no one he could talk to.

All at once the murder of Posy McManus came back to him with jolting force. *One improbable crime?* his mind screamed. *Oh, no. It's two crimes now.* Sweat broke out on his forehead.

How in God's name could this be? Amanda's little girl had the makings of a mass murderer.

The right thing to do would be to immediately alert his captain to what was on those surveillance tapes. He should further advise him of the ghastly similarities to the unsolved murder in the park. Let his superior notify Kurt and Amanda. Dump the whole mess into Fitz's lap.

But he couldn't. He cared about Amanda, and he was just now starting to realize how deep those feelings ran.

She had figured out Kurt was having an affair with Carolyn Devonshire this morning. He didn't think she could handle finding out about Lorna on the same day. Scratch that; he wasn't sure she could handle finding out about Lorna ever.

It was only going to be a matter of time before his captain and Kurt Dale both started asking him what was on those surveillance tapes. Blaze didn't have the faintest idea how he was going to tell them.

As Bebe awoke from her afternoon slumber, the first thought to drift into her mind was of Lorna. Not what she had seen on that dreadful tape this morning, but what the child had said to her last night: *I love you and I don't want to hurt you.*

All at once her resolve to tell Amanda began to crumble. She had no doubt of Lorna's sincerity when she voiced that threat. Once she saw that tape this morning, little doubt remained that Lorna was fully capable of retaliating for any perceived slight.

Blaze was the law, and it was his responsibility to impart the devastating news of Lorna's acts upon her parents. Bebe was not going to do it. She had no interest in risking her life.

Bebe thought again about the strange woman who'd come calling this morning and the gift she left for Lorna. Any manner of conspiracy theories began dancing through her mind. She wondered if someone had wanted the DA dead and they found a way to get Lorna to kill her. Perhaps the gift was supposed to be some kind of reward for a job well done. This thing could be much bigger than Bebe knew, and she had to try as best she could to keep herself out of harm's way. She could not be sucked any further into this raging shitstorm.

Bebe also realized her anger with Blaze had faded. While she still thought dragging her into that horrid little room and playing that hellish movie was a colossally cruel thing to do, she could understand why he'd done it.

Upon learning the identity of Carolyn Devonshire's killer, Blaze must have been panic-stricken. He could not very well run to his superiors with this newfound information. Amanda and Kurt were his friends, or at least Amanda was. Bebe could understand Blaze wanting to protect her.

The *perp,* as Blaze would call her, was no ordinary person. It was his good friend's seven-year-old little girl. That was a terribly heavy burden to carry alone. She resolved to call him this afternoon to try and smooth things over. He must be beside himself with worry over what Bebe would do with the unwanted knowledge he had saddled her with.

She was a little depressed to realize that though her anger with the good detective had diminished, so had her romantic feelings. Making her watch that tape had changed her view of Blaze in a very fundamental way. Bebe didn't think she could ever go back to the warmth she felt before he made her sit through that miserable thing.

Bebe had no idea how Blaze spent the rest of that long morning. If she'd known, Blaze would not be the only person her feelings would have changed toward.

Bebe needed to decide if she was going to tell Blaze about the strange woman who came to call at her shop this morning. She just didn't know how much farther out on a limb she was willing to walk. Telling him about Lorna's late-night visit was completely out of the question.

Bebe sighed forlornly when she thought of the long and unpleasant conversation which lay ahead. She wished she could just jump in her car and leave town rather than face all the horrors recently foisted upon her. She wished with profound sincerity she had chosen anywhere on the map besides Alder Lake to call home after she left Royce.

Bebe glanced at the clock and reluctantly threw the covers off her body. She hated climbing from the cocoon of her warm bed and facing the rest of this long and stressful day. Amanda was due in to work in less than an hour and there would be too many questions to answer if she arrived and found the store locked up tight in the middle of a weekday afternoon.

She plugged all of her telephones back in and raised the shades. While she was driving to the shop she turned her cell phone back on, though she didn't listen to any of Blaze's pleading and apologetic messages. She would deal with him later. First she had to try to act normal around Amanda; a performance that should make her worthy of an Academy Award.

Bebe thought about adding yet another lie to the growing pile she was harboring. She pictured that house of cards tumbling over once more, as it grew ever taller with each new story she felt forced to fabricate.

She need not have worried about trying to hide her guilt from Amanda. Her friend did not show up for work that afternoon. The message she left claiming to have a sore throat sounded oddly subdued.

Bebe would not be the only one struggling to hide her guilt, or fabricating tales in the long days ahead.

CHAPTER 21

The convenience store clerk looked nervously out the door again. The weird boy had been out there for over ten minutes, and the clerk wasn't sure if he should call the police.

What looked like maybe the worst case of dandruff in the history of mankind seemed to plague this strange kid. It was more than just the gray particles floating lazily around his head that worried the clerk, however. There was something wrong with the kid's eyes. They were lit up like a kaleidoscope. *Drugs,* the clerk thought. *LSD or something.*

While he pondered just what drugs the strange kid outside his store might be abusing, the strange kid was pondering how to get a very nice vampire couple to his current location. Finally, inspiration struck.

Francis Barclay walked into the convenience store and approached the clerk. He wasn't terribly surprised to see fear flood the man's eyes. He knew he wasn't looking so hot these days. How good can you look when you have been dead for over two hundred years? He hoped there would be no unpleasantness. He was blissfully unaware that the man behind the counter had his finger resting lightly on a panic button, and if he showed the slightest hostility the police would be summoned immediately.

"Forgive me, sir," Francis began, "but have you any parchment and a quill I might be able to use? I apologize, I have no coin with which to compensate you."

A puzzled frown creased the clerk's brow. "Have I any what? Is this some kind of joke?"

Now Francis was the one who was puzzled. He knew that in this era people spoke quite differently than when he was human, but parchment and quill were still a necessity. He knew this since there was an entire aisle dedicated to them in that enormous shopping village he had stayed in.

He saw a pad of sticky notes and a pen—one of those wonderful self-inking quills, to his mind—on the counter. He pointed at them. "May I have a piece of that very small colored parchment, and the use of your writing instrument with the ink inside?"

With the tips of his fingers the clerk pushed the pad and pen toward his terrifying customer.

"Many thanks, kind sir. Can you tell me please, what is the name of this town?"

"Umm… uh…" For a minute the clerk could not even remember it. Finally it came to him. "Vista Park," he stammered. His lips felt numb.

"And the name of this thoroughfare?" Francis pointed out the window toward the street.

"Thorough what?"

"The roadways. Have they names?" Francis asked patiently.

"Oh, you mean the intersection. It's Busey and Second."

Francis took the pen and the sticky note. He wrote down the information after verifying the correct spelling of the street name with the clerk. He pulled the piece of paper from the pad and put it in his pocket.

Thanking the dumbfounded clerk a second time, Francis turned to leave. His eyes were drawn to a large candy display and he licked his lips.

He turned back to the clerk. "I realize, having no coin, this is a foolish question, but may I have one of these sweet bars? I ask only because I am very hungry and am unable to pay for a proper meal."

The clerk nodded and waved toward the display. "Take whatever you want, dude."

"Truly?" Francis asked. The most grisly smile the clerk had ever seen broke out on his pale face. Particles of ash swirled around him as he grabbed hastily for the treats. He stuffed a handful of candy bars into his pocket and finally left the store.

As the boy walked outside, the clerk saw what looked like hundreds more of those weird looking flakes float off of his hand. He almost screamed when it appeared that half of the kid's hand floated away with them.

Once he was gone, the thunderstruck clerk walked around to the front of the counter and squatted down. He moistened his finger with the tip of his tongue and picked up a couple of the particles he'd mistaken for dandruff. They smelled burned. In fact, his whole store had a vaguely sweet, charred stench to it.

He wasn't surprised when the next customer who walked in wrinkled his nose and asked, "What was for lunch? Barbequed hobo?"

Francis Barclay walked up the block to a fast food restaurant, where he found minimal shelter from the disfiguring breeze. He sat outside at a plastic table and chairs. He had to wait nearly twenty minutes for his hand to reform. When it finally did, his ring finger was only half formed, the pinky not at all.

He tried to ignore the curious stares from people and kept his deformed hand hidden from view under the table. God, how he hated this world.

Once he realized the last two fingers were not coming back, he walked behind the building where no one on the street could see him. He hoped none of the employees would choose the next few minutes to exit the restaurant from the rear door.

He summoned Samantha. Her lovely golden glow emerged just as a small child dining with her parents stood up on the booth where they were seated and looked out the window.

"Pretty!" the little girl exclaimed, smiling and pointing at the dog.

Her parents looked briefly in the direction the child pointed. They were not high enough to see what she was looking at and dismissed it.

A few moments later the little girl cried, "Doggie! Pretty doggie!"

With a tired smile, her mother told the child to sit down and finish her hamburger.

Francis patted Samantha's head and endured a kiss on the face. He fortunately did not realize that her lapping tongue had taken a huge chunk of his cheek with it.

Samantha's tail wagged busily. She was clearly happy to see him.

"My faithful Samantha," he said lovingly, and scratched behind her ear. "It is time to bring me the people."

Samantha voiced a low, respectful "woof." She seemed to be aware they were in a much more public venue than where she was usually summoned by her master for a meeting, and that it was broad daylight. Discretion seemed in order.

Francis tucked the sticky note with the location of the convenience store into her collar and told her to bring it to Lorna's new guardians.

As the last of Samantha's golden light faded and she set off to deliver his message, Francis hoped the couple would come to him by nightfall.

As he had feared, his tenuous limbs were beginning to fail. He sensed his time on earth was once again growing extremely brief.

CHAPTER 22

Amanda Dale sat on the front steps of her house. There was a suitcase on the walkway before her. On the days she worked, childcare was arranged for her children. Despite not going in to Curious Curios and Collectibles today, Amanda still dropped Nate off at daycare and allowed Lorna to stay at a friend's house. She did not want them to witness what was coming next.

She glanced at her watch. Seeing the time, she expected Kurt home any minute. The suitcase she had packed was for him.

When he pulled into the driveway, Amanda rose from the steps and walked toward him, pulling the suitcase behind her.

Kurt stepped from the vehicle and took in his wife's pale face, the puffy circles beneath her eyes and the grim expression on her face. He knew at once she had found out about the affair. He did not, however, understand the significance of the suitcase.

Not knowing what to say to her, his mind unable to manufacture a single plausible excuse, he opted for acting like everything was normal. He asked, "Aren't you supposed to be at work?"

"You can't stay here tonight," she declared, ignoring the question.

Suddenly the presence of the suitcase became crystal clear. His eyes displaying the classic deer in the headlights stare, Kurt looked at her for a long moment before replying, "Look, I don't know what Bebe told you, but it's not what…"

Amanda cut him off. Her eyes flashed with both anger and surprise. "Bebe? What does she have to do with this?"

Kurt stammered, "Uh…well, nothing I guess."

With a sick feeling in her stomach, Amanda realized Bebe was aware of her husband's affair. She wondered if Blaze had been the source of that knowledge. She also wondered bitterly just how long her friends knew about it, and when they planned on telling her.

"Exactly how many people in town, besides my best friend, know you were fucking the DA?" Amanda asked.

Kurt flinched. "Oh, God," he sighed, running a hand over his face. "Amanda, I swear to you I never meant for this to happen!"

Amanda's jaw worked. She was fighting back tears, resolved not to cry until she was back in the house. "No, Kurt. You never do. I really would have thought after being accused of killing your last mistress… or was Tina Hilliard even the last one? Well, never mind, it doesn't matter. I really would have thought you would have lost your taste for this kind of thing. Guess I was wrong."

"I have to tell you something," Kurt sputtered.

"I have no interest in anything you have to say anymore. Blaze says you didn't kill the Devonshire woman. You aren't even a suspect. Honestly, I hoped it was you. You wouldn't have been able to fight the divorce I am going to file for nearly as strenuously from behind bars."

With that she rolled the suitcase down the driveway and turned on her heel to go inside.

Kurt started after her. She stopped and spun on him. "You set one foot in this house tonight, and I swear I will dial 911 and claim domestic violence."

Kurt stopped. "What are you going to tell Lorna? She's going to wonder where I am."

"How about the truth? Her father is a lowlife scum, and I finally kicked his ass to the curb. Wonder if your daughter will think it was as long overdue as I do."

Kurt's jaw fell open in shock. He cried helplessly, "Amanda, please. Don't drag the kids into this. I am begging you."

"I'll tell Lorna any damn thing I choose. Your days of asking for consideration of any kind are over. Just get the fuck out of here. I can't stand to look at you anymore." She went inside and slammed the door.

Kurt stood on the front steps uncertainly for several minutes. Finally, he walked back to his car and heaved the suitcase inside. He had tried to tell her about Francis Barclay, and the very real possibility that he had returned again, but Amanda was in no frame of mind to listen to anything he had to say. Kurt knew his wife would have thought he had invented the story, lying just to try and stay in the house.

He swiped angry tears from his eyes as he backed out of the driveway.

His whole world had unraveled in a single afternoon. The full weight of what had just happened with Amanda was beginning to sink in. He sobbed out loud, "I wanted to break up. I tried! I never meant for this to happen." But he understood none of that would even matter to Amanda.

Kurt knew in his heart he'd exhausted his quota of forgiveness from his wife and his marriage was over.

As he drove slowly toward downtown in search of a hotel, thoughts of custody battles, child support, and moving out of his beautiful house overwhelmed him. He needed to pull over to the side of the road. His eyes were too blurred from tears to even see where he was driving.

Amanda told Lorna her father was working on a case and wouldn't be home. Lorna accepted the explanation for Kurt's absence without question, but she looked troubled. Neither she nor her mother ate much of their dinner. Amanda ended up scraping most of it into the garbage disposal. She never followed up with Lorna about her new hairdo as she had planned.

In fact, Lorna felt like her mother was looking straight through her all evening. She didn't seem to see her at all. Lorna had a feeling her mother wasn't being completely honest with her about where her daddy was, and she wanted to ask questions. In her mother's current mood, she knew she would get scolded if she did.

Kurt called around seven o'clock and told Amanda where he was staying. He asked what she told Lorna about his absence, and Amanda grudgingly gave him the story. When he requested to say goodnight to his daughter, there was no response. Amanda simply called Lorna to pick up the extension.

Once the kids were in bed and Amanda had some time to herself, she went into the den and closed the door. She dialed Bebe's number.

She'd been feeling guilty all day because of what had happened with Blaze that morning. He was her best friend's man. She had even been the one to set them up.

All her life Amanda had been a pretty girl. When she was young, there had been occasions when a friend's boyfriend would hit on her. She always prided herself on being a loyal friend and never going near any boy who was seeing someone she knew. She couldn't believe she had done this now. Not to the best friend she ever had, and certainly not with an officer Kurt worked with. Her guilt had absolutely nothing to do with being a married woman. Understandably, she felt no loyalty to her husband right then.

She was actually sorry Blaze hadn't been able to get her out of the damn jeans. She felt like she had earned the right to sleep with someone else. After fifteen years of being faithful to a man who never was, she deserved to finish what they started this morning. Unfortunately, thoughts of Bebe weighed heavily on her mind.

Bebe picked up the phone on the third ring. "Hi, sweetie. The sore throat better?"

Amanda hesitated. "I didn't actually have one. I lied. I couldn't come in today because I kicked Kurt out of the house. Guess I didn't want to leave that message on your answering machine."

Her friend didn't sound terribly surprised. "I'm sorry, hon."

"So, how long did you know about it?"

Bebe gasped. "I… well. Oh, Amanda, you must hate me."

"Of course I don't hate you. I would just like to know how long you knew Kurt was cheating on me and why you didn't tell me."

"Blaze and I saw them together last week. I wanted to tell you, but…"

"But what, Bebe? Why didn't you?" Amanda heard her voice rising and struggled to keep her emotions in check.

"Because Blaze thought we shouldn't. You know, because of the kids and all. We didn't want to hurt you." Her voice caught on the word *kids.*

Though Amanda felt terribly betrayed, she found it pretty hard to hold on to too much righteous anger with the image of her legs wrapped around her best friend's beau still dancing through her mind.

Her voice sounded far more tired than angry when she scolded, "You should have told me."

"I know, honey. I'm so sorry. If I had it to do over again, I would have."

There was silence on the line for a few moments. Finally Bebe asked, "How did you find out, anyway? Is it because Kurt's a suspect in her murder?"

"No. I figured it out on my own. You would be amazed at how much practice I've had making these deductions over the years. And Kurt isn't a suspect according to Blaze." Amanda winced when she said the detective's name.

"You talked to Blaze today?" Bebe asked. Her voice suddenly sounded strange. It sounded somehow ominous, when she asked, "Did he tell you anything about Carolyn Devonshire's murder?"

Amanda wondered why Bebe would ask that. Was it just curiosity about the murder, or something else? She had already told her Kurt wasn't a suspect. What else was she wondering?

"Like what, Bebe? He wouldn't tell me anything more about a case than he would you." Amanda knew she sounded oddly defensive but couldn't help it.

There were so many lies between them, so many unspoken truths that could have destroyed their friendship. Neither woman wanted to stay on the phone any longer. The conversation was like trying to negotiate a field teeming with land mines. Neither woman knew which way to step to avoid an explosion.

Bebe said she was sorry again for not telling her about Kurt. Amanda said she was sorry she lied about having a sore throat. They said they loved each other and hung up. Both women were crying as they put down the phone.

Ben and Lily Jarvis entered the intersection written on the sticky note found tucked in Samantha's collar into the GPS. The location was just over thirty miles from their home.

Both dogs were in the back seat, craning their heads out the rear windows and enjoying the breeze.

Lily was worried. "What if this is some kind of setup, and we're driving into the trap of a vampire hater luring us to our deaths?"

Her husband looked more amused than scared. "Really, Lily? They sure went to an awful lot of trouble if all they want to do is kill us."

"Maybe, but if we get there and anything looks hinky, promise me you will turn the car around immediately."

Ben patted her knee reassuringly.

When the GPS informed them, "You have reached your destination," Ben guided the car to the curb.

They took in their surroundings. On one corner stood a convenience store. Across the street was a strip-mall with a bagel place, dry cleaner, and a hair salon. Ben started to open the car door when Lily put a restraining hand on his arm.

"Wait. We don't know where we are supposed to go. Shouldn't we wait for whoever put that note in Samantha's collar to contact us? We have no further instructions."

"Honey, you watch too many movies. We aren't dropping off ransom money. We don't need instructions. Let's just get out of the car and start walking the dogs up the block. Whoever set this in motion will find us. Think of it as an adventure."

Lily still looked concerned as she opened the car door and stepped out.

They walked the dogs up the block and crossed the street. As they walked past the strip-mall, Samantha began wagging her tail excitedly. She voiced two happy barks, and then yanked the leash toward a boy who materialized from the back of the building.

Lily and Ben exchanged a glance as a teenager with long, stringy hair lumbered toward them. The approaching stranger smiled happily. He reached out for Samantha, who was tugging on her leash to greet him.

Lily noticed the missing digits on the newcomer's hand and winced. She took in his disheveled appearance and the bits of ash floating about his body. A moment later she was assaulted with the smell of him, and took an involuntary step back. She moved behind her husband, pulling Lionel with her. He did not appear anxious to get too close to the stranger, despite his new sister's enthusiasm.

Ben was struggling to keep a pleasant smile on his lips. In the face of that god-awful odor wafting off the boy, it wasn't easy.

"Hello," he said, offering his hand to shake. "I'm Ben, and this is my wife, Lily."

The boy reached out to take the man's offered hand with a look of embarrassment. As he extended his right hand, it turned to particles and over half of it floated away in the breeze. Lily cried out in horror. Ben put a reassuring hand on her arm to quiet her.

"How long have you been dead, young man?" Ben asked.

Francis Barclay looked relieved. "A long, long time. Centuries, in fact." He looked around nervously, as the relentless wind blew his hair back from his face. His chin began to crystalize and disappear into the air before them. Francis put one hand to his face and groaned. This was new.

He asked, "Sir, have you a conveyance we can take shelter in? If I stay out here, I fear I may disappear altogether. I will explain everything I can, but I don't have much time left."

Ben pointed across the street and began leading the boy toward the car. Lily grasped her husband's hand hard enough to grind his knuckles painfully together. He endured the pain without complaint, and squeezed back reassuringly.

Once they were settled into the car, Lily in the back seat with the dogs, Ben and Francis up front, Ben asked, "Has Samantha been dead that long too?"

The boy shook what was left of his head. "No. Samantha died only a few years ago."

"How did she come to be your dog?" Ben looked puzzled.

"I had to return once before. It was then that I turned her."

"May I ask why you would turn a dog?"

"It was not intentional. I thank you for providing her with care. She is a good dog. Perhaps she will stay with you when I am gone."

"Gone? Where are going?" Lily asked from the back seat.

"Let me explain…" Francis began.

He spoke to Ben and Lily Jarvis for over an hour. He started with the murder of his family centuries before, and then went on to tell them why he had awakened from the dead the first time. He told them about Lorna and how she had been turned when he kidnapped her.

"You sure make a lot of progenies by accident," Lily observed uncomfortably at this point in Francis Barclay's narrative.

"Indeed, my lady," Francis agreed mildly. He then told them about what Lorna had done to fulfill her need for blood, and the reason why he had enlisted their help.

"She has killed," Francis said softly.

Lily exclaimed, "Oh my God! That poor child!"

Samantha whined, putting a paw on Lily's arm. She seemed to agree that Lorna's plight was a bad one.

"Does anyone know she is vampire? Or what she has done to survive?" Lily sounded anguished.

"I do not know. I am certain her parents are not aware of it. However, now that she has killed twice, it is only a matter of time before someone discovers not only what she has done, but what she is as well. This is why it is imperative she be relocated to your home at once."

"I have never heard of a vampire child whose parents were mortal. I'm unfamiliar with any minors turned like this." Ben sounded alarmed.

"Her parents must be told," Lily said firmly.

Francis shook his head. "That would not be wise. Her father is a lawman. He should have been killed five years ago. Unfortunately, I failed."

Ben and Lily exchanged an uneasy glance.

"You're not planning on going after him again, are you?" Ben asked uncomfortably.

"No, sir. I do not believe I was summoned back this time to continue avenging my family's murder. That has lost its priority in my heart. Now my only concern is the welfare of the child."

Once Francis had finished telling them the sad history that brought him back from the dead a second time, he informed them that his current body was not going to last very much longer. It would be up to them to rescue his child.

Ben tried to place a reassuring hand on the boy's shoulder. He hastily pulled his hand back when it seemed to go right through what lay beneath the shirt sleeve. For one alarming moment the cloth flattened, as though it no longer housed an arm at all.

"I… I'm sorry, Francis," Ben stammered, staring in awe at the sleeve where the boy's arm had disappeared beneath his grasp.

Francis offered a small smile. He appreciated how kind these people were being to him. Sitting beside him in a car with no open windows couldn't be easy. The smell of his burned body must be making them sick, yet they endured without complaint.

Francis tentatively asked how they procured their own supply of blood without harming anyone. Ben explained his profession and told him about the stash they kept in the basement.

Francis thought this ingenious. He had a wistful moment, wishing his parents had considered such a career path. Things would have turned out so differently for everyone.

Not knowing who they would be coming to meet today, Ben had thoughtfully brought some blood with them in case there was a vampire in need. It was hidden beneath the spare tire. When he offered it to Francis, he accepted gratefully. He didn't feel that he needed the blood at this point, but to not accept might have appeared ungracious.

They were fine people. Francis was satisfied that he had succeeded in securing the safety of his blood-child, and a great burden was lifted from his heart. He knew that this time, when he returned to his eternal slumber, he would finally rest in peace.

CHAPTER 23

Feeling like a registered sex offender, Bebe parked her car across the street from the elementary school playground and waited in the shade for the children to appear.

She had no idea what time recess was, but she had an unpleasant errand to attend to, and she was determined to put it behind her.

Bebe waited for about twenty minutes before being rewarded for her patience by the sight of children spilling out into the yard.

She began walking toward the chain link fence that separated the youngsters from the outside world and scanned their faces.

Spotting Lorna seated on a bench with two other girls at the northeast corner of the small play yard, Bebe walked the perimeter of the fence until she was directly in Lorna's line of sight. As soon as the girl saw her, Lorna's face lit up in a sunny grin and she waved.

Bebe manufactured a smile that felt about as real as wooden teeth, and motioned for the young girl to follow her. It appeared Lorna had done a pretty respectable job of covering the scratch on her face with an eccentric new hair style. She wondered what Amanda had made of her child's new 'do.

When Lorna rose from the bench, Bebe searched the yard for adults. She was relieved to see the only one present was preoccupied with cleaning a spilled juice box from a child's shirt. Bebe walked as far to the other side of the yard as possible from where the woman was located and waited for Lorna to join her.

When the child approached, Bebe motioned for her to be quiet. Lorna nodded and reached through the fence to take Bebe's hand.

Bebe grasped Lorna's fingers briefly, fighting the wave of revulsion she felt at her touch. She would never be able to escape the image of Lorna on that tape murdering the DA. It was forever burned into her heart. She felt nothing besides fear and loathing for this demon masquerading as a little girl.

"Hi, Lorna," she said. "I only have a minute, and I don't want anyone to see me here, so listen carefully, okay?"

Lorna nodded.

"I managed to get everything clean except your shoes. Those, I pitched. You know the window you climbed in the other night when I took you home?" she asked her.

Again, Lorna nodded.

"I'll leave the clothes in a bag outside that window tonight after midnight. Make sure you bring them in before your folks wake up, okay?"

Lorna replied, "Yes," and started to ask Bebe something.

Bebe held up a hand to stop her. "Also," she continued, "somebody dropped off a gift for you at my store, and they asked that I give it to you. I don't know who it's from. I will leave it in the bag with your clothes."

Lorna smiled. She appeared happy that someone had left her a present. Once more, she opened her mouth to speak.

Bebe cut her off again. "And, one last thing, Lorna. I kept your secret, so I expect you to keep mine. If you tell anyone I helped you the other night, I will deny it. I could go to prison because I pulled your behind out of the fire. Do you understand that?"

The smiled faded and tears filled the little girl's eyes. "I'm sorry, Bebe, I never meant to…"

When Bebe cut her off one last time, it was with great fear that she spoke the final words she needed to. She was determined never to be Lorna Dale's savior again. Better to be killed by her, than to spend the rest of her life under the thumb of a monster.

Bebe said, "Don't you throw me under the bus, little lady. I'm telling you the same thing you told me; I love you, so I don't want to have to hurt you either. Got it?"

Lorna's eyes flew open in shock and tears spilled down her cheeks. She nodded her head soberly.

"Good. I have to go now. Dry your eyes before you go back."

As Bebe turned to walk away Lorna called out to her in a small, unhappy voice, "Bebe, wait!"

She stopped and looked back at the girl.

"I'm still me," Lorna whispered. "I just want you to know that. I'm still me."

Bebe thought her heart would break at the desperate look in the eyes of this child she had once loved so much, and now could only fear. She turned and walked away.

Aching from the encounter, Lorna watched Bebe cross the street. She dried her eyes and started slowly back toward the other children.

Bebe wasn't terribly surprised to see Blaze standing in the doorway of her shop when she heard the bell over the door offer its melodic little jingle. He stood there with a hangdog expression, unsure if she was going to order him to leave. Bebe hadn't gotten around to calling him yesterday.

She smiled as warmly as she could muster and waved him inside. "Don't worry, I won't bite."

The way his presence always seemed to fill a room still made her feel a little breathless. Before she could allow herself to feel the annoying response from her loins which always seemed to accompany Blaze's appearance, Bebe reminded herself of the airless little room he had forced her into the previous day, and the charming movie starring her best friend's daughter, he had forced her to sit through.

"Bebe, I am so sorry. I don't even know what to say," Blaze began.

She held up a hand to stop him. "No apologies, please. Look, I understand why you showed it to me. I guess you didn't feel like there was anyone else you could trust."

He exhaled a harsh breath. "I was so afraid you were never going to talk to me again. Or worse, report me to the department. Honestly, I can't blame you if you do."

"I would never get you into trouble like that. I just hope you realize I am the wrong person to ask for any advice on how you're supposed to handle this. I love Amanda, and I loved her kid too."

Blaze did not miss the past tense in that sentence. He also felt a terrible pang of guilt at the mention of Amanda's name. "So where does this leave us?" he asked miserably.

Bebe wouldn't meet his eyes. "I think until this whole situation is resolved, we shouldn't see each other. I don't know what's going to happen to Lorna at this point, and I doubt you do either. I don't want to be in the middle of it anymore."

"I never meant to put you in this position, Bebe. You will never know how much I regret showing you that video."

Bebe waved her hand impatiently. "I said no more apologies, okay? What's done is done. Wasn't it you who told me you can't put the toothpaste back in the tube?"

Blaze smiled humorlessly. "Yeah, wasn't that like a hundred years ago, when we saw Kurt walk out of the hotel with the dead DA?"

"Our first date. It does feel nearly that long ago now, doesn't it?" Bebe looked wistful.

Blaze took her hand. "Can I call you when this whole thing is over?"

"I honestly don't know, Blaze. It's sweet of you to ask, but you have much bigger things to worry about right now than you and me going steady."

Blaze looked even more depressed when he nodded and let go of her hand. "Don't suppose you would give me one last hug for the road, would you, pretty lady?"

Bebe leaned momentarily into his embrace. She was so stiff that Blaze felt like he was hugging a piece of steel. In a way, he was. Bebe was one tough cookie.

He left the shop feeling as though he'd probably blown the best thing to happen to him since moving to Alder Lake. Bebe was a very special lady, and Blaze realized that he was right up there with Kurt Dale when it came to sabotaging relationships.

He felt a little ashamed of the relief that washed over him when Bebe had ended things between them. She made it sound like it was only for the time being, but Blaze thought he saw something a little more permanent in the lady's eyes.

The vision of Amanda, breathless and aroused, had not been very far from his thoughts since yesterday. He somehow felt a little less guilty for those musings once Bebe gave him the heave-ho.

It wasn't like he believed it was now perfectly okay to have these feelings for a married woman. It just made them seem a little less sordid with Bebe out of the mix.

Once again, he could hear his mother's disapproving voice in his mind. *I never knew I raised such a schmuck, Medwyn.*

He thought miserably, *Neither did I, Mama. Neither did I.*

As the meeting between Francis Barclay and the vampire couple who would soon be his progeny's new guardians drew to a close, Ben Jarvis asked, "Where have you been staying?"

Francis responded vaguely, "I have managed to find lodging most evenings."

Lily closed her eyes in silent horror. She knew what was coming next.

"And where will you stay tonight?" Her husband inquired.

"I've not located anywhere yet. Once the wind settles, I will take my leave. I am sure you are anxious to return home."

Ben shook his head. "Nonsense. You'll stay with us tonight. We have a guest room I'm sure you'll find quite comfortable."

He cast a reassuring look in the rearview mirror at his wife's troubled face.

"I do not wish to be any imposition."

Ben waved a hand. "You're not. Besides, we have a great deal to discuss about the child. It only makes sense that you stay with us tonight, right, Lily?"

Lily attempted a smile that looked more like a grimace, as she nodded her acquiescence.

Trying to improve the mood in the car, Ben offered, "My wife is a wonderful cook. She's making lasagna for dinner tonight. I'm sure it's been awhile since you've had a good home-cooked meal."

"Thank you kindly, but I need little food now." Pulling one of the candy bars taken from the convenience store out of his pocket,

Francis remarked, "Except for these sweet bars, I find I have lost my appetite."

The doctor in Ben burst forth, as he launched into a vigorous lecture on the dangers of too much sugar. When he caught the exaggerated roll of his wife's eyes in the mirror, he abruptly ended his discourse with a mumbled apology.

Lily shook her head as he started the engine and turned the car in the direction of home. He was happy to see a small smile dance across her lips.

Even Francis was smiling. He commented, "It wasn't the sugar that killed me."

Blaze drove home after leaving Bebe's shop. He needed to figure out what to do. He advised the secretary at the department that he would be working in the field on the Devonshire case and could be reached by cell phone.

It was on that device that Kurt Dale called him. He inquired if Blaze had viewed the surveillance tapes from Carolyn's murder yet.

Blaze was surprised at how smoothly the lie flowed from his lips, as he told the other detective there had been a problem with the equipment and the tech guy was working on it. He said he should be able to see the footage first thing in the morning.

If Captain Fitzgerald called and asked the same question, he would have to think of another story. He was banking on the fact that Kurt had enough trouble in his personal life right now to bother checking up on this fabrication.

"I'll call you once I've watched them," Blaze offered, trying to end the phone call.

"Okay. Call my cell phone. Or you can reach me at the Ramada downtown. I'm staying there for the time being," he admitted dejectedly.

Blaze felt a sharp stab of guilt at the momentary glee he felt from Kurt's revelation. "I spoke to Amanda," he said. "She mentioned she knew about you and Carolyn."

"Did you tell her? I know it wasn't from Bebe," Kurt asked bluntly.

Blaze was instantly defensive—probably too defensive. "I didn't have to. She figured it out all on her own. Your wife is not a stupid woman."

Kurt was surprised at the other detective's emotional reaction. "You think I don't know that?" he responded, equally as defensive. "I'm just trying to figure out where she heard about it so I can do damage control. Do you know who might have said something to her? I am trying to keep the story off the front page of the goddamn newspaper. "

"I have no idea. Like I told you before, Kurt, I can't worry about your marriage. I have two murders to solve." With that Blaze offered a hasty goodbye and hung up the phone.

After Blaze disconnected the call he sat with the phone in his hand for several minutes. He was fighting the urge to call Amanda. It didn't take long for him to lose that battle. He felt vaguely unnerved at the way his heart sped up when he heard her voice on the line.

"Hi," he said tentatively, "I was just calling to see how you're doing. I spoke to Kurt. He told me he was staying at the Ramada."

Ignoring the guilt rising in her chest like bile, Amanda asked him, "Would you like to come over tonight for a glass of wine after the kids are in bed?"

"Isn't that a bad idea?" Blaze wondered out loud.

"Probably," she conceded, "but I need a friend. You're still my friend, aren't you, Blaze? Or did we completely fuck that up too?" She sounded like she was about to cry.

"Of course I am," he reassured her.

He decided not to overthink it. He tried to tell himself that he wasn't looking forward to seeing her. He tried to tell himself he wasn't hoping to hold her in his arms again, but he knew better. He tried to convince himself he was just going over there because she needed a friend. Of course, he knew better about that too.

He also tried very hard to forget what he knew about Lorna for the time being. He would never admit, especially to himself, that his newly discovered feelings for Amanda Dale had taken priority over everything else in his life—even his obligations as a police officer. He was in way over his head, yet he just kept letting the tidal wave take him further under.

Blaze knew there was no way he was going to tell Amanda about Lorna's crimes tonight. Not after she had just thrown her husband out. To hit her with such devastating news on the heels of that would be cruel, he rationalized. Tonight he would be her friend, he promised himself. There would be nothing more to it. Of course, we all know what happens to the best laid plans, don't we?

CHAPTER 24

Lily made dinner, and even their strange houseguest managed to eat a small piece of lasagna. Francis also devoured two helpings of the tiramisu she made for dessert. Somehow, Ben managed to restrain himself from preaching about the perils of sugar.

Once the meal was consumed, and the dogs had been walked and settled down with their chew bones, Ben and Lily sat with Francis in their living room to discuss the fate of Lorna Dale.

Ben had printed all of the newspaper articles he could find about the two murders which had taken place over the past week in Alder Lake.

There was no doubt in any of their minds, it was the child, Lorna, who was responsible for both. They understood exactly what had compelled her to commit such unspeakable crimes; she was starving.

Ben Jarvis knew it was only a matter of time before somebody figured out that the little girl was not only the perpetrator of those crimes, they might also realize she was a vampire as well.

This could have unimaginably dire and far-reaching consequences. To Ben's way of thinking, the fate of all vampire-kind now hung in the balance. If little Lorna Dale's true identity was discovered, then how long did any vampire have before they were exposed as well?

It was Francis Barclay who first brought up the idea of kidnapping her.

Lily vehemently rejected this notion, insisting there must be another way. She argued that her parents had to be brought in and involved in any decision about the child's future.

"Her mother and father must already know what she is," she declared. "There is no way she could have kept it from them all this time. We cannot just take her."

After hours of discussion and analysis of all possible options, Ben realized the potential consequences from contacting the child's parents were simply too great to risk.

Eventually Lily acquiesced, as she had so many times before in her marriage. She trusted Ben's decisions on most subjects. She had, after all, allowed him to turn her when she was barely a woman herself. However, on this issue she was deeply troubled.

Once they had settled Francis Barclay in the guest bedroom and were lying side by side in their bed, she asked, "How are we going to explain a child living with us to everyone?"

"We'll think of a suitable story, Lily. That's the least of our worries."

"True. Explaining the story to our friends when it airs on Dateline will be much more difficult. Though, I'm sure Keith Morrison will give us the chance to explain when he interviews us from our cell. He seems like a very reasonable man."

Ben laughed softly and took his wife's hand in the dark. "Honey, that won't happen."

"Seriously, Ben, I know we have to help that little girl. But do you realize what you're planning is a felony? If we get caught we'll go to prison. How are we going to survive if that happens? We rely on your profession to get blood honorably and humanely. If we're incarcerated, we die."

He squeezed her hand tighter. "I do realize that, darling, I just can't think of another option. I don't see how we can leave a seven-year-old vampire with no blood-guardian. Her maker is dead. He won't be around to help her much longer. Look at what she has done to survive. Do you see any way she can continue her life in that town after she has murdered two people? I don't. Can you think of another way to save her?"

Lily sighed. "I don't know, but sacrificing our own lives for a stranger seems a bit extreme."

"If you have a better idea, I am open to suggestions. I believe the risk we take trying to talk to the child's parents is far greater than the one we would take attempting to remove her from Alder Lake. It's far too dangerous when we have no idea how they would react."

"Her parents will want to protect her. They will want to help her, Ben."

"Her father is a police officer. If that child gets caught—and it is only a matter of time before she will—then she is the one who dies. And won't that be our fault if we don't do something to save her? I can't live with that on my conscience. Can you? The way I see it, we're all she's got."

It was from this passionate speech that Lily finally ceased voicing her objections and agreed to help her husband kidnap Lorna Dale.

Francis Barclay lay awake in the most comfortable bed he had ever slept in. His faithful dog slept beside him on the coverlet. He reached out in his mind to speak to his child.

In Alder Lake, fifty miles away, Lorna heard his words in her head. She smiled and sat up in bed.

Father, where are you? I need you. I know I shouldn't be, but I'm hungry again. Not food hungry, but the other one… you know.

Yes, child. I know. You absolutely must not find anyone to feed on tonight. You must be strong, just until morning. Can you do that for me?

Lorna was elated. *Father, will you be here in the morning?*

Her happiness weighed like a stone against Francis Barclay's heart. He knew he would never see the vampire child he had created ever again.

I have found people to help you. They will come for you in the morning. Tell me where your schoolhouse is located. Will you be there in the morning hours tomorrow?

Lorna told him what time she would be at school, and gave him the name of the one she attended.

She was starting to get worried. *Father, you will be coming with these people, won't you?*

With a heavy heart, Francis explained to her that he wasn't sure his body could make the journey. He told her she would have to trust the man and woman he was sending for her.

Lorna brightened a little when he told her that Samantha would be with them. He knew how much she loved the dog.

What Lorna did not know, was now that the plan to save her was in place and there were earthly vampires to care for her, Francis Barclay's work was done.

He planned to tell the couple where they could find Lorna in the morning. After that, he would simply walk outside, allowing the wind to carry him away and return him to the ashes he had risen from.

Francis Barclay never was one for long goodbyes.

Amanda wore a floor-length lounge dress when she opened the door to Blaze. She made sure both children were asleep before she went into her bedroom and pulled the dress from the closet.

While she had been wearing pants all day, the decision to change into more accessible attire was not a subconscious one by any means. Amanda was a practical woman, so she didn't bother trying to justify this wardrobe change by telling herself the dress was more comfortable, or any nonsense like that.

She brushed her teeth, freshened up her makeup and fluffed her hair. As an afterthought, she spritzed a little perfume in the hollow of her throat. After only a moment's hesitation, she removed her bra.

While Blaze may have tried to convince himself tonight's visit was completely innocent, Amanda had no such illusions. She had not invited him over because she needed a friend. She needed much more. She needed revenge on a husband who had lied and cheated on her for all the years of their marriage, and Blaze was going to help her realize that end.

She wasn't exactly sure when she had made that decision. It might have been as early as yesterday morning when Blaze put her up against the wall and then couldn't get her out of the damn jeans. Or it might have been as late as today when he phoned to check on her.

It didn't really matter anyway. She only knew that at some point her guilt over messing around with her best friend's beau had been trumped by her anger at Kurt, and she was damn well going to do this.

She had wanted this man for a long time; as far back as the Christmas party three years ago. She never once acted on those feelings—never even permitted herself the luxury of a single daydream about what it might be like to feel his hands on her body. She never allowed those desires to even see the light of day.

When she thought about how blatantly Kurt pursued every woman who ever tickled his fancy, it made her blood boil. Not even being wrongly accused of one mistress's murder, and the public humiliation which followed, was enough to stop his miserable womanizing. The possibility of losing her, God knew, was not motivation enough. Even the prospect of losing his children in a nasty custody battle couldn't keep his dick in his pants.

Amanda was not only going to give her husband a taste of his own medicine, she was honestly curious to know how it felt to act with such wanton disregard of one's marriage vows and succumb to the most basest of desires.

Amanda opened the front door and ushered Blaze inside. Taking his hand, she led him past the living room and into the den. She closed the door and turned the lock, then poured two glasses of wine. Blaze felt electricity when her fingers brushed against his hand as she handed him the wine.

Amanda led him to the couch against the back wall and curled up next to him, her body exquisitely close.

He started to ask, "Did you tell Kurt to go stay at a hotel or did he…"

"Let's not talk about Kurt, okay?" Amanda placed one cool hand on the side of his face and ran a manicured fingernail gently down to his lips.

He took her hand and kissed the palm. "We don't have to talk about Kurt, but we need to talk about something, 'cause I can't think straight when you touch me like that."

She gave him a coy glance. "Did you ever think maybe that was the point?"

She watched him take a long drink of wine, then peeled the glass from his fingers and leaned against him. On the wings of a sigh, Amanda softly breathed his name.

Blaze felt that whisper linger in his ear and shiver down his back. He pulled her into his arms.

He had no trouble at all divesting her of her clothing this time around.

As Blaze made the sweetest love to Amanda she had ever known, she hoped he didn't see the tears as they ran down her cheeks—even as she came.

While Blaze made love to Amanda on the couch in her den, Bebe Sugars approached the house through the backyard. She stood outside the window of that very room, oblivious to the passionate storm raging within.

Bebe had come to return Lorna's clothing; the outfit she had worked so diligently to clean, erasing any sign of the child's murderous rampage.

Taking great care to be quiet, Bebe tucked the bag out of sight, behind a shrub below the windowsill.

The shade was blessedly pulled. She could not see the most egregious of betrayals being committed against her just a few feet from where she stood.

She was greatly relieved to be rid of that bag of clothing, as well as the dog figure the weird lady had forced her to take. More importantly, she was now shut of Lorna Dale's misdeeds.

Perhaps it was intuition, or maybe the heat between Blaze and Amanda was so intense it travelled right through the drawn shade and closed window beyond, but something made Bebe pause as she was leaving.

Not knowing exactly why she felt compelled to do so, Bebe walked around to the front of the house. When she saw Blaze's car parked in the driveway, she put a hand to her mouth, stifling a gasp.

For a moment she reasoned that he must be there delivering the devastating news about Lorna. But if that were the case, wouldn't Kurt's car be there too? Surely Blaze wouldn't tell Amanda her daughter was a murderer without Lorna's father present.

Bebe didn't kid herself for long. This was more than just an officer delivering bad news, or even a friend offering comfort. Amanda was not the only one with a healthy dose of woman's intuition. Bebe knew exactly what Blaze was doing there.

With a bitter taste in her mouth, she made her way back to the car. She tripped once because her vision was blurred by tears and she couldn't see where she was walking.

The tears weren't of jealousy—at least not entirely. She felt a numbing sense of betrayal, mingled with hollowing rejection from a man she'd been trying to build a relationship with until just this very afternoon.

She wasn't sure where the pain of her best friend's treachery ended and the pain of being forsaken by Blaze began.

Why, she wondered, was it so easy for him to jump into Amanda's bed, when he would barely give Bebe a kiss goodnight after their dates?

While Bebe's feelings for Blaze may have cooled after he dragged her smack into the middle of Lorna's drama, it didn't make this startling revelation hurt any less.

By the time she drove home, Bebe's pain had turned to white-hot fury. The murderous little Lorna used her for a get-out-of-jail-free card the night she murdered the DA. Her boyfriend had given her front row seats to the movie from Hell, and then ran to her best friend's bed for solace within hours of their break-up.

Bebe had just left an abusive husband and a disastrous life in Michigan with a dream of starting over. Alder Lake was supposed to be her second chance at happiness, a brand new life. What a joke.

She wondered how Amanda would face her at the shop after this. She wondered how Amanda could have even done this in the first place.

Then it hit her. She had done it because payback is a bitch, and Amanda Dale needed revenge. Blaze just happened to be the most convenient tool available for her to avenge fifteen years of infidelity.

Bebe marveled at how Kurt Dale had managed to singlehandedly ruin her life with his cheating.

One day she saw him walk out of a hotel arm in arm with Carolyn Devonshire. From that moment on, the man had become like a disease. A fast-spreading infection which had taken over every corner of her life and destroyed every relationship she'd managed to build.

Blaze and Amanda—now that was something Bebe hadn't seen coming. It certainly hadn't been going on for long. In fact, tonight was probably the first time.

It's not like they'd been sneaking around at hotels the way Kurt had. That wasn't what was going on here.

It really wasn't terribly hard to figure out how it happened. Blaze needed comfort. The videotape of Lorna had completely unraveled him. And, Amanda, having learned her husband cheated again, needed vengeance. It was the perfect storm.

Bebe wondered if Blaze had told Amanda about what her precious daughter had done to Kurt's mistress. Probably not. She couldn't imagine Amanda falling into bed with the bearer of those awful tidings.

Bebe had never felt so alone. Not even when she first moved to town and didn't know a soul. God, what she wouldn't give for those days again. It would beat the hell out of being forced into a web of lies and secrets for crimes she had nothing to do with. Why was she being forced to pay the price for Kurt Dale's infidelity and Lorna Dale's violence?

If she never had to look at any of them again, it would suit her just fine.

The problem was Amanda worked in her shop and Bebe needed the help. If she fired her, it would leave her with only the stupid teenage twit to help run things. She wasn't going to shoot herself in the foot because she was angry. Kurt Dale had taken enough from her. She wasn't going to let him take the good hired help too.

Bebe knew only one thing for sure: just as Amanda's marriage to Kurt Dale had ended this day, so had her friendship with Beatrice Sugars.

CHAPTER 25

Lorna did not think it possible that her mother could be any more preoccupied than she had been the last few days. She was wrong. When she woke up for school the morning after her blood-father had come to her with news of the people who would help her, Amanda did not even hear when Lorna asked if she had seen her purple sandals. She had to ask the question twice before her mother's eyes focused on her.

Her mother answered rather dreamily, "Oh, I think I saw them by the back door."

Lorna had never seen her quite like this before. She seemed to be floating around the house like a disembodied spirit rather than walking the rooms like a solid human being. It was weird.

Since Lorna was rather preoccupied herself, she didn't spend too much time thinking about her mother's oddly ethereal behavior.

Lorna had completely forgotten about Bebe telling her she was going to leave the bag with her clothing by the window last night. She left for school, leaving it waiting patiently below the window outside the den.

She was very curious and very excited about the people her blood-father said were coming to give her blood today. It was a good thing too, because she was getting awfully hungry again. While she would never admit this to anyone, she had acquired a taste for not only blood, but for killing as well.

Despite the terror she had felt right after committing these horrific acts, there was a compelling excitement that accompanied the encounters like an invited friend.

She wondered if she would hunt with these new people, and the idea sent a shiver of delight through her.

The only thing that darkened her excitement was when her blood-father told her he may not be coming with them. She desperately needed to see him.

Lorna was looking forward to seeing Samantha again. The dog had been a most beloved friend, and even though it had been years ago, she still remembered being devastated when her mother told her Samantha died.

While she was curious to know how the dog had come to be with these new people, and how in the world she was still alive, Lorna did not asked these questions of Francis Barclay. Last night didn't seem like the right time.

The logistics of where and how she should meet up with the new people was his only priority.

Her father was concerned Lorna would not be able to escape the school easily. She explained about a side entrance where she could leave undetected. She said that she would tell her teacher she was suffering from a stomach ache about twenty minutes before recess. She would ask to go to the nurse's office while everyone was in class and the hallways deserted. She gave him the time.

Francis Barclay had passed this information on to Ben and Lily. The plan was arranged.

Readying for today's dangerous mission, Lily coiled her long, black hair into a bun at the back of her head and covered it with a baseball cap. She donned oversize sunglasses and was attired in all black clothing.

Ben, having called in to work claiming a family emergency would keep him away for a few days, was decked out in similar fashion.

While they ate a rather subdued breakfast, Francis informed the Jarvises that he would not be going with them to collect the child. He would in fact be leaving for good this morning.

They accompanied him outside, Samantha and Lionel at their side.

Francis appeared to shimmer in the early morning sunlight. He appeared far less substantial than he had seemed even the night before. The landscape behind him could now be vaguely observed right through his body.

After more assurances from Lily and Ben that they would see to Lorna's safety, they bid him farewell. Holding hands, they watched as he walked off into the sunlight.

There were tears pooling in Lily's eyes as she observed his hair blow about his head like a halo, then disintegrate into fine grains of dust. It swirled off into the air above him. Soon his whole body appeared to swirl like the funnel of a tornado, as the rest of him was swept up into the air.

Just before he blew apart, he raised what remained of his arm in a final wave. Then he was gone. Samantha whined low in her throat. Ben reached down absently to pat the dog's head.

Enrico Vasquez stood with a puzzled frown on his face. The janitor, who had become so fascinated with Lorna all those months ago when he saw her enter the restroom with a fire extinguisher, was once again wondering what she was up to.

Just as he had done months before, Enrico watched Lorna from the shadows. She was hurrying down the isolated hallway toward the school's side exit.

As she reached to push the heavy door open, he sprang from his hiding place and grabbed ahold of her arm.

"Hey, where do you think you're going? You can't leave by yourself. Why aren't you in class?" he demanded.

Lorna jumped. "Let go of me!" Her voice shook with fear. "Um… my mom is picking me up. I don't feel well." She tried to pull free of the janitor's grasp, but he held tight.

"Why isn't she picking you up out front?" he asked suspiciously.

"You better let go," Lorna growled. "I'm warning you."

Enrico began pulling her in the direction of the principal's office. He would let them sort it out. He had no intention of letting this weird little girl run away. Who knew what she was capable of? If she would clean a grown woman's clock in the middle of the day with a fire extinguisher, he was convinced, whatever today's plans included, they were sure to be nefarious.

Enrico was stunned when all of a sudden he was no longer able to keep herding the child toward the office. She had stopped walking and was now yanking her arm back with all the force she could muster.

Enrico couldn't believe she was actually winning this weird tug-of-war. He must have outweighed the kid by over a hundred pounds, yet he could no longer budge her even a single step.

When he opened his mouth to tell her to stop fighting him, he slammed it shut with a jaw-rattling snap.

Her eyes were aglow with a deep, baleful brilliance. They looked almost ready to burst into sapphire flames as they bathed the wall beside them in an eerie blue light.

"What the…" he began.

Lorna took advantage of his momentary distraction to pull free from his grasp. She raced for the door.

Enrico stood paralyzed, with his mouth hanging open, watching her.

Escaping through the side entrance, Lorna immediately spied a silver SUV idling at the curb. There was a woman in black clothing and a baseball cap waving her over.

Lorna ran to her. "Hurry," she gasped, "the janitor is chasing me!"

The lady threw open the back door and lifted Lorna inside, before jumping into the passenger seat. As she was slamming the door closed, she yelled, "Go, Ben, go. Now!"

Ben Jarvis jammed his foot on the accelerator. The sound of burning rubber filled the neighborhood as he sped down the street. Sparing a look into the rearview mirror, he caught sight of a dark-skinned man running after the car.

Enrico Vasquez, having finally managed to get his body moving again, was giving chase. He recognized the vehicle as a late model Lexus. He tried to read the license plate number, but it was illegible. He could only make out the first number, a three, before it disappeared around the corner.

Ben Jarvis, thinking ahead to this very scenario, had smeared the license plates with mud before they left this morning. He had considered removing them altogether, but if a police officer saw them driving with no plates, he knew it would arouse far more suspicion than if they were just dirty.

Enrico charged back into the school and stormed the principal's office. Someone had to be told.

Once he explained what he had just witnessed, the school secretary informed the principal. The principal in turn called Lorna's parents to find out if one of them had picked up the child or authorized someone else to do so.

It took only a few minutes before the police were notified that Lorna Dale had been kidnapped.

Once they were safely on the interstate, Ben and Lily introduced themselves to their new ward. Ben told Lorna that they, too, were vampire, and they had been sent by her maker to help her out of the trouble she'd gotten herself into.

This was the first time Lorna ever heard the word vampire in relation to herself. She was flabbergasted.

"What do you mean, *you too,* are vampire? I'm not a…" Her voice trailed away, as the full impact of what Francis Barclay had truly done to her all those years ago hit home for the first time.

"No wonder Bebe was so scared of me." She began to cry.

Lily reached back to pat the little girl's leg. She gave her husband a worried glance. "Sweetie, you didn't know you were a vampire?"

Lorna shook her head. "No. I knew I was… well, different, and there's the blood thing, but I didn't know I was anything like that."

She was growing increasingly upset by this news. "Carolyn Devonshire was right, I am a monster!" she wailed.

Ben and Lily both shouted, "No!" at the same time.

They exchanged another look.

Lily said, "We are not monsters. Vampires are still people, Lorna. We just have different needs than other humans. We are civilized and we live our lives just like everyone else. Apart from, well… *the blood thing*, as you called it. Aren't you just like all your friends? You go to school, and you do the same activities, right?"

"Yes, but I… well… I did some really bad things. I don't think other kids have ever done what I did."

When Lorna dropped her eyes, Ben replied, "It's okay, Lorna. We know about the bad things. That's why we're here. That's why Francis Barclay sent us for you."

"Is he…" Lorna began.

Lily reached into the back and patted her knee again. "Yes, honey. I'm sorry. He went away this morning. He wanted to stay, but he couldn't make it any longer. He needed to ensure that you were taken care of, and then he had to return to… well, wherever he lives now," she finished awkwardly.

Lorna swiped tears from her eyes. "What about Samantha? Where is she? Father said I could see her."

At this, Lily brightened. "Oh, you will! Samantha lives with us, and we have another dog too. His name is Lionel. I think you'll like him very much."

"So we're going to your house?" Lorna asked.

Lily nodded.

"Okay, but I have to be back before school lets out. I'll have to come up with a real whopper of a story to explain where I was. I told my teacher I had a tummy ache, so maybe I won't get into too much trouble."

Lily looked at Ben with alarm.

He cleared his throat. "Well, Lorna, your father thought, given what you had to do to get blood, it might be best if you came and stayed with us for a while."

Lorna's eyes opened wide with surprise. She looked back and forth between them. "Stay with you? You mean like live at your house? My mom and dad won't let me do that."

"Sweetie, do they know what you are? Or what lengths you went to for blood?" Lily asked.

"Of course not! No one knows about that except my blood-father and now you. But my parents won't let me stay with you."

Ben began to say something about going to jail for committing murder.

Lily slapped his arm and shook her head. "We'll talk about this later," she replied firmly, "after we have had some lunch and have fed."

"Who do we feed from?" Lorna asked eagerly.

More troubled glances were exchanged in the front seat.

"Well, we don't feed off of anyone. We have blood at the house. All different types. We can let you try them, and you can pick out the one you like best. I like A positive," Ben replied.

"A, what?" A puzzled frown creased Lorna's brow.

"It's a blood type. There are several different kinds. They all taste a little different. We will find the one you like best."

"Who do you get it from?" Lorna asked curiously.

"Many different people. I'm a doctor, Lorna. I founded a blood bank. People donate their blood."

"Wow! They give it to you without even putting up a fight or anything?" Lorna marveled at this.

Ben took the next several minutes to explain to Lorna how a blood bank worked. He told her the donors were unaware that some of their blood ended up in the Jarvises freezer. He imparted how dangerous it could be to their survival if anyone were to learn about that. He also pointed out what a good thing it was because no one was ever harmed or killed for their blood.

Lorna seemed oddly disappointed at this news.

CHAPTER 26

When Kurt took the call from Lorna's school, he felt like the person on the other end of the line was speaking in some foreign language he could not decipher.

After identifying herself as the school principal, the woman asked him if he had picked his daughter up, or if he had sent someone else to come get her.

Before Kurt's brain could even begin to compute the question and formulate a response, the caller went on to say that if he had indeed sent someone else to fetch Lorna, he had violated the school's policy on authorized persons who were permitted to take the children off of school grounds.

She was in the middle of saying something about the proper location to collect a child being the front of the school in the designated parking lot, and not from the side entrance, when Kurt cut her off.

"What are you talking about?" he asked, completely perplexed.

"Lorna was seen leaving school in a silver-colored SUV. We are trying to find out who picked her up."

Kurt was not overtaken by panic yet. Given the current climate between he and Amanda, it was possible she had made previous arrangements for Lorna to spend the afternoon with a friend, or sent someone else to pick her up and just never mentioned it to him. When he glanced at his watch and realized it was far too early for his daughter to be out of school, alarm began to slowly seep up his spine with the cloying stickiness of spilling molasses.

"Let me call my wife," he responded and disconnected the call.

Amanda was baking brownies and singing along with the radio when the phone rang. She woke up feeling quite domestic and wanted to make a treat for Lorna. Blaze too, if he would be stopping by later, as she hoped.

She couldn't remember the last time she felt inspired to bake something special for Kurt.

Everything she felt upon waking up the morning after committing her first act of adultery was wonderful. She not only felt sexually sated in a deliciously feline sort of way, she felt pretty—beautiful, even. When was the last time Kurt made her feel that way? When was the last time she'd felt even a fraction this desirable or this happy in the last fifteen years of marriage?

What began as payback against her philandering husband had blossomed into something quite unexpected in Amanda's heart. While she always had a genuine affection for Blaze, Amanda didn't realize how deep that affection ran.

It far exceeded merely using him to extract revenge against Kurt. She realized that the warmth she felt for Blaze was somehow cleaner and purer than any emotion she had felt for the man she married, since the first time she discovered he'd been unfaithful.

As she marveled at these newfound emotions, the phone rang. Her good mood shriveled, and the smile fled her face when she saw who the caller was.

"What is it, Kurt," she answered, not bothering to mask her annoyance as she turned down the radio.

"Did you send someone to pick Lorna up from school?" Kurt's voice was tense with barely concealed worry.

"Pick her up? It's not even noon. She won't be out for three hours yet. I'm not working today, so I'll get her myself."

He explained about the school's disturbing phone call, claiming Lorna had been seen leaving the school in a silver SUV.

Amanda felt a cold and overwhelming terror course through her entire body.

"I… I don't even know anyone with a silver car. Who do we know with a silver SUV, Kurt?" she stammered.

"Shit!" Kurt cried, panic finally seizing him entirely in its steely jaws. "Meet me at the school. Now!"

Amanda turned off the oven and grabbed her car keys from the hook by the door. She did not even bother with removing her apron before speeding out of the driveway and racing toward Lorna's school. Her heart was hammering in her chest and she was breathing in shallow little gasps.

Somewhere inside her mind, she wondered if this was punishment for what she had done last night. In nearly the same breath, she knew if that were true, Kurt's sins would have caught up with him long before now and he would have burst into flames years ago.

Kurt alerted Captain Fitzgerald to the situation. Four squad cars were already waiting for him at the school by the time he arrived. Detective Blazer was not among them. This wasn't considered a violent crime yet, and he would not be alerted to the events surrounding Lorna's disappearance until later in the day.

Blaze was, once again, suspiciously absent from his desk, claiming to be working in the field for a second day on the Carolyn Devonshire case. In truth, he was hoping if he stayed out of sight, he would also be out of mind. He desperately needed to buy some time before his captain started asking questions about those damning surveillance tapes.

That wish would be granted very shortly, as Carolyn Devonshire's murder would take a distant back seat to the kidnapping of Lorna Dale.

A statewide Amber Alert was issued, and the now familiar gathering of news vans and reporters once more blanketed the steps of the police department, the school, and the front lawn of the Dale home. Their presence only served to exacerbate the bitterness Amanda felt for Kurt, as it brought back unpleasant and painful memories of the last time their home drew a media swarm.

For Kurt, the media's convergence on his home was a frightening reminder of Francis Barclay, and the inconceivable horror that he might be back in Alder Lake. His terror only intensified as he wondered if Barclay was connected to his daughter's disappearance.

He was going to have to tell Amanda about it now. He found the prospect of sharing this bitter revelation with his wife almost as frightening as discovering Lorna had gone missing.

Enrico Vasquez was interviewed first at the school, and then dragged down to the station and interrogated for several hours there. He emerged as a suspect practically the moment he started spouting off about Lorna and the fire extinguisher. He couldn't seem to stop talking about the incident and what he had observed on that long-ago afternoon. He wisely kept the detail about her eyes glowing to himself.

The fact that he was the last person to see Lorna, and the one to report her missing, did nothing to help eliminate the police's suspicions. Everyone was having a hard time believing the story he was telling. If it were true, they all wondered, why not report the incident to the school back when it happened? How much credibility could he have when he claimed to have left a woman passed out on a bathroom floor without going for help?

The authorities were less convinced of his guilt only after he passed a polygraph test and willingly gave a DNA sample. However, he remained on the police's radar as a person of interest in the case.

A wiretap was placed on the Dales' home phone in the event someone called with ransom demands. With little to go on, all Kurt and Amanda could do was wait.

Officers were constantly in and out of the house. Two of them had the annoying task of shooing the press away from the front door.

Amanda desperately wanted to call Blaze. For obvious reasons she didn't. She asked Kurt tentatively, "Shouldn't Blaze be brought in?"

"They aren't considering it a violent crime at this point. Let's hope it doesn't turn into one." He sighed miserably.

"Since when isn't kidnapping a violent crime?" she asked, frustrated.

"Amanda, there is something I haven't told you. With everything that's been happening, there hasn't been a good time to bring this up."

She scowled at him. "If it's about another woman, honestly, Kurt, I couldn't care less anymore."

Kurt closed his eyes briefly at the dull lack of emotion in his wife's voice when she spoke of his infidelity. "It's nothing like that. It's about Francis Barclay."

Amanda's eyes flew open in shock. "What in God's name could you possibly want to tell me about him?" she exclaimed. "Look, Kurt, if this is some stupid ploy you've dreamed up to scare me into letting you come back..."

"It's not. I swear! I never even wanted you to know about this. I think it might have something to do with Lorna's kidnapping, though."

Amanda put her hands up to her face and gasped in horror. "No, that can't be, Kurt. Why would you even think such a thing?"

"Because the death of both Carolyn and the woman in the park were just like the ones Barclay committed all those years ago. The method was the same as Tina Hilliard and the rest of Barclay's victims. Only now he's even more violent then he was before. He's literally ripping out the throats of his victims."

Amanda glared at her husband. "You are a fucking liar!" she roared.

Just then Blaze appeared before them. His expression was grim. "He isn't lying," he declared soberly, "however, the killer was not Francis Barclay."

Blaze removed a DVD from his shirt pocket. "I need to show you both something. Do you have a DVD player?"

Amanda, looking bewildered, pointed to the one in the living room.

Blaze shook his head. "In private. Do you have one in your bedroom?" he asked cryptically.

Ben Jarvis turned on the television. He watched in astonishment the media coverage Lorna Dale's disappearance had spawned.

Regularly scheduled programming on all the local networks was interrupted to broadcast the Amber Alert. Every channel was saturated with ongoing coverage from the police department, the school and the Dale home.

He snapped the television off before either Lily or Lorna could see what was going on.

They were in the backyard playing with the dogs when Ben rushed out to the driveway and pulled the car hastily into the garage. Thank God he had muddied the license plates. Apparently, the janitor had not come out of the school in time to see Lily, so they had absolutely no description of the people involved in the child's abduction. They only had a description of the vehicle and the first number of the license plate.

Lorna was so happy to see Samantha, that for a little while she forgot she was in a strange place with people who had no intention of returning her to the only home she had ever known.

She looked like a normal, happy child out back playing with the dogs. Even Lily seemed to be more relaxed and enjoying herself, now that they were safely back in their home.

Ben didn't realize how tense he had been once they spirited Lorna away from her school. He was convinced they would be caught every step of the way. The entire drive was spent checking the rearview mirror and expecting to see flashing red lights behind them. He couldn't believe it, but somehow they had managed to get away with this.

Lily prepared club sandwiches for lunch. Both she and Ben were relieved to see Lorna eat heartily.

While they were expecting a period of adjustment, they did not expect the first hurdle to present itself so quickly. They encountered it right after lunch, when Ben brought blood up from the basement so they could feed.

There were four blood types for Lorna to choose from. When she lifted the first plastic bag to her lips, she took one sip and crinkled her nose in disgust. "Yuck! It's cold," she complained, dropping it and crossing her arms stubbornly over her chest.

Ben and Lily's eyes met for a brief troubled moment, before Lily suggested, "I could warm it up. Would you like that?"

Lorna slid the bag across the table to her with one outstretched finger.

As she carried it into the kitchen, Lily called over her shoulder for Lorna to bring her the other bags as well. She would heat all of them in hopes that at least one of the blood types would appeal to the child.

She fished a double boiler out of a cabinet and placed the blood on the stove to warm. The Jarvises owned a microwave oven because no modern kitchen came equipped without one, but they rarely used it. Lily preferred cooking the old fashioned way. She thought everything tasted better without involving the microwave.

Once the blood was heated, Lily poured the bags into three pretty bone china mugs. She took a small taste of one before carrying them out to the dining room on a silver tray. She had to admit, the child was right. It really was much better warm. Why had she never thought of this before?

When Ben saw the nice cups and the silver tray, he quipped in an exaggerated English brogue, "Oh, look. It's high blood time at Buckingham Palace."

Lily gave him a stern glance and shook her head. Making sure Lorna would drink the blood was no laughing matter.

They held their breath and awaited Lorna's verdict when Lily placed the first mug on the table before her.

Lorna wrapped both hands around the cup and took a small tentative sip. She nodded and smiled. Ben and Lily breathed a huge sigh of relief. They had weathered the first storm.

Lorna only needed to try two different blood types before declaring herself a B-Positive girl.

As Lorna sipped from the half-full cup of blood, Ben was vaguely distressed when the girl commented, "Tastes better when it comes right from the people, you know?"

An officer was shooing away a reporter from the side of the house when he spotted a paper bag lying below the window. He donned cotton gloves and carried it inside. He handed it to his superior officer, who examined the contents.

When he saw it appeared to be a little girl's clothing, he radioed the detective assigned to the case immediately.

The detective told him to put it aside to be taken to the crime lab for analysis.

Once Kurt and Amanda led Blaze upstairs to their bedroom and shut the door, he sat them down on the bed.

He looked at Amanda. What she saw in his eyes sent a shiver of fright through her.

He began, "This is the surveillance tape from the courthouse the night Carolyn Devonshire was killed. It shows her murder."

Amanda gasped, "I don't want to see that!"

Blaze looked at her pityingly. "I am so sorry, Amanda. You have to. You should have seen it before now. I just didn't have the heart to show it to you. To either one of you." He glanced at Kurt.

"If Francis Barclay didn't kill her, then who did, Blaze? And why should Amanda have to see this? She doesn't have the stomach for this kind of thing." Kurt said, placing an arm around his wife's shoulder. He shot her an annoyed glance when she pushed it away.

In a small, scared voice, Amanda asked, "Does this have something to do with Lorna?"

Blaze scrubbed at his face with his hand. "It has everything to do with her. There really is no easy way to tell you this. Lorna killed Carolyn Devonshire."

Kurt flew up from the bed, thundering, "Are you out of your mind? Is this some kind of sick joke?"

Amanda sat in stunned silence, looking pleadingly at Blaze.

He looked back at her with such tenderness it made her heart ache. Ignoring Kurt entirely, Blaze said softly, "You have no idea how sorry I am to have to show you this."

He walked to the TV. "You should both be prepared. It's not easy to watch." He was still looking at Amanda when he said, "Please forgive me."

Kurt began vehemently arguing, as Blaze turned on the television and inserted the DVD into the player. "There must be some mistake," he cried helplessly as Blaze hit the play button and stepped out of the way of the screen.

You could hear a pin drop as they all watched in silent horror as the grainy video came to life, and little Lorna Dale walked into the courthouse.

When the tape was finished, Amanda sat with her hands balled into fists and held against her mouth, as if to silence the screams trying to escape.

Kurt's face was ghost-white. He turned to Blaze and asked, "Who else knows?"

Blaze averted eye contact when he answered, "No one. I haven't even told Captain Fitzgerald." A brief image of Bebe vomiting into the wastebasket in the interrogation room flooded his mind, and he quickly pushed it away.

"Did either of you have any idea she was capable of something like this? Or why she would do it?"

Kurt shook his head. "Of course not! We..."

Almost too softly to be heard, Amanda said, "Because she's a vampire."

Kurt turned on her. "Oh, no she isn't! Don't you ever say that again!" His voice sounded menacing.

Blaze put a restraining hand on his shoulder. "Let her talk, Kurt."

"It's not true!" he hollered.

Amanda looked at her husband with a mixture of pity and disgust. "It is true and you know it. Why else would she kill a woman in the exact same manner Francis Barclay did? Why else would she kill at all? What little girl does something like this? We should have known all along, Kurt."

"No, Amanda! No! Our daughter is no such thing. There has to be some logical explanation for this." Kurt glared at his wife.

Amanda continued, unrelenting, "Barclay turned her into one five years ago when he took her. There have been so many signs. We just ignored all of them."

Amanda ticked each one off on her fingers, as she said, "Sucking on your bloody tissue from the shaving cut. Eating bugs in the backyard. The raw steak. All of it. We just never wanted to face it. What was it you said? *She's a weird kid.* Remember that? Well she wasn't weird until that monster got ahold of her. He did this!"

Kurt looked at her, shocked. "She ate bugs in the yard?"

Amanda nodded miserably. "And not when she was a toddler either. When she was old enough to know better. I never told you about that, but it happened more than once."

Blaze interjected, "Look, I don't know about this whole vampire thing. Kurt, I know you think this Barclay guy is back. But we have to deal with the facts here. Is there anyone else who might know, or even suspect, Lorna killed the DA? If someone else knows, that might be who took her."

Kurt and Amanda could think of no one. Both were trying very hard to digest the gruesome display just witnessed on that tape, not to mention the very real possibility their daughter was indeed a vampire.

"In order to try and contain this, Kurt, I think you better call Fitzgerald. Ask him to assign me as lead detective on the case. As Lorna's father, he will do what you ask."

Kurt agreed. He braced himself to make the call. When the captain asked him why he wanted Blaze to lead the investigation, he lied, claiming he was afraid the kidnapping might be connected with one of his old cases from when he worked in the violent crimes division.

Fitzgerald accepted this explanation without question and granted Kurt's request. He informed the detective who had been originally assigned as the lead that Blaze would be taking over. He told him to brief Blaze as soon as possible and get him up to speed.

The detective called Blaze and told him about the bag of clothing found by the window.

When Blaze looked in the bag and recognized the clothing as the same pieces worn by Lorna Dale when she murdered the DA, he asked the officer who found it to show him where the bag had been discovered. He requested the man bring over a fingerprint kit, and he managed to pull a perfect thumbprint from the windowsill outside the den.

Blaze personally took the bag to the crime lab. He ordered the bag tested for prints, and the clothing inside for DNA. He asked for the tech to put a rush on it.

He told her it had to do with the disappearance of Detective Dale's daughter. She dropped everything else she was doing and began working on it at once.

While awaiting the fingerprint results, Blaze met with the detective for the briefing. It was then he learned of the janitor's story about Lorna and the fire extinguisher.

When he questioned Kurt about the incident, he remembered it with vivid clarity. In fact, Kurt recalled the entire afternoon, including having sex with Carolyn Devonshire in a hotel room, and being late to pick Lorna up from play rehearsal.

He could not believe his sweet little daughter looked him straight in the eye that day and asked him to give Kelly Winter a ride home, all the while knowing she had left the girl's mother unconscious on a bathroom floor.

Kurt Dale realized he did not know his daughter at all. She was the person he loved most in this world. He'd raised her since birth, so how could he possess absolutely no knowledge of who she truly is. Or *what* she is, for that matter.

Kurt knew vampires existed. He'd done battle with one personally five years before, so he could not afford the luxury of denying their existence. He just refused to embrace the notion that his Lorna could be one of those vile creatures, no matter how much evidence existed to support such an unfathomable and horrid explanation for the wretched crimes she'd committed. His little girl could not be a vampire.

CHAPTER 27

One summer, about twenty-five years before Beatrice Sugars ever heard of a town called Alder Lake, she took a temporary clerical job in the mayor's office in the small Michigan town where she lived.

Royce was between jobs at the time, a not uncommon state of affairs, and they needed the money.

The position required Bebe handle campaign funds, and as such, a prerequisite of her employment was being fingerprinted.

It was from that long ago, all but forgotten job, her fingerprints were entered into the national AFIS database, where they lay dormant and unnoticed for over two decades.

The fingerprint tech called Blaze on his cell phone. She excitedly told him she found a match for the print he pulled from the windowsill of the Dale home. There was also a match to one print found on the bag containing Lorna's clothing. They were from the same person, and that person lived right in Alder Lake. The DNA results from the clothing would take a few days and would yield nothing when they did finally come in. All the evidence had gone down the drain in Bebe's washing machine.

As Blaze hurried to the lab to collect the print results and get ready to go haul someone in for questioning, he hoped with all his heart it was the same person who had taken the little girl, and she would be found unharmed.

You could have knocked the detective over with a feather when he saw the name of the person whose fingerprints were pulled from the window.

Trying not to betray his complete and utter dismay, Blaze asked the tech, "You're sure about this?"

She led him to the computer and showed him the inlay of the thumbprint he pulled. When she superimposed the simulation of Bebe's print from the AFIS database over the top, he could see it was a one hundred percent match.

He thanked the technician and left the station with a heavy heart and churning stomach.

He wondered if after he'd shown Bebe that dreadful tape, she had somehow gotten the idea into her head to kidnap Lorna and stop the child before she could hurt anyone else.

But he knew that wasn't it. Bebe was no kidnapper. He knew she had nothing to do with Lorna's disappearance. What he could not begin to understand was how on earth she had gotten her hands on the clothing Lorna was wearing the night she murdered Carolyn Devonshire.

After delivering the news to Kurt and Amanda Dale that their daughter was a cold-blooded killer, Detective Medwyn Blazer did not believe there could ever be a conversation to follow he would ever dread as much.

He was wrong. Topping the list was the one he was now on his way to have with his ex-girlfriend.

Just shoot me now, he thought ruefully, as he pulled into a parking space in front of Curious Curios and Collectibles.

When Bebe heard the bell above the door, she was not overjoyed to see who graced the entrance to her shop. A war of conflicting emotions raced through her as Blaze closed the door behind him.

He glanced around the shop to see if there were any customers who would overhear their conversation. Seeing none, he seemed to read her mind, as he stated, "I'm probably the last person you want to see, huh?"

Bebe offered a small wintry smile. "No. That would be Kurt Dale. But you're a pretty close second."

He tried to smile back and found he couldn't quite manage it. "When I tell you why I'm here you may wish I was Kurt. I'm here in an official capacity, Bebe."

She looked at him with a worried frown. "More about Lorna, is it?"

Blaze nodded. "I have to ask you a rather difficult question."

Now completely frightened, Bebe walked past him and turned the sign in the window to *Closed.* She locked the door. "Okay. What's the question?"

"How did you come into contact with the clothes Lorna Dale was wearing the night she killed Carolyn Devonshire?"

Bebe grabbed the counter for support, inhaling sharply. She was suddenly dizzy.

Blaze reached out to take her arm and steady her. Concerned, he asked, "Should we go sit down in the back?"

Bebe nodded and allowed him to lead her by the elbow into the back room. Before he sat down he brought her a glass of water from the tap in the bathroom.

She looked up gratefully and took a long draught from the glass.

Clearing her throat, she told him, "The night Lorna killed Carolyn Devonshire she showed up here and begged me to help her. I was working late that night, if you remember."

Blaze was stunned. "You knew she killed the DA? Why the hell didn't you tell me about this?"

"Of course I didn't know. All Lorna told me was that she was in trouble. Judging by all the blood she brought with her, it was bad trouble. I asked her repeatedly what had happened and she refused to say anything."

"After I showed you the tape, you still didn't think you should mention her visit?" he fumed.

"Lorna threatened to hurt me if I told anyone she was here that night. After viewing the lovely tape you couldn't wait to share with me, I thought she would kill me if I breathed a word of it to anyone."

Blaze looked at her doubtfully. "She showed up here late at night, covered in blood, and offered no explanation whatsoever?"

Bebe sounded exasperated as she replied, "I'm telling you, she never said a word about Carolyn Devonshire. I didn't know what happened or where all the blood came from. She certainly never told me she'd killed anyone. The only thing I am guilty of is giving her something to wear and washing her clothes. How did you find out I even had them?"

"Your fingerprints were on the bag and on the Dales' windowsill. Why on earth are your prints in the national database anyway? Do you have a record you never told me about?"

Bebe rolled her eyes. "Why, yes. I used to rob banks in my spare time for fun and profit. I got caught once or twice," she replied dryly.

"Seriously, Bebe, why are your prints on file?"

"About a thousand years ago I took a job working in the mayor's office. Had to get printed in order to work there."

"Ah." Blaze nodded. "Why did you leave a bag full of clothing from a crime scene under their window?"

"I told Lorna I would put her clothes there after I washed them, along with the little statue that was in the bag with them. She was supposed to bring it inside. Why did you test the bag for fingerprints? How did you even know it was there?"

Blaze raised his eyebrows in surprise. "You're cluelessness about what goes on in this town never ceases to amaze me. You haven't by chance seen the news today?"

Bebe shook her head, bewildered. "Nope. Been here all day. What is it now?"

"Lorna is missing. She was kidnapped from school earlier this afternoon."

"What? Oh my God! By who?"

"We don't know. I was hoping the bag of clothes would lead me to the guilty party, but I'm guessing you don't have her locked up out back?"

Bebe could not mask her irritation. "No, Detective, afraid not. Is this the part where you read me my rights and arrest me as an accessory after the fact, or whatever the hell you law types call it?"

He squeezed her hand. "No one's arresting you. You kept my dirty little secret, so I will keep yours. Thanks for not ratting me out to my superiors about the tape. By the way, Kurt and Amanda have seen it now. They know what Lorna did."

"Speaking of dirty little secrets, does Kurt know who you were keeping company with last night?"

Now it was Blaze's turn to look like he was going to faint. His eyes flashed with guilt. "Oh, Bebe. I would ask how you knew, but I'm a trained detective. Guess you saw my car when you were dropping off the clothes last night."

"Uh-huh. Aren't you going to tell me it's not what it looks like?"

Blaze looked at her levelly, saying nothing.

"Yeah," Bebe replied, "that's what I thought. How long has this been going on?"

In my dreams for roughly the last three years, Blaze thought. He prudently did not voice this out loud.

He said, "If you're wondering if I was seeing her while you and I were together, then the answer is no. Of course not."

Bebe rose and turned her back on him so he wouldn't see the tears threatening to fall again.

Once she had regained control of her emotions, she turned back. Her expression had hardened once more. "I guess you probably want to know about that statue in the bag."

Though Blaze had seen it, he hadn't given it a second thought. He placed far greater significance on finding the clothing Lorna wore the night she killed the DA.

He told her, "I saw the statue, but didn't give it much thought. I was more concerned with the clothes. Why did you give that thing to her?"

Bebe proceeded to fill him in about the woman who left the dog statue for Lorna and the odd conversation they shared. She chastised him for not running it for prints.

While Bebe's fingerprints might be on the dog, there could be at least one more person's on it as well.

As Blaze was readying to leave, Bebe cautiously laid a restraining hand on his arm. "Can I ask you something?"

He looked apprehensive. He knew what the question was likely to be, and he didn't want to hurt her any more than he already had.

"Did you have feelings for her even when you were seeing me? Is that why you would never let things get further than a little kissing between us?"

Blaze put his hands on Bebe's shoulders. "I didn't honestly know I had feelings for her until a couple days ago. If you and I kept seeing each other, I probably still wouldn't know. She's a married woman, after all. I blew it with you when I showed you that tape. I saw it in your eyes when you broke up with me."

"That only half answers my question."

Blaze sighed. "Bebe, I don't know why things didn't go any further with us. It just wasn't the right time. Not after seeing Kurt and Carolyn Devonshire together. And not with everything else that's been swirling around since we started going out. Murder and mayhem aren't really conducive to romance."

"Well, forgive me, Blaze," she said more sharply than she intended, "the way I see it, all the same crap is still swirling around now. It didn't seem to stop you from hopping into Amanda's bed."

For this, Blaze had no answer. She was right. He wasn't going to insult her further by offering any lame excuses. He said only, "I'm sorry I hurt you, Bebe. It was never my intention."

His words only served to make her angrier. "Well, how about Amanda?" she spat. "Is she sorry she hurt me too? Did she ever pause for a moment before fucking you to ask herself, gee, how would Bebe feel about this?"

Blaze's eyes hardened. "You would have to ask her that question. You may want to keep in mind, the lady just found out her seven-year-old daughter is a murderer, and now the child's been kidnapped. You and I are probably not the first things on Amanda's mind right now."

Bebe was ashamed of herself. She supposed in light of the circumstances she must sound awfully selfish. Her anger crumbled, and she stammered an apology.

Blaze's eyes softened. He leaned down and kissed her on the forehead before hurrying out the door to his car.

This time he saw the tears as they spilled down Bebe's cheeks. Oh, how he wished he hadn't.

CHAPTER 28

Amanda locked herself in the bathroom with her cell phone and sent a text message to Blaze: *I have to see you. Please.*

He responded immediately, *How?*

She wrote back, *I will think of something. Stay by your phone.*

When she emerged from the bathroom, she found Kurt at the desk in the den. "I have to go to the drug store."

He looked at her, puzzled. "Now?"

She didn't meet his questioning gaze, as she mumbled, "Female emergency."

He handed her his car keys and told her, "You will never be able to get your car out of the garage with all of those reporters. I parked on the street."

She took the offered keys and left out the back door. She walked all the way around the back of Russell and Darlene's house before doubling back up the street to where Kurt was parked. It was the same route Bebe had used the night before. Amanda somehow managed to escape without alerting the press to her presence.

Once she drove a few blocks, she pulled over and texted Blaze again with her location.

He responded at once, *My house?*

On my way, she replied, pulling away from the curb.

Blaze parked on the street in front of his house and left the garage door open. When Amanda pulled up, he motioned for her to pull into the garage.

He had learned his lesson about what could happen when cars were left out in driveways for all the world to see.

Once Amanda pulled the car inside, Blaze lowered the door and went to her.

She practically fell into his arms as she threw open the car door.

"I'm so glad you called," he said against her neck. "I thought you would hate me for allowing what happened between us last night, without telling you what I knew about Lorna." Blaze sounded anguished.

Amanda pulled out of his embrace and looked at him. "First of all," she said, "let's get something straight. You didn't *allow* anything. Last night happened because I planned for it to happen. You didn't have a lot of say in the matter. Secondly, the fact that you DIDN'T show Fitzgerald that tape says a whole lot more about your feelings for me than anything else does."

Blaze breathed a huge sigh of relief. "Then we're okay?"

She answered the question with a kiss.

He asked her if she wanted to come inside. She declined, telling him about the lie she told Kurt to get out of the house.

Amanda climbed back into the car, promising to get in touch with him when she could. Before backing out of the garage, in a solemn voice, she told him, "Find my baby, Blaze. Bring her back to me." She left without waiting for a response.

Amanda drove home thinking about secrets. When Blaze asked her if they were okay, she didn't really answer that question.

She was thinking about how he had kept what he knew about Kurt and Carolyn Devonshire from her. Then he kept the considerably worse secret about Lorna. Maybe if he had told her before today, her daughter wouldn't be missing now. She wondered if that crossed his mind.

Amanda sincerely hoped someday she would have the luxury of being able to have a long conversation with Blaze about keeping secrets. About what the cost would be to their relationship if he kept any more. Whether he was doing it out of some misguided attempt to spare her feelings, or because he didn't think she was strong enough to handle the truth didn't matter. If there was still any relationship left between them at the end of this nightmare, it was a talk she intended to have. There would be no more secrets.

Of course, now wasn't the time. Now the only thing that mattered was finding her daughter.

When Amanda arrived home she parked around the block and entered the house through the back door. She wished the damn reporters would get tired and go away.

Kurt was waiting for her. If he wondered about the absence of a bag from the drug store, he did not say so. He told her Captain Fitzgerald wanted to have a press conference in which they would plead to Lorna's captors for her safe return.

Kurt remarked, "I don't think those things ever work, but I suppose we better do it."

Amanda agreed. Her only stipulation was that the conference be held at their home. She didn't want to have it at the police station. More bad memories.

The ghost of Tina Hilliard once again whispered in Amanda's ear, as she remembered standing by Kurt's side at the police department during another press conference held five years before. She still cringed when she thought about that humiliating morning when Kurt publicly proclaimed he was innocent of the crime after his mistress was found murdered.

Kurt passed along this request to Fitz, and half an hour later, both the captain and Detective Blazer arrived at the Dale home. A bank of microphones were set up on the front lawn.

Fitzgerald began the press conference by assuring the public that every resource was being expended to locate Detective Dale's daughter. He talked about the Amber Alert and urged anyone with information to call 911.

He then introduced Blaze as the lead detective on the case and turned the mike over to him.

Blaze explained they had begun an exhaustive search for any silver Lexus SUV with a license plate number beginning with the number three that was registered within a forty mile radius of Alder Lake.

In actuality, the search of the DMV records was for a silver Lexus with a license plate that began with the number three or the number eight, just in case the janitor had made a mistake. Enrico Vasquez didn't strike Blaze as being the most reliable witness.

Too bad that search radius had not been just ten miles wider. The search would hit a dead end by nightfall.

Once Blaze was done fielding what questions he could, he turned the mike over to Kurt and Amanda, who did the obligatory impassioned speech, begging for Lorna's safe return.

Enrico Vasquez was hauled in for questioning two more times and given another polygraph. He passed a second time.

The statue Bebe put in the bag with Lorna's crime scene clothing was dusted for prints. There were no usable ones found. Not even Bebe's were on the little dog.

The case was growing colder by the minute, and as day one turned into day two, Kurt and Amanda Dale were growing frantic.

Amanda allowed Kurt to move back into the house. They were united in their grief, and they had to make decisions together. However, that first night when Kurt went to their bed, Amanda went into Lorna's room and slept there. Not only didn't she want to sleep beside her husband, she wanted to feel as close to her daughter as she could. The agonizing pull she felt in her heart found little solace there, but it was all she had.

The sleeping arrangements stayed that way, though there was little sleep to be had on that long and miserable first night without their daughter, or the second night, or the third.

Search parties were formed. Every friend, neighbor and co-worker offered to help. Strangers came out en masse to help scour every inch of town.

Bebe put aside her jealousies and brought over food. She called Amanda daily and offered what little support and encouragement she could.

Then there was the requisite candlelight vigil held at the church.

This proved too much for Amanda, who refused to attend. She hissed at Blaze on the phone, "Why does everyone keep acting like she's dead? She isn't! I would know if she was. Lorna is still alive. She's out there somewhere. Find her, Blaze, please find her," she wept.

There were no leads at all. Lorna Dale had disappeared into thin air.

CHAPTER 29

On day five after Lorna's disappearance, Blaze sat Kurt and Amanda down for a very difficult talk. As was his style, he did not mince words.

"I have to turn over the surveillance tape of Carolyn Devonshire's murder to Fitzgerald," he told them.

Amanda cried, "No! You can't do that!"

Kurt was adamant when he said, "Over my dead body! I will never let you show the tape to anyone."

Anticipating this vehement response, Blaze allowed them to have their say without reaction.

When they were done yelling at him, he said, "Let me explain to you why I have to do this now. Will you let me do that without interrupting?"

When Kurt began to argue, Amanda placed a stiff hand on his arm. "Kurt, let him talk."

He quieted and waved a hand at Blaze to go on.

The detective told them, "I am under pressure from everyone to solve Carolyn Devonshire's murder. I am being asked a lot of questions about the surveillance video that I can't put off answering any longer. This is going to go one of two ways: I can either go to Fitz with the tapes myself, or he is going to go to the courthouse and get another set of copies. If that happens, I will be fired for withholding evidence. Either way, he's going to find out who killed Carolyn Devonshire. There is no way to keep this from getting out."

Kurt ran a hand through his hair. "But, Blaze…"

Blaze held up a hand to stop his argument. "Kurt, you know what I am telling you is true, so let me ask you both something. Would you rather have strangers assigned to the case to find your daughter? Ones unfamiliar with your fears about what she might truly be? Or do you want me on it; a family friend who is aware of Francis Barclay and whatever role he might play in all this?"

He let them digest that before continuing, "Because, if I don't come forward with the tapes now, I will be fired and possibly tried for obstruction. If that happens and they find Lorna, she will be in the hands of strangers at the juvenile detention center with no one on her side. You won't have any access to her. I am going to be her only hope. I can't help her if I am not the one in charge of the case when they bring her in. I have stalled as long as I can. No one knows I have even seen the surveillance tapes yet. They believe I dropped everything to focus on finding Lorna since the day she went missing, so the delay was understandable. It's not anymore. They expect me to work the Carolyn Devonshire murder case, and solve it if I can. I have to tell Fitz."

Kurt sighed miserably and looked at Amanda. "He's right. One way or another Fitz is going to get his hands on the tape. We have no choice. Better he hears it from Blaze than someone else."

Blaze looked at Amanda.

With tears in her eyes, she nodded. "Okay, then. I guess there is no choice. No way out of this. You better protect my little girl if they get their hands on her, Blaze. Swear to me!"

Kurt demanded, "I'm going with you when you tell Fitz. He'll understand why you came to me with the information first. I have to do whatever damage control I can for my child, Blaze, so don't argue with me on this, okay?"

Blaze reluctantly agreed.

As Amanda watched them walk out the front door, she felt more helpless than she had in her entire life. She only hoped Blaze would be the one to find Lorna. If someone else did, she feared they would crucify her.

Captain Fitzgerald had seen a great many things in his thirty years in law enforcement. What he saw on the surveillance tape that Blaze claimed to have spliced together only that morning rocked him to his core. He was rendered speechless. He looked from Blaze to Kurt and then back at the now dark TV screen. He opened his mouth to speak but couldn't seem to form any words yet. He remembered with vivid clarity the pastel yellow sweater his wife had purchased for Lorna Dale on the day she was born.

The silence grew awkward. Finally Blaze broke it by saying in the most professional voice he could muster, "Sir, how do we handle this? What with the perpetrator being not only a minor, but the daughter of one of our own?"

Kurt bristled at having Lorna called *perpetrator,* but what could he say? There was no argument he could find to defend her against that title.

Captain Fitzgerald slowly began to get his wits about him. "First of all, Kurt, I am sorry as hell about this for you and Amanda. Do we know if her kidnapping is connected to that crime?" He hooked a finger in the general direction of the TV screen.

"We have no leads on who took her or why," Blaze said.

"Kurt, can you excuse us? I don't want to discuss Carolyn Devonshire's case in front of you, in light of this... ah, new information." Fitz once more waved at the TV and wrinkled his nose like he just smelled something rank.

Kurt wanted to argue but knew it was useless. He rose and left the room.

Once he closed the door behind Kurt, Fitz said, "Okay, so the Devonshire case is solved. Now we need to decide what we're going to release to the public. Since the crime was committed by a minor, we can withhold her name."

Blaze asked, "Even from her husband? He's going to want to know who did it."

Fitzgerald was thoughtful for a moment. "Yes," he finally nodded, "even from him. Do we know of any motive for why that child would have done this?"

"No, sir," Blaze replied. He was thinking more about protecting Amanda than Kurt when he remained silent about Kurt's relationship to the deceased. What good would it do? The case was, after all, solved. Creating even more media fodder was the last thing any of them needed.

Blaze went on, "I believe, based on the manner of death, Lorna Dale is probably responsible for the Posy McManus murder as well. I will have the DNA results shortly. I am confident the DNA found on Carolyn Devonshire will match what was found on the McManus woman."

Captain Fitzgerald was once more dazed from shock. "Jesus, Blaze! She's just a little girl! Why would she do this? How could she do it? She's so tiny. How did she overpower two grown women? That tape is unbelievable. I never would have believed this if I hadn't seen it with my own eyes."

Blaze agreed. He'd kept his anxiety hidden going into this meeting. He was terrified his captain would have many more pointed questions pertaining to what the hell took him so long to view the tapes.

Fitz might still raise those questions once he had some time to recover from the horror he'd just witnessed. For now, Blaze was relieved to have dodged a bullet.

Another press conference was scheduled as soon as the DNA results for Carolyn Devonshire was in, and Blaze's suspicions confirmed. This one, carefully worded and blessedly brief, gave no opportunity for the assembled reporters to ask any questions.

The only speaker was Captain Fitzgerald, who in a cautiously crafted speech, announced that the guilty party in the murders of both the DA and the woman in the park had been identified. The current location of the suspect was unknown. A massive manhunt was underway. As the suspect was a minor, the name would not be released. He left the podium immediately after making this announcement and locked himself in his office, where a bottle of scotch waited in the bottom drawer of his desk.

As he poured a drink, he wondered why Detective Dale always seemed to end up in the middle of a shitstorm and dragging the whole department down with him. He was growing weary of the Dale family's never-ending drama.

He adored Detective Blazer. The man had no crazy wife, no felonious children, and kept his penis where it belonged. There was not one shred of drama in his personal life to splash all over and muddy the department.

Little did Fitz know, his sterling opinion of Blaze might change drastically in the coming months.

Everyone held their collective breath as they awaited the evening news. They wondered if some sharp reporter would link the disappearance of Lorna Dale to the missing underage suspect in the murder cases. No one did. Not even the most savvy of reporters would have dreamed sweet little Lorna Dale was a cold-blooded killer.

CHAPTER 30

As the days stretched into weeks, Ben Jarvis traded in the silver Lexus for a black Audi. He worked diligently to establish some sense of normalcy to their lives.

He and Lily dealt first with Lorna's anger and denial, then with her depression, and finally with a grudging acceptance of the situation she had gotten herself into. The acceptance came only after Ben was forced to show her Captain Fitzgerald's latest press conference from a YouTube video.

When she heard the captain say the suspect was underage and missing, all color drained from her face, as the truth hit home. Everyone back in Alder Lake knew what she had done. She was no longer sweet little Lorna Dale, everyone's favorite child. She was now a wanted felon.

She wondered what her parents must have thought when they learned of her crimes. She'd never been in trouble a day in her life. Discovering she killed two people must have crushed them. She missed them terribly and longed for things to go back to the way they were before she had gotten into this mess. She missed her school, her friends, and her little brother. The homesickness kept her awake at night. Lily sat up with her in the dark doing her best to offer comfort.

Eventually, Lorna's hair was lightened and cut into a new style. Ben brought home colored contacts for her to wear, and Lily took her shopping for a new wardrobe.

Ben's family was well-connected. There were few, if any, crucial items they could not obtain or did not have a resource for. Ben's father put him touch with someone who could produce new identification and provide all the necessary documentation to back it up. Lorna Dale was not the first vampire to ever require this unique service, though she was most likely the youngest.

While it took some time, eventually Lorna was provided a new name and social security number. She remained mercifully unaware that the identity she assumed once belonged to a girl from Wichita, who perished in a fire when she was the same age as Lorna.

There was one brief moment of comic relief when Lorna learned what her new name would be: Amy Louise Cox.

"Louise?" she asked, wrinkling her nose. "My middle name is Louise? Who would do that to a kid?"

Finally, she was enrolled in a small and very expensive private school at the edge of town, where the Jarvises hoped they had altered her appearance enough that no one would recognize her from the massive media coverage her disappearance had provoked.

Lorna's presence in their household was explained to friends and acquaintances with a vague story about Lily's niece having to come live with them because her mother had taken ill.

Despite all the precautions taken to ensure Lorna's identity would never be exposed, Lily was constantly on edge and in fear of capture. She could not even go to the grocery store without looking over her shoulder and jumping at every shadow. Each time the phone rang her heart leapt into her throat, wondering if this would be the call that ended it all.

The call never came, and the shadows she jumped at never jumped back. They had gotten away with it. They had succeeded in saving Lorna Dale from the law. Now the only question was whether they could save her from herself.

Eventually Kurt Dale returned to work. Walking by Carolyn Devonshire's office every day served as a constant and piercing reminder of his daughter's crimes, and worse, of her disappearance. He requested his office be moved out of the courthouse and back into the police department.

Though there was little space available, and the move was inconvenient, Captain Fitzgerald authorized it.

A few weeks after Kurt returned to work, so did Amanda. She had lost weight, and the circles beneath her eyes attested to how little sleep she was getting.

Bebe was grateful to have her back. She tried her best to overlook the bitterness she felt about what had transpired between Amanda and Blaze. She had no idea if they were still seeing each other. Since Kurt was living back in the house again, she didn't think it likely.

The two women were no longer close. The Sunday night dinners ceased altogether. The best that could be said for the relationship was that each treated the other with respect and gentleness. There was a mountain of unspoken emotions standing like an ocean between them. The road back to each other was going to be long and painful, if it could ever be found at all.

Unbeknownst to Bebe, Amanda was preparing to talk to Kurt about divorce. She wanted to file for one right away, and she wanted him out of the house. Still sleeping in Lorna's bedroom at night, she and Kurt spoke little. Amanda found the silence in the house since their daughter's disappearance positively claustrophobic.

Despite Bebe's belief to the contrary, Amanda and Blaze were still very much an item. It was to him she ran every time the quiet in the house overwhelmed her. Amanda's only relief from the overpowering grief of Lorna's absence was found in the detective's bed, which she frequented often.

Kurt remained unaware his wife had taken a lover. He did not know where she went at night, and he never asked. Every day that passed without Amanda asking him to leave provided him with a small glimmer of hope the marriage could still be salvaged.

He had stopped holding out any hope at all that his daughter would be found. Unlike Amanda, he was unconvinced she was still alive.

He was trying his best to move on with his life, though he had no idea how to even begin rebuilding it. Everything had blown up, and he did not have a single clue how to heal his heart or start a new journey without his daughter. He did not believe there was any way to put back together the fragments of his shattered world. Most mornings he was astounded to wake up and discover his heart still beating. He was pretty sure he would die in his sleep from the unbearable pain of it all.

Eventually he spoke to Fitz about making an appointment with the local psychologist the department contracted with, and Fitz authorized that too. Kurt began weekly therapy sessions. He did not tell his wife.

Bebe and Amanda spoke little of Lorna, and they did not talk about Blaze at all. Just before Amanda returned to work, Blaze revealed that Bebe was aware of what had happened between them right before Lorna went missing. He did not, however, mention that Bebe had aided Lorna on the night she killed Carolyn Devonshire. True to his word, he was keeping her dirty little secret, even from Amanda.

"How did Bebe find out about us?" Amanda wondered.

"I told her," Blaze lied.

"Why would you do that? You had to realize it would just hurt her feelings."

"I thought she should know there's no chance of us having a future together," Blaze explained. "I didn't want her to hold on to any false hope. She needed to let go so she could move on and find someone else."

Amanda thought it sounded like a noble thing to do, if it was the truth. Yet something about the explanation bothered her. Wasn't Bebe the one who ended things between them in the first place?

If Amanda wasn't so consumed with a nagging and constant fear for Lorna's safety, she probably would have seen through the thin veil of Blaze's lie immediately.

She also knew that protocol dictated she say some word of apology for moving in on her best friend's beau, but she never did.

These days Amanda saw very little of anything going on around her. She had very little interest in other people's expectations of how she should behave. She lived in a constant haze, floating through the days in a bubble of terror. Every ring of the telephone caused her heart to cease up in her chest. Every waking moment was spent in fear that the bubble would burst with the discovery of her daughter's lifeless body.

Each second was torture, with the same questions buzzing endlessly through her mind: Where was she, was she being cared for, was she alone, did the person who took her know she was *special?*

Special was how Amanda referred to Lorna's condition. The word vampire tasted bitter on her lips and would not be uttered. Even though she knew in her heart that wretched word was what her little girl had become, she just could not bring herself to say it—couldn't even think it. *Special* worked just fine when any description was required, be it verbal or in the privacy of her own thoughts.

She wasn't sure Blaze really believed any of it was true. He may have just been humoring her to spare her any further grief. He always listened patiently whenever she brought it up, and promised he'd never stop looking for Lorna, nor do everything in his power to bring her safely home.

Blaze would never speak of the true feelings he held in his heart about Lorna to the woman he loved. He believed the child was probably dead. The case was ice cold, and barring some miraculous new lead, they had absolutely no idea where to look for her at this point.

Another thing he would never tell Amanda was that a very small part of him was just a wee bit relieved the murderous little girl was out of their lives. While he may have fallen in love with her mother, Lorna Dale scared the hell out of him.

It was a rare night on which Amanda cooked dinner anymore. They had been eating a lot of takeout since Lorna went missing. So Kurt was surprised, and quite pleased, when Amanda told him not to pick anything up for them. She would be preparing a meal. What he didn't know was the reason why his wife had suddenly donned her apron again.

When they finished eating, Amanda said, "We have to talk, Kurt." Her voice was tinged with regret.

He looked at her warily. Before she could say what he feared was coming, he rushed to speak first. "Amanda, I don't think we should make any decisions about anything until Lorna is found. We have to stick together for her sake. At least until we know what we're dealing with when she's returned."

He hated the pity he saw in his wife's eyes. He never thought he would long to see her eyes blazing with fury at him again, but now he did. This was so much worse. When she was mad it meant she still cared.

Amanda sighed. "I agree with you. And when we find Lorna we will deal with it together. That doesn't mean you and I have to stay together in the meantime, though."

Kurt sounded frantic and lost. "I don't know how to be without you. I can't go through all this without you. I know what a lousy husband I've been, but I can change, Amanda. I'm trying. I am even seeing a shrink. Please just give us one more chance. Especially now."

Amanda was startled to see her husband crying. She couldn't recall the last time she'd seen him in tears. She was further startled to realize how completely unmoved she was by those tears.

She patted his hand like she was comforting a stranger. "I think it's good you're talking to someone, Kurt. I hope it helps you. But, the truth is, I've fallen in love with another man."

He swiped at his eyes with the back of his hand and glared at her with a completely stupefied expression. It might have been comical under other circumstances.

Amanda waited for Kurt's response to this stunning revelation.

When he didn't say anything, just kept staring at her, dumfounded, she asked, "Did you hear what I said? I'm in love with someone else."

"Who?" His eyes narrowed with suspicion. He hoped like hell she was just saying this to hurt him the same way she had been hurt so many times in the past by his infidelity. He couldn't for the life of him think when she would have found the time to see anyone, let alone fall in love. Their lives had been completely derailed by Lorna's disappearance and the horrible knowledge of her crimes. When, he wondered, would Amanda have found time to go find someone else?

"You're not going to like this," Amanda said regretfully. She was trying her best to look sympathetic. However, it was rather difficult to maintain a contrite expression while relishing the tiny bit of evil glee she was feeling from finally turning the tables on him. She couldn't help enjoying the complete and utter disbelief she saw in his eyes.

"Who is it?" His shock was starting to be replaced by anger.

"It's Blaze. We've been together since just before Lorna went missing."

Kurt's jaw fell open. "Blaze?" he whispered doubtfully.

"Didn't you wonder where I've been going all these nights this past month?"

"You said you needed air," he said stupidly.

Amanda smiled sweetly. "I did."

Kurt looked at her with a mixture of fury and skepticism. "I don't understand. Isn't Blaze dating Bebe? How did you end up together if he's seeing your friend? That doesn't make any sense."

"I'm sure to you it doesn't. In your mind, only you can have relationships outside of our marriage. You never thought I would do it, did you?"

"I don't know what I thought. I know I treated you like shit. So, this is payback, right? You're just trying to hit me where it will hurt the worst? Fine, you succeeded. Are you happy? Now tell me it's not true."

When Amanda said nothing, he searched her face for the truth.

The look in her eyes said it all. Amanda wasn't making this up to hurt him. She really was having an affair with Medwyn Blazer.

An uncontrollable fury washed over him. For the first time in fifteen years, Kurt Dale was afraid he might strike his wife. He rose from the table with such force he sent the chair flying backward. It crashed against the island in the kitchen.

Amanda gasped. Kurt saw fear leap into her eyes.

He glared down at her, his jaw set. "You better break it off, bitch. You will not humiliate me this way. No one else better know about this bullshit either, or so help me I will kill you. Do you hear me? I will kill you! I'm surprised Bebe hasn't killed you already, or doesn't she even know?"

Amanda took in Kurt's balled fists, his red face, and the vein pulsing in the middle of his forehead. He had never called her a bitch before—at least not to her face. For the first time in the history of their marriage, she was truly afraid of her husband.

She didn't answer his last question. Judging by the look of him, anything she said would be enough to send him over the edge and erupting into violence.

He stormed from the kitchen and she heard the front door slam. Moments later his car roared to life and peeled out of the driveway.

Oh, shit! Blaze! Amanda thought with dread. That was probably where Kurt was going. She grabbed the phone and dialed Blaze's number with shaking fingers.

"Hi, honey," he answered the phone.

"Blaze, are you home?"

"Yes. You coming over? I picked up that wine you like."

"You have to get out of there right now! I told Kurt about us. I think he's gone out looking for you."

Blaze was quiet for a minute. "You told him?"

"Yeah, and he's furious. You have to get out of there!"

"Amanda, settle down. I can deal with Kurt. He doesn't scare me."

Amanda slapped her leg in frustration. "Now is not the time to have a pissing contest with him. I have never seen him this mad. I thought he was going to hit me."

"Did he?" Blaze asked, his voice growing tight with anger.

"No, no, of course not," she said hastily. "But, he's positively livid. I don't know what he's capable of. Please just get out of there until he calms down."

"I am not leaving my house, Amanda. Trust me, I can handle Kurt."

"He's a cop. He carries a gun," Amanda continued, trying to speak some sense into him.

"I do too, babe," Blaze laughed.

The good humor in his voice infuriated her. He wasn't taking this seriously. "Men!" she cried in frustration and hung up the phone.

Kurt did not confront Blaze. He was mad, not stupid.

He went to Smokey's Tavern and ordered a double whiskey. And then another. And another.

CHAPTER 31

Two months after Lorna's disappearance, just when Ben and Lily Jarvis believed the worst was behind them, Lorna began acting out. She was getting in trouble at school and having tantrums in the house almost daily.

Finally, she snuck out of the house in the middle of the night. Brazenly walking into a homeless shelter, Lorna fed on a man deep in a drunken stupor. She did not kill him. In fact, he never even awakened when Lorna sank her fangs deep into his wrist. He mumbled something unintelligible and rolled over, completely unaware of her presence. But it scared the hell out of Lily and Ben.

Lorna made no effort to hide her transgression from them. She was no longer concerned with concealing her activities by climbing surreptitiously out of windows. In fact, Lorna stole Lily's cell phone from its charger before turning on the light in the foyer and simply walking out the front door.

She called the house phone once she had finished committing the deed. "Can you come pick me up? It's a long way to walk back, and you probably don't want to risk anyone seeing me on the streets this late, do you?" she asked an alarmed Lily.

It was nearly dawn. Both Lily and Ben had been sound asleep when the phone rang. They hastily dressed and drove to the shelter, where Lorna sat patiently on the steps waiting for them.

When they questioned her about why she had done such a thing, when her needs were well met by the blood in the freezer downstairs, she shrugged. "I just felt like it."

"Lorna, you can't do things like this!" Lily exclaimed. "What were you thinking? Are you deliberately trying to get caught?"

Lorna looked at her tolerantly. "What's the big deal? I didn't hurt him. The guy never even knew I was there. Sometimes I miss biting. It's not just about the blood, though it's way better when you get it right from a person. You should try it some time."

Ben erupted in anger. "You don't need to bite, young lady. What you need, we provide, and you get more than enough blood right at home," he fumed.

Lorna began to sob. "You never hunted. You don't know what it's like. Sometimes I just want to."

"Well you can't!" Ben roared.

When Lorna began to argue further, he warned, "Enough! There will be no more talk of this, and if you ever do it again I will lock you in your bedroom at night. Don't think I won't. We risked everything to save you. This is how you repay us?"

The incident was not repeated, but Ben took to working longer hours, leaving Lily to deal with Lorna's issues. After much coaxing, Lily finally persuaded the child to open up to her. The problem was obvious. She missed her mother.

Through a tear-choked outburst, Lorna asked Lily how she expected her never to speak to her mother again. She simply couldn't do it.

The more Lily insisted it was out of the question, citing all the reasons why, the more Lorna begged, pleaded and wailed. She even went so far as to threaten another late night visit to the homeless shelter.

She stopped short of calling her parents without Ben and Lily's approval. She wasn't blind to the fact that they had risked a great deal to save her and she didn't want to get them in any trouble. She just wanted to hear her mother's voice. The homeless shelter incident had been Lorna's misguided attempt to try and get Lily and Ben to send her back home.

It took two weeks of this behavior before Lorna finally wore Lily down. She convinced her that a two-minute conversation could do no harm. At the very least, it would let her mother know she was still alive.

"Doesn't she deserve that much?" Lorna asked.

It became increasingly evident that Lorna was not going to stop acting out, nor was she going to cease asking Lily to contact her mother. Lily knew it was only a matter of time before Lorna quit asking and called Amanda Dale herself. Lily was frankly surprised the girl hadn't done so already. She and Ben made no effort to hide their cell phones from the child. And what if they did? A telephone was not so difficult to find, even for a seven-year-old. Lorna had proven to be very resourceful when she needed to be. Then the police would show up on their doorstep and it would all blow up in their faces.

Finally, against her better judgment, Lily gave in. She purchased a disposable cell phone with cash and took Lorna to the park to place the call. She did not tell her husband.

She sat rigid and vigilant while Lorna dialed. She was ready to disconnect the call at the first word she deemed dangerous. She had schooled Lorna on what she was allowed to say and what she wasn't. If the child crossed the line, the call would be terminated.

Lorna understood her limitations. She threw her arms around Lily's waist in gratitude.

When the call came in to Amanda's cell phone, she was wandering around the grocery store, aimlessly throwing things into her cart and trying to remember to buy diapers for the baby.

Kurt had moved out this past weekend. Amanda promptly retained an attorney, who agreed to file the divorce papers and see that Kurt was served by the end of the week.

Tonight the baby was with Kurt. When the phone rang, Amanda fished it out of her purse and looked at the number. It wasn't one she recognized.

"Hello," she answered listlessly, grabbing a box of cereal off a shelf.

"Mom, it's me!" The unmistakable sound of her daughter's voice filled her ear.

Amanda shrieked and dropped the cereal box to the ground, unnoticed.

Gripping the phone so tightly it would later leave marks, she cried, "Oh dear God! Lorna! Honey, where are you? Are you alright?"

Lorna started to cry at the sound of her mother's voice. "Mommy, I'm okay. I'm so sorry for everything."

Amanda struggled with the hysteria trying to overtake her. She took in two deep breaths and steadied her voice. "Sweetheart," she said, "I need you tell me where you are. Do you know?"

Lily gave her a warning look, and Lorna nodded at her. "Mom, I can't. I don't have much time. I just wanted you to know I'm okay. Is Daddy with you? Can I talk to him?"

Lily looked nervously around the park and tapped an imaginary watch at Lorna. "Hurry up," she whispered.

Amanda heard that whisper. "Honey, who is that? Is that the person who's got you?"

"Mom, I…"

"Lorna Marie Dale, you put that person on the phone right now, do you hear me, young lady?" Amanda demanded.

An order, when delivered in the *mom-voice,* left absolutely no room for defiance.

Since birth, Lorna had never disobeyed that voice, and she had absolutely no intention of starting now. She held the phone up to Lily like it was hot. "Sorry," she apologized, wide-eyed. "You better talk to her. Don't hang up or she'll kill me!"

Lily looked like a deer caught in the headlights. She could hear the woman through the phone saying, "Hello, hello? Is anyone there?"

Lily closed her eyes, regretting ever having allowed Lorna to place this call in the first place.

She sounded weary when she put the phone to her ear. "Hello, Mrs. Dale."

Amanda slid down the shelf with the cereal boxes and collapsed to the floor. She clutched the phone even tighter to her ear.

A woman walked by. She looked at Amanda curiously and then promptly hurried away.

Amanda forced herself to sound calm. If she was hysterical, she was going to lose the one and only chance she might have of ever seeing her daughter again.

"Hi," she said, "thank you for talking to me. Is my daughter alright?"

"Yes, she's fine. I can't talk to you. I have to go."

The woman sounded scared to death. Her voice was light and fragile. She did not sound like a menacing kidnapper.

"Wait! Please don't hang up," Amanda cried. "Please, just tell me why you took her."

Lily still sounding weary and dreadfully afraid, whispered, "Because she was in trouble—terrible trouble. We had to get her out of there or she wouldn't have survived."

Amanda felt all the strength leave her body. Did this woman know what Lorna had done? She wondered if she also knew what her daughter had become. That she was *special.*

Amanda said, "I know she was in trouble. But what do you mean she wouldn't have survived? Why wouldn't she have survived?"

"I cannot talk to you. If my husband found out I let Lorna call…"

Amanda asked, "Who's your husband?"

Lily drew in a shuddering breath. "I've said too much already." Lily punched the button savagely, disconnecting the call.

Lorna looked at her awestruck. "You just hung up on Mom," she said soberly. "No one hangs up on Mom."

When the phone began to ring in Lily's hand, she pitched it into the bushes and began to cry. She grabbed Lorna's hand, hastily pulling her toward the parking lot.

Lorna felt sad and elated all at the same time. Just hearing her mother's voice was enough to make everything that had happened in the last two months seem like a nightmare she might still be able to escape.

She felt terrible Lily was so upset, though. Lily had been very good to her. She never wanted to hurt her this way.

"I won't tell Ben, I swear!" Lorna promised in an effort to say something to make Lily feel better.

Once settled in the driver seat, Lily turned sideways to Lorna. "I know you won't, honey. But we can't ever do this again. It's just too dangerous."

Lorna started to weep. She asked Lily, "You really do expect me never to see my parents again, don't you? This isn't just temporary until what happened blows over, is it?"

Lily covered the little girl's hand with her own. "No, it's not temporary. What you did won't blow over, Lorna. Don't you see that? The only way we can protect you is by keeping you here with us. You are safe, you are in school, and you don't have to resort to… well, to extreme measures for blood. Your life is here now."

Lorna dissolved fully into tears and fell against Lily. "I want my mommy," she bawled with such gut-wrenching anguish it broke Lily's heart. She held the child. Soon she was sobbing again herself.

Lily Jarvis was starting to realize that while Lorna was safe with them, she was also completely broken-hearted. This was not going to go away. It wasn't something the child would one day get over. Lorna would never adjust to this new living arrangement. Before the child grew any more desperate and took matters into her own hands, Lily was going to have to do something. And Ben wasn't going to like it.

Amanda tried redialing the phone number the call had originated from several times. There was no answer. She fled the grocery store leaving the half-full cart still in the cereal aisle.

By the time she reached Blaze's house, she was crying uncontrollably. She hammered on the front door and burst inside the minute he opened it. He couldn't understand a word she was saying. Only, with great effort, did he finally manage to calm her down enough to extract the story from her.

Once he understood, he held his hand out. "Give me your phone."

Amanda handed it over. Blaze retrieved his own cell phone and called someone on speed dial. When the call connected, he said, "Cheryl, it's Blaze. Give me the dispatch supervisor."

He waited less than a minute for the transfer to connect. Once the supervisor was on the line, Blaze told her to run a reverse directory search for the phone number Amanda received the call from. She said she would take care of it and call him back with the information.

While they waited, Blaze asked Amanda, "Don't you think you better call Kurt and tell him?"

"I will," she snapped, a little more irritably than intended. "Let's find out who owns that phone first."

The news that it was an untraceable cell phone with prepaid minutes did not surprise Blaze at all.

Amanda was not in the least bit disappointed at the news. She told him, "If Lorna persuaded whoever she's with to let her call me once, she can do it again. That lady didn't sound like a kidnapper. She sounded scared half out of her mind. She had this sweet little feminine voice. At least we know Lorna is okay. My baby is okay, Blaze," she cried, throwing her arms around his neck.

Something in Amanda's description of the caller reminded Blaze of the dog statue and Bebe's description of the woman who'd delivered it. Their demeanors sounded suspiciously similar. He was pretty sure whoever gave Bebe that dog now had Lorna.

When Amanda called Kurt, she relayed the conversation with Lorna and the kidnapper in far less detail than she had with Blaze. Things between them had been terribly strained, and they were only going to get worse when he was served with divorce papers. She knew Kurt needed to be told Lorna was okay, but she didn't want to stay on the phone with him any longer than necessary.

The first thing Kurt asked was if Blaze ran a reverse on the number. Amanda handed the phone over to Blaze and let him explain about the disposable cell phone.

Kurt was none too pleased to hear Blaze's voice. There was little love lost between them after Kurt learned of his wife's relationship with the other detective.

While he never confronted Blaze directly, the tension between the two men was thick enough to cut with a blade.

Kurt would not have gone so far as to say Blaze stole his woman. He did believe, however, that Blaze had taken advantage of Amanda when she was at her most vulnerable. Kurt never would have believed it was his wife who had been the pursuer.

Once they had performed the requisite duty of informing Kurt of the good news, Amanda turned to Blaze and asked him what they should do now.

"There isn't much we can do besides wait until they call again," he replied.

And they would not have to wait for long.

CHAPTER 32

The morning after Lily allowed Lorna to phone her mother, she dropped her at school and then promptly drove back to the park.

She doubted if the phone she'd chucked into the bushes would still be there. It was a pleasant surprise to discover it had not been stolen and was still lying right where it landed the day before. She would not have to try and find Amanda Dale's phone number through directory assistance.

Lily went to the mall and bought three more disposable cell phones with prepaid minutes. Again, she paid cash.

Taking the phone number from the first phone, she called Amanda using one of the new ones.

This time Amanda was much calmer. She had experienced the first good night's sleep she could remember since before her daughter vanished. Knowing Lorna was alive was all she needed to finally sleep through the night. She possessed every confidence they would call again.

Amanda carried her cell phone throughout the house. It never left her pocket. While she was feeding the baby his breakfast, it rang. She snatched it up immediately.

"Hello," Amanda answered cautiously.

"Mrs. Dale? We spoke last evening."

"Thank you so much for calling back, Mrs…?

Lily closed her eyes. God, she had to be careful. This lady was going to trip her up if she didn't watch every word.

"My name is not important. Please don't try to get me to reveal information that I cannot. If you do it again I will hang up, and you will never hear from me or Lorna again. Do you understand? Just listen to me, alright?"

"Of course. I'm sorry," Amanda said affably.

"Are you aware of what Lorna did before we removed her from Alder Lake?" Lily asked pointedly.

"You mean the… the criminal things?"

"Yes, I am speaking of the crimes. Do you know why she committed them?"

"Because she had to, or at least she thought she did," Amanda answered carefully.

"That's exactly right." Lily was relieved to hear that Amanda seemed to understand. It meant she at least suspected something was amiss with her daughter.

She continued, "Mrs. Dale, your daughter needs you, but it is not safe for her to return to Alder Lake. Your husband is a policeman. Does law enforcement know what she's done?"

"They do," Amanda answered truthfully. She hastily added, "We can protect her."

"You see, that's where you're wrong. She has certain needs now. If Lorna is locked up, even for a short amount of time, without the ability to have those needs met, she will die."

Amanda sputtered, "What are you saying? That's insane."

"No, Mrs. Dale, it's not. Any type of jail or detention center is equivalent to a death sentence for Lorna."

Amanda sat down heavily in a chair. Obviously this woman knew Lorna was *special.* It appeared she had a much better understanding of what her daughter's needs were than Amanda did.

"Okay, I think I understand what you're saying," Amanda answered. "Now may I ask you a question?"

"Go ahead," Lily's voice sounded wary.

"How do you know so much about Lorna's special needs?"

"Because, Mrs. Dale, I have the same needs myself."

Amanda gasped. Her composure abandoned her completely. She stammered, "Jesus Christ, are you a… are you a…"

Lily was horrified at how frantic the other woman sounded. How was she ever going to accept what Lorna had become if this was her reaction?

"Yes. I am vampire too. It was Lorna's maker who sent us to help her. She wouldn't have lasted without guidance. Her maker is gone now."

Amanda could barely breathe, as she asked, "Was her maker Francis Barclay?"

Lily was surprised Amanda knew this. "Yes, he was. Barclay returned from the grave a second time only to secure guardians for his progeny. He told us about the reason for his first visit. I assure you, there was no malice this time."

Amanda's voice caught with fear. "Where is he now?"

"Gone. He died again. He was only able to stay for a very brief period of time."

"You're sure?"

"You have nothing to worry about, Mrs. Dale. He's gone. We didn't think you even knew Lorna had been turned."

Amanda was in shock. Through numb lips, she replied, "We didn't know. Not until she… not until after she…" The sentence was left unfinished.

Lily finished it for her. "Not until she killed."

"Yes. Not until then." Amanda's voice shook.

"With us, she will never have to do anything like that again. We have what she needs. The… the blood. No one dies for it."

"Blood?" Amanda felt sick. "How do you get this blood?" she asked, her voice dripping with disgust.

"Forgive me, but that is none of your business. The only thing you need to know is that we obtain it lawfully and humanely. Now let's talk about Lorna."

"I want to see her," Amanda said stubbornly. She was expecting an argument.

"She wants to see you too. Because I care about her, and cannot stand to see her so unhappy, I am going to arrange it. You see, Mrs. Dale, I'm not the enemy."

"No? You kidnapped my daughter. You will forgive me if I'm having a little trouble feeling the love," Amanda retorted.

Lily sighed. "You still don't get it, do you? Lorna needs me. She needs me every bit as much as she needs you. You may not like that, but it's a fact. Now, do you want to see your daughter or not?"

Amanda was overjoyed. She couldn't believe it. It sounded like the woman was really going to allow her see Lorna.

"Yes, I want to see her. Please. Just tell me what you want me to do." She would promise the woman anything at this point.

"If I allow you to see Lorna and you double-cross me, you will never see your daughter again, do you understand?" Lily asked.

"I understand. I won't betray your trust."

"You must come alone. If the law is with you or hiding in the bushes, and I get arrested, you should know that I too would die if incarcerated. I have never fed from a live human. Not once since I was turned ten years ago. I don't expect you to care about my wellbeing, but if you care about Lorna's, and you truly understand what she is now, you will realize she needs me."

"I do realize that. I know you are trying to help her," Amanda agreed vehemently.

"Your husband may not come with you," Lily demanded.

"I will come alone. I promise."

"You must tell no one, not even him. When I decide on the place I will call you back with details. Be ready to leave at a moment's notice. I won't wait."

"Alright. I'll be ready. Thank you for doing this! Thank you so much for taking care of my little girl."

The phone disconnected.

Amanda would do as she was told. She would tell no one about the phone call. Not Blaze and not Kurt. She intended on keeping her word. She would show up to the meeting alone.

She had no intention of leaving her child in the care of that woman, however. *That vampire,* her mind spat like a vile curse. The word alone made Amanda's skin crawl.

She was sure there must be some cure for it. Amanda thought being vampire was an affliction—some type of disease that with the proper treatment could be cured. *Vampireitis* she thought and laughed like a loon.

Lorna might be one today, but Amanda would see to it that her child did not stay that way. Lorna was hers. When she went to this meeting, it would be with every intention of bringing her little girl home and healing her of this dreadful infection.

CHAPTER 33

For two days Amanda waited. She was beginning to think the woman must have changed her mind and was not going to contact her again.

Lily very nearly did change her mind. It was only Lorna's continued desperation that convinced her to go through with it.

She knew there was every possibility the woman would double-cross her. Had she been in Amanda Dale's shoes, she would do anything to ensure she got her child back. She was not anticipating this to play out as planned. There were so many risks.

She had tried to impart on Lorna's mother the belief that the little girl would be in danger without Lily. She wasn't sure she'd succeeded.

There were several precautions she planned on taking. She hoped they would be enough to guarantee her anonymity and avoid capture.

First, Lily rented a motel room for two nights. She paid with cash and used an assumed name. She made sure the room was on the ground floor, with a parking space directly in front. The motel was ninety miles from where they lived. It was even further from the Dales' home. Amanda would have over one hundred forty miles to drive in order to see her daughter.

Next she rented a nondescript compact car. She performed the same camouflage Ben had done on the Lexus, muddying the license plates. She left it parked a few blocks away from their home where Ben wouldn't see it.

Samantha seemed to understand what they were saying when they spoke to her. Lily planned to bring the dog with them to stand sentry outside the motel room door. She would leave her with instructions to bark like crazy if she saw anyone approaching.

She would back the rental car into the space directly in front of the room. The keys would be left in the ignition, ready for a fast getaway if one was needed.

Her personal cell phone would remain home. She watched enough TV to know her movements could be traced if she brought it. Only the disposable ones would accompany them to this meeting.

Her husband seemed aware of her heightened anxiety. He attributed it to Lorna's morose behavior these last few weeks, and did not ask her what was wrong.

Once Ben left for work, Lily called Lorna's school. She said the child was feverish and would be absent today.

When Lorna finished breakfast, Lily finally told her she was taking her to see her mother.

Lorna was ecstatic. She threw her arms around Lily, crying, "Oh thank you, Lily! Thank you, thank you!"

"Lorna, I know you're excited, but you have to remember this is a very dangerous thing we're doing. So, when I tell you it's time to go, there can be no arguments. We must leave immediately. Do you understand?"

Lorna nodded solemnly. "Yes, Lily, I do."

"If you try to go back to Alder Lake with your mom, well, the police already know what you did, and they won't understand. I don't have to remind you of what would happen if you're locked up with no access to any blood."

Lorna's eyes opened wide with fright.

Lily hastily added, "I'm not trying to scare you. I just want you to realize what could happen if you take it upon yourself to leave with your mother. You would find yourself starving again in a matter of days."

Not trying to scare her? Who was she kidding? Lily was trying to put the fear of God into the little girl. It was the only way to ensure she would cooperate.

Once she had dispensed with these final admonishments, Lily sucked in a deep breath and dialed Amanda's phone number. She used the second disposable phone, her goal being to never place more than one phone call on each. While they weren't supposed to be traceable, she was taking no chances.

Amanda did not balk when Lily told her the location of the meeting. She was so relieved to hear from her, she would have been willing to board a plane across the world if that's what it took to see her daughter again.

Lily gave the address of a convenience store located less than a mile from the motel. She planned to make sure Amanda arrived alone to the first stop. If everything still looked safe at that point, she would direct Amanda to the motel.

Amanda immediately dropped her son off at daycare. She didn't know what fresh hell might be waiting for her ahead, so she texted Kurt to pick Nate up from daycare later.

When he called to press her for details about why she couldn't pick him up herself, Amanda did not answer the call. Nor did she pick up the phone when Blaze called.

Explanations for her unexplained absence could wait until she and Lorna were safely back in Alder Lake. If things went the way she planned, they would be home by nightfall.

Just before leaving Amanda hid one final precaution inside the sleeve of her blouse.

Lily sat parked across the street from the convenience store with Lorna and Samantha in the back seat. She had issued a stern warning to Lorna a few moments before: When she saw her mother, she better fight whatever urge she might have to yell or jump from the vehicle and approach her. One false move and the meeting was off. There would be absolutely no contact until they were at the motel.

Lorna solemnly nodded her acceptance. She gave Lily a description of her mother's car.

When it entered the parking lot, Lorna leaned over the seat. "That's her!" she exclaimed.

Lily's prediction had been correct. Lorna's first instinct was to fly from the vehicle and run to her mother. Samantha, sensing what the girl was getting ready to do, positioned herself between Lorna and the door.

Lily spared a glance in the rearview mirror to make sure Lorna wasn't making any move to exit the car. She saw Samantha herding Lorna away from the door. *That is one amazing dog,* she thought.

Lily turned around and growled at Lorna, "Settle. Right now."

Lorna immediately sat still and stopped trying to push past the dog.

Lily trained her eyes on the child's mother. She watched as Amanda Dale exited the vehicle and hurried into the store.

It appeared the car Amanda arrived in held no other occupants, unless they were hiding on the floor or in the trunk. No cars entered the parking lot behind her.

Satisfied Amanda had complied with her instructions so far, Lily pulled the third disposable phone from her purse.

She dialed Amanda's number. Putting the car in gear, she pulled away from the curb as she waited for the call to connect.

"Hello," Amanda answered breathlessly. Her voice was a coiled spring of sheer tension.

"Ask the clerk for directions to the Peachtree Motel on Highway 14. Come to room nine," Lily instructed and hung up the phone.

She wanted to give herself a few minutes to get Lorna settled into the room, Samantha outside the door, and herself situated in front of the window so she could watch Amanda's arrival.

Once at the motel, Lily removed Samantha's leash.

"If you see anyone coming near this room, bark like crazy. Okay, girl?"

Samantha woofed once. She got it.

Lily herded Lorna inside the room and saw to her preparations.

Amanda waited impatiently for a customer to finish purchasing a pack of cigarettes. As an afterthought, the guy added a pack of gum and began fishing change out of his pocket. He was discussing last night's football game with the clerk. Amanda fought the urge to smack him.

When he finally left, Amanda asked the clerk for directions to the motel. He explained there were several turns, and it would be easier if he drew a map.

She waited anxiously for him to finish.

What felt like an eternity later, he finally handed her the paper and tried to explain where the motel was.

Amanda wrenched the scrawled map from his hand. She bolted toward the car, calling an abrupt word of thanks over her shoulder as she ran.

As Amanda pulled up to the motel, Lily watched nervously through the partially drawn curtains.

Amanda pulled in next to Lily's rental car. As she flung open the car door, she saw a dog standing guard in front of room number nine. She paused for a moment to look at her.

Samantha wagged her tail happily and started barking.

Amanda gasped, *Oh my God! That looks exactly like Darlene and Russell's old lab. The one Russell thought was turned into… Oh, no. It can't be!* she thought.

Sparing one final troubled look at the dog, Amanda raised her hand to rap on the door. It was opened before she could knock, and Lorna launched herself into her mother's arms.

Lily abruptly closed the door and shot the bolt as soon as the woman was inside.

Amanda wrapped her arms around Lorna and began weeping. Lorna was sobbing just as hard. Awkwardly, Lily stepped in between them. She gently pried Lorna out of her mother's embrace.

"Mrs. Dale, would you mind opening your blouse? I need to make sure you aren't wearing a wire," she said apologetically.

Amanda took in her daughter's captor as she unbuttoned her blouse. Amanda figured she stood two or three inches taller than Lorna's kidnapper and she easily outweighed her by ten pounds.

She was shocked to see how petite the woman was. She did not appear to have any weapons. Amanda thought she might be able to get Lorna out of there without even having to unlimber what she had brought with her for protection.

Once she stood with her blouse open, proving she was not wired, she looked at the woman. "Okay?"

Lily nodded.

Amanda hastily redid her buttons and knelt down to look Lorna over.

Lily retreated. She sat at a small desk in the corner of the room to allow them time to enjoy their reunion.

Amanda was shocked to see her daughter's transformed appearance. The kidnappers had certainly done an admirable job of disguising Lorna's identity. Amanda examined Lorna closely to make sure she was unharmed. The little girl endured the inspection, while chattering wildly about seeing Samantha again, the other dog Lionel, and her new school.

Her mother was only listening with half an ear. She was gauging the distance between herself and the door, trying to decide if now was a good time to sweep her daughter up and run like hell.

The woman didn't look like she was tensed for battle. Amanda thought she looked pale and frightened.

Lorna asked, "Mommy, did you see Sammie? Doesn't she look amazing? Not dead at all."

While extremely curious about the dog, and how on earth that could actually be her neighbor's long-dead pooch, right now the only thing that mattered was getting Lorna the hell out of here. All questions would have to be asked later. She was going to make a run for it.

Still smiling at Lorna, and nodding her head as the child prattled on, Amanda began stroking her hair and leading her ever so slowly by the hand in the direction of the door.

Lily was gazing out the window. When she glanced back, she was dismayed to see Amanda and Lorna were now several inches closer to the door than they had been only seconds before.

She leapt from the chair, closing the distance between them with startling speed.

Amanda pushed Lorna toward the door, yelling, "Run, baby, run!"

Amanda could not believe how freakishly fast the kidnapper had bridged the space between them.

Lily grasped Lorna's wrist with unintended force, and the child yelped in pain.

Amanda yanked the sleeve of her blouse up, and Lily saw the blade of a very large knife.

She flung Lorna to the floor and grabbed Amanda's arm. The rubber band holding the blade in place snapped and Amanda wielded it by the handle.

Lily grabbed for it, immediately slicing her fingers with deep gashes.

She did not feel the pain as blood began to rain down her arm. Her fingers grew too slippery to keep any purchase on the knife.

Amanda screamed at Lorna again, "Run!" as she waved the knife in Lily's face.

Because of the fear and sudden adrenaline rush, Lily felt her fangs pop free. Her eyes took on a sinister golden glow. It was a glow Amanda remembered with vivid clarity from Francis Barclay. Only the color was different. The terror it inspired, however, was exactly the same.

Amanda screamed and turned toward her daughter. Lily was on her instantly.

They struggled briefly for the knife. Lily bent Amanda's fingers back and the knife clattered to the floor.

Lorna was cringing in terror, her arms wrapped protectively over her head to avoid being hit, as her mother and Lily tumbled to the floor beside her.

Seeing Lily's fangs, Lorna had no control over her own. They popped free, and her eyes changed. Suddenly the dreary motel room was bathed in eerie light.

The two women crashed into an end table. A lamp fell and hit the carpet with a heavy thud, inches from where Lorna sat cowering. The child screamed in terror.

Lily rolled on top of Amanda, struggling to pin her arms. By now the pain from her cut fingers was screaming agony, as she tore the damaged flesh even further in the brawl.

Amanda glanced up and saw Lily's razor-sharp fangs. She looked to her daughter and saw the exact same thing.

The sight of those twin pairs of Dracula-like fangs snapped the last of Amanda's sanity. She let loose a bloodcurdling scream.

"Don't you bite me! Don't you dare bite me!" Amanda shrieked hysterically.

"What? No one is going to bite you," Lily tried to yell above the woman's horrified screams, but Amanda was too far gone to hear anything. Lily kept trying in vain to pin the woman's flailing arms.

With a banshees howl, Amanda wrenched Lily's cut fingers toward her own mouth.

"I will bite you, you bitch! I am going to bite you! See how you like it!" she screeched.

Lily cried out in pain. "No, no! Oh, God, don't do that!" she panted, trying desperately to pull her hand free of Amanda's grasp.

It was too late. Amanda thrust Lily's bloody fingers into her mouth and bit down hard enough to make her scream.

With strength Amanda could not believe this petite little woman possessed, Lily sprang up from the floor, pulling Amanda to her feet with her.

Once standing, Lily slapped Amanda across the face in an effort to quell her frenzy. She shoved her head down, yelling, "Spit! Spit it out!"

Amanda, at last stopped fighting. Lily's blood was smeared across her face and chin. Amanda looked at the woman with dawning horror, as she tried to spit out the blood still in her mouth.

With a mewl of disgust, Amanda wiped blood from her lips with the back of one shaking hand. She was trembling uncontrollably. The smack across the face Lily delivered hadn't been necessary. All the fight went out of Amanda when she saw the look of abject terror flood the other woman's face when her blood passed Amanda's lips. All at once Amanda's knees unhinged and she crumpled to the bed.

Ignoring her bleeding hand, Lily ran to the bathroom. She drew a glass of water from the tap and hurried back into the room.

Sloshing water over Amanda's arm, she forced the glass into her hand. "Rinse it out! You have to rinse it out!"

Amanda swished the water around in her mouth and spit it onto the floor. She repeated this two more times until the foul taste of Lily's blood was nearly gone.

Lorna rushed to her mother's side, her eyes two huge saucers of fright. At least they were no longer glowing. When Lorna saw Lily's bloody fingers she began to cry.

Lily returned to the bathroom and wrapped her hand in a towel. When she approached the bed, Amanda's arm was wrapped protectively around her daughter. She looked dazed.

Lily's fangs had retracted, and the eerie glowing light extinguished from her eyes. Amanda felt a fleeting hopefulness. Perhaps the whole miserable encounter was nothing more than a fear-induced hallucination.

She knew better. She'd seen Francis Barclay's eyes aglow in the field behind her house five years ago and remembered mistakenly believing she'd hallucinated him too.

Today she'd seen her daughter's fangs, as well as a dead dog barking and wagging its tail outside. These were no hallucinations either.

Lily sat down next to them. She looked at Amanda sympathetically. "We have to go now," she replied, placing a firm hand on Lorna's shoulder.

"Is… is what happened here going to, um… Is it going to affect me in some way?" Amanda looked at the woman pleadingly. The fear Amanda saw in the woman's eyes when she bit her fingers was even more frightening than seeing her fangs had been. Amanda couldn't believe she had actually bitten a vampire. That was certainly a new twist on an old story.

"I really don't know," Lily replied truthfully. She had a fleeting memory of telling Francis Barclay he sure made a lot of progenies by accident.

"You can't just take her again," Amanda sobbed and reached for Lorna.

"Mrs. Dale, you heard what she said. She's in school; she has a stable home. She's in far less danger with us than she would be back in Alder Lake. We will be in touch with you again. Please, let's not have any further unpleasantness today."

Amanda had begun to feel queasy. There was simply no fight left in her. She feared if she attempted to take Lorna again, the woman would tire of brawling with her and drive those razor-sharp fangs into her throat, ending the battle once and for all. She did not plan on meeting the same fate as her husband's old mistress, Tina Hilliard. She did not plan on dying in this motel room. She would never be able to get Lorna back if that happened.

Amanda looked at her daughter with an agonizing longing. "Swear to me you will stay in touch with me?" she pleaded with Lily.

"I will. I have to now," Lily said forlornly.

Amanda didn't like the sound of that.

Lily left them to rinse off Amanda's knife in the bathroom and place a clean towel around her wounded fingers.

She tidied up the room as best she could. She was grateful the heavy lamp had not broken when it fell to the floor in the struggle. The shade was slightly out of true, but she didn't think the motel staff would even notice it.

The blood was another story altogether. Some had soaked into the ridiculously thin carpet. There wasn't anything she could do about that. She threw the bedding over it and hoped some hotshot police officer wouldn't be called in to take a sample for DNA testing when the motel staff saw the blood.

While Lily's DNA profile was nowhere on file now, she figured that could change in the coming days if Amanda Dale ever figured out where to find them.

Life had suddenly become even more complicated. *Ben is just going to love this,* she thought sarcastically and rolled her eyes.

With her fingers split to ribbons and in need of stitches, she had little choice but to confess to her husband how they'd spent the afternoon. The ramifications of today's rendezvous could affect Ben too. He would have to be told.

The two women walked out of the motel room together with Lorna between them.

Lily looked over at Amanda. "Do you feel well enough to drive?"

Amanda cast a concerned glance at Lily's hand. "I might ask you the same question. Can you drive with your hand so badly injured?"

They both said they could manage. Lily had a lot of explaining to do to her husband. So did Amanda. In fact, Amanda had quite a lot of explaining to do to both a husband *and* a boyfriend. It was going to be a long day.

ONE YEAR LATER

The cloud of gossip which had been swirling around Blaze and Amanda for quite some time was finally beginning to wane. The couple had provided the town with several months' worth of steamy rumors. They started when Blaze put his house on the market and moved in with Amanda.

Not only did Amanda leave Kurt for a fellow detective, (a black man, no less!) they'd secretly married, and were living in the very house she'd shared with her husband for years. The shame of it all!

Of course, who could blame the woman for having a nervous breakdown and running wild like that. She was really never the same after her little girl was kidnapped.

As far as the town knew, Lorna Dale had never been seen again and was presumed dead.

At last, there was a new bit of salacious town gossip for tongues to wag about: The Pattersons' daughter, Trish, had turned up pregnant. What made the story noteworthy was that Trish was a sixteen-year-old high school student; the father, a twenty-eight-year-old musician. He was the drummer for Candy and the Canines.

And it got even better! Mr. and Mrs. Patterson wanted to see the man arrested for child molestation. Their daughter wanted permission to marry him.

This little gem of wickedness had blessedly pulled the staring eyes off of Blaze and Amanda. The town grapevine, that insatiable beast, had the Patterson family to feed it now. Blaze and Amanda were old news.

The couple wished the Patterson girl and the musician well. Should the young man not go to prison, and a wedding take place, Amanda swore to send a gift.

They were in a good place. Blaze's house finally sold, and they were able to pay Kurt off for his half of the value of his former marital home. The court decreed Amanda must cash him out in the divorce settlement if she wished to remain in the house.

Kurt had been patient about the money, for which Blaze and Amanda were both grateful.

They finally shared that long-awaited conversation about keeping secrets—the one Amanda was so adamant they must have. Only it was she who turned out to have the biggest secrets to tell.

In their six months of marriage, things between them were very good. Bebe had attended the wedding. Kurt had not.

Kurt no longer lived in Alder Lake. He was working for the police department in the city where his daughter resided under an assumed name.

While Captain Fitzgerald would never tell anyone, he signed the form authorizing Kurt's transfer with something approaching elation. Then he drank a healthy belt from the bottle in the bottom drawer of his desk. Things were definitely looking up.

Though they spoke little, Amanda thought Kurt was doing well. Last week, when she and Blaze had dinner at the Jarvises, Lorna mentioned Kurt was seeing someone.

Lily pulled Amanda aside later in the evening and whispered that his new girlfriend looked young enough to be his daughter. Lily saw the young lady at his house the last time she dropped Lorna off for a visit.

Amanda wasn't surprised. She had noted with some amusement, the gray at Kurt's temples was suspiciously absent last time he came to pick Nate up for the weekend.

Love was certainly in the air for everyone, it seemed. Even Bebe had met a gentleman online and seemed to be enjoying some long overdue romance in her life.

She sounded almost giddy when she spoke of him at La Travisa last Sunday, where she and Amanda dined after they closed the shop.

When his wife looked up at him in the darkness of their bedroom, Blaze saw only her eyes. Amanda's once lovely cat-green eyes, were now a deep and disturbing aquamarine color. The exact same shade as her daughter's.

They glowed like two disembodied orbs, hovering just below his shoulder. Blaze had never quite gotten used to the way they glowed in the dark, and it always gave him a start. That disturbing jolt, however, did not stop the now familiar, yet, somehow morbid arousal he felt beneath the sheet, as Amanda drove her fangs into the sensitive flesh between his neck and shoulder. She bit him there so the bite marks would not show above his collar.

Blaze knew the sex that followed would be very good. It always was on the nights Amanda drank from him, and he could taste his blood still warm on her lips.

About the Author

Krystal is the author of two previous novels and numerous short stories. She lives in the Pacific Northwest, where she is working on her fourth book, *Phone Call from Hell.*

Visit the author's website:
http://www.darksidestories.com

www.ingramcontent.com/pod-product-compliance
Lightning Source LLC
Chambersburg PA
CBHW030424310726
48979CB00009B/1608/J

* 9 7 8 1 9 4 1 5 3 6 5 2 0 *